SHAKING EVE'S TREE

THE JEWISH PUBLICATION SOCIETY

 PHILADELPHIA   NEW YORK   5750/1990

SHAKING EVE'S TREE

SHORT STORIES OF JEWISH WOMEN

edited by SHARON NIEDERMAN

ALSO BY SHARON NIEDERMAN

*A Quilt of Words: Women's Diaries, Letters & Original Accounts of Life
in the Southwest 1860–1960* (Johnson Books, Boulder, 1988)

Copyright © 1990 by Sharon Niederman

First edition   All rights reserved

Manufactured in the United States of America

Library of Congress Cataloging in Publication Data

Shaking Eve's tree: short stories of Jewish women/edited by Sharon

Niederman.—1st ed.

p. cm.

ISBN 0-8276-0356-8 (cloth)

ISBN 0-8276-0369-X (paper)

*1. Short stories, American—Jewish authors.   2. Short stories,
American—Women authors.   3. Women, Jewish—Fiction.   4. Judaism—
Fiction.   I. Niederman, Sharon.*

PS647.J4S54   1990

813'.01089287—dc20   *89-78487*

                                                              CIP

Designed by Adrianne Onderdonk Dudden

CONTENTS

ACKNOWLEDGEMENTS

This book is the work of many people. Special thanks to the hundreds of writers who submitted stories for consideration — may you keep writing and may there be increasing opportunity for you to be heard. I want my friends and those close to me to know how vital their faith and encouragement have been to the creation of this book. Thanks and blessings to Rabbi Lynn Gottlieb, Demetria Martinez, Elizabeth Roll, Janet Voorhees, Sallie Janpol, Kathy Matthews, Maryhelen Snyder; my partner, Jim Burbank; my parents, Ann and Jack Niederman; the Nahalat Shalom Rosh Hodesh group; and the Lama Foundation. Thanks too to my editors, Diane Levenberg and Sheila Segal and to Elissa Biren and Diane W. Zuckerman of the Jewish Publication Society.

Many of the stories collected in SHAKING EVE'S TREE: SHORT STORIES OF JEWISH WOMEN appeared previously in publications. The editor gratefully acknowledges the cooperation of editors, agents, and the authors.

"The Tornado Watch Cookbook" by Carol K. Howell was originally published in *Redbook*. Reprinted by permission of the author. Copyright ©1986 by Carol K. Howell.

"Children of Joy" by Joanne Greenberg was originally published in *Hadassah* and was also published in RITES OF PASSAGE by Holt, Rinehart and Winston. Reprinted by permission of The Wallace Literary Agency, Inc. Reprinted by permission of the author. Copyright ©1966 by Joanne Greenberg.

"Deeds of Love and Rage" by Marsha Lee Berkman was originally published in the *Sonora Review*. It also appeared in *Lilith*. Reprinted by permission of the author. Copyright ©1984 by Marsha Lee Berkman.

But let me impress just one thing upon you, sister . . . Your imagination and your emotions are like a vast ocean from which you wrest small pieces of land that may well be flooded again. That ocean is wide and elemental, but what matter are the small pieces of land you reclaim from it. The subject right before you is more important than those prodigious thoughts on Tolstoy and Napoleon that occurred to you in the middle of last night. . . .

Etty Hillesum
An Interrupted Life:
The Diaries of Etty Hillesum 1941 – 1943

INTRODUCTION

Just a decade ago, the question, "Why are there no women Shake-speares?" triggered ardent debate between feminists angry about the censorship of women's art and traditionalists who believed women couldn't really write great literature. Yet looking at American fiction since World War II, we might ask: Where are the great Jewish women writers? Where are the female Bellows, Roths, Hellers, Mailers, and Malamuds? Why is a thorough, serious examination of the American Jewish experience from the female point of view missing from the library shelves?

Although we have a blooming garden of Jewish women writers, only a handful have chosen to address in their fiction the historic, moral, folkloric, practical, philosophical, and psychological issues of the Jewish condition. Considering the number of writing women who are Jewish, the absence of their story from the postwar literature of exiles and outsiders is astonishing. Jewish women's fiction has been primarily assimilationist, without addressing the issues of assimilation. In few works do we find the consciousness of being female and Jewish raised in ways fundamental to the story.

Contemporary fiction by Jewish women writers who acknowledge their Jewishness *at all* falls into four categories.

First, there is the confessional writing of highly successful, popular authors such as Erica Jong and Nora Ephron, who epitomize the quick, witty, sarcastic, brittle voice that has become identified as *the* voice of the urban woman writer. Their characters are assimilated, and their tangential Jewishness provides a rich source of humor. Isadora Wing, the protagonist of *Fear of Flying,* and Rachel Samsat, the protagonist of *Heartburn,* might have gone to the same school—Bennington. The plots revolve around their sexuality and their relationships with men — the basics explored by so many female writers in the attempt to reveal and comprehend the rules and taboos that have diminished women's ability to know themselves.

Another type of popular Jewish woman writer is represented by Belva Plain, whose generation-spanning, rags-to-riches epic, *Evergreen,* goes straight to the heart of the American dream. Characters who just happen to be Jewish rise from the status of struggling immigrant outsiders to become wealthy, influential insiders, with all the pressures and heartaches that such a journey entails. Jewish family sagas can now be found on the historical romance fiction rack as well.

The third group also writes about the immigrant experience but from a different perspective. Short story writers Tillie Olsen and Grace Paley give insight into the secular Jewish immigrant experience as their characters of three generations weave in and out of the world of Jewish memory and values. With its clear social consciousness, their work is a foundation of feminist Jewish fiction.

The fourth type, those who write openly about their femaleness and their Jewishness, often focusing on these two aspects of existence as their characters' primary concerns, are producing feminist Jewish fiction. This genre has emerged within the past dozen years with the support of magazines such as *Lilith* and *Sinister Wisdom* and with the publication of many of the writers included in this anthology whose work both delivers and encourages the authentic expression of Jewish women's experience.

What is meant by the term "feminist Jewish fiction?" It is fiction that probes the experience of being Jewish *and* female from the Jewish female's point of view. It goes beyond admitting to the Jewishness of the characters or creating a setting with Jewish reference points; it explores the ramifications of Jewish identity and heritage, particularly as manifested in family, or surrogate family, relationships. Feminist Jewish fiction tears away at the veils of invisibility and the art of camouflage. This emerging genre raises heartfelt issues previously ignored, dismissed, or deliberately masked.

The essentially conservative expectations of Jewish women within the Jewish community, the inhibiting power of stereotypes and the lack of a real place for women's self-expression within the tradition are some of the reasons why, until recently, Jewish women have rarely written about being Jewish.

It's difficult to become a writer, a woman writer. To arrange one's life for writing, often at sacrifice; to believe in one's work when there may be little or no support; to commit to one's own imaginative processes when real life pushes women toward committing far more strongly toward other people's endeavors — these acts essential to becoming serious about one's work require a strength that few writers believe they possess and that they must improvise, like their stories, as they go along.

The traditional Jewish woman, by and large, could not afford or accommodate the rebellious imagination required to create serious fiction. (And if she found herself on a life path leading toward writing, she generally shed her Jewishness.) As Adrienne Rich writes on the conflict between writing and the female role:

". . . if the imagination is to transcend and transform experience, it has to question, to challenge, to conceive of alternatives, perhaps to the very life you are living at that moment. . . . Now, to be maternally with small children in the old way, to be with a man in the old way of marriage, requires a holding-back, a putting-aside of that imaginative activity, and demands instead a kind of conservatism. I want to make it clear that I am not saying that in order to write well, or think well, it is necessary to become a devouring ego. This has been the myth of the masculine artist and thinker; and I do not accept it. But to be a female human being trying to fulfill traditional female functions in a traditional way is in direct conflict with the subversive function of the imagination. The word traditional is important here. There must be ways, and we will be finding out more about them, in which the energy of creation and the energy of relation can be united." [1]

[1] Adrienne Rich, "When We Dead Awaken: Writing as Re-Vision," *On Lies, Secrets and Silence: Selected Prose 1966–1978* (New York: W.W. Norton & Company, 1979) p. 43.

Certainly, women of traditional Jewish background received education and encouragement to accomplish—within the limits of what the culture judged good for husbands and children. To subordinate their talents to family and community; to go so far but no further—*or else*—these unspoken commandments kept Jewish women from exploring the truths of their lives. What was true for women in the majority culture was intensified and more strongly enforced for Jewish women, who were taught to be responsible for saving their people from total destruction and given the arena of the family in which to perform this miracle.

Jewish women have been leaders and key articulators of feminism, their names becoming household words in the 1960s and 1970s. For Jewish women who identified with feminism, claiming female identity became paramount and Jewishness was frequently pushed aside, if not abandoned. How could a woman be a feminist, someone struggling to move beyond the limits of the traditional female role, and at the same time embrace Judaism, a patriarchal religion that denied women full participation? Women could not read from the Torah or count in a *minyan* or become rabbis.

But feminism has touched Judaism, and now a fair place for women is being created within the tradition. Women are reclaiming ancient ceremonies, such as the celebration of Rosh Hodesh (the New Moon), writing feminist Haggadahs, and crafting rituals that express women's spirituality in a Jewish context. They are also graduating from mainstream rabbinical schools in ever-increasing numbers. With the emergent support for women's participation both in the synagogue and in the new sisterhood of Jewish women's groups, women writers are freer to explore Jewish female experience.

Another reason for our prolonged literary silence was the internalization of ugly stereotypes. As long as we were labeled the Jewish Princess or the Jewish Mother, as Marjorie Morningstar or Sophie Portnoy, repellent from the tops of our frosted heads to the tips of our frosted toes, we felt ashamed. We often chose to pass, whenever possible, rather than admit who we were, in life or in literature. Like all minority members, we were bred on put-downs. We were too loud, too pushy, too intense. We spoke too fast, our hair was too unruly, our skin not the right shade. We learned that our natural state was unacceptable, from society as well as from our own community. And coming from the post-Holocaust generation, we had the special awareness that stereotypes can kill. Many of us responded by trying to become Jewish and not-Jewish at the same time: We loyally admitted our ethnicity at the Seder and on the High Holy Days but tried to ban our Jewish personal characteristics from social and professional relationships. Our experience differed from that of our brothers, who gathered strength to tell their story from their inherited position within the community.

Facing disapproval from within the community and lacking the community's support to face the outside world's criticism, Jewish women writers chose to create characters who either were not Jewish or were not "too Jewish." They created characters whose Jewishness was as elusive as they wanted their own to be. Feminist Jewish writers are now beginning to expose the stereotypes instead of hiding from them. Lynn Freed's "Foreign Student" is a story that dissects the stereotype of the Jewish American Princess, and Marcia Tager's "Cousins" describes the bitterness that can result when a young woman rebels against her Jewish family's stereotypical expectations.

While there exists a tradition of Jewish women writers and poets, until recently most of their works were lost—out of print, untranslated from Yiddish. We may have come across a name, a fragment, a poem now and then, a flash of light, but that's all. The fortunate have, at best, their grandmothers' sepia photographs and a few stories of immigrant life told, with tea and honeycake, on a rainy childhood afternoon.

»«

The theme of *Shaking Eve's Tree* grew out of the material submitted. Most of the manuscripts were concerned with how to be a mother and how to be a daughter—how to balance tribal affiliation with personal integrity. This tension is expressed with unusual poignancy in two mother-daughter stories—Carol K. Howell's "The Tornado Watch Cookbook" (originally published in *Redbook* with much of the Jewish content omitted) and in "Deeds of Love and Rage" by Marsha Lee

Berkman. And as the assimilated protagonist in Laurie Colwin's "A Big Storm Knocked It Over" contemplates her new pregnancy, two provocative personal mysteries—her vestigal Jewishness and her irrepressible sexual curiosity—remind her that not even marriage and motherhood can guarantee emotional security in this complicated universe.

While much feminist fiction has focused on female sexuality and the examination of romantic relationships with significant others, Jewish feminist fiction seems primarily concerned with clarifying relationships between parents and children. If we have rejected or been rejected by our family, we are now concerned with making peace and finding a place there. Bette Howland's "The Life You Gave Me" and Libbi Miriam's "Taking the Bus" both deal with adult children facing painful relationships with their aging parents and learning to say goodbye. Grace Paley's "Zagrowsky Tells" shows the parental relationship from the point of view of a grandfather who learns to love his daughter's inter-racial child and so overcomes his own racism. Tradition assists the development of inter-generational understanding in Joanne Greenberg's "Children of Joy," where a young woman who idealizes the shtetl past of her grandmother and great-aunts is set straight with affection and humor, and in Gloria L. Kirchheimer's "A Case of Dementia," where a sophisticated lawyer casts a Sephardic spell on her mother.

The protagonists of the stories in this book insist on acceptance for themselves. Lesléa Newman's "The Gift" traces the childhood and young adulthood of a Jewish lesbian woman as she reconciles her Jewishness with her sexual identity. "A Leak in the Heart" by Faye Moskowitz shows the struggle of an immigrant woman for self-forgiveness after the death of her infant daughter.

Some of these stories show women returning from exile to make peace with the denied and neglected parts of themselves from which they have run. "A Gift for Languages" by Sharon Niederman tells of a Berkeley professor, overwhelmed by the death of a beloved mentor, who is no longer able to deny her Jewish roots. Often through a crisis—death, illness, pregnancy, divorce, separation, or another life cycle transformation—these characters learn a new truth that changes them and brings them to a clearer self-definition that includes acknowledgement of their origins.

The theme of individuation is found in E.M. Broner's "The Dancers," a story about separation between mother and daughter, and Zena Collier's "Passage," which tells of loss of innocence as a fourteen-year-old girl learns at the Seder table the truth of her family's past as it leads to the family's dissolution.

The stories in this collection move through a vast imaginative and geographic territory — New York City, suburbia, California, the Midwest, the old country, Israel, England, and South Africa. They present a variety of women's voices, of both well-known and emerging authors: some identify primarily as Jewish writers, others explore Jewish issues as one of numerous concerns. The stories are told from the points of view of characters of many ages and varied social status, demonstrating the variety of Jewish women's experience. Some of these stories have appeared in national publications, others in little magazines, and others are making their first appearance in print here.

Until now, our experience has remained invisible, as invisible as the white letters of the Torah, those letters around the black script that tell the missing stories of our foremothers. As Jewish women scholars and rabbis are now beginning to decipher the white letters of the Torah, contemporary women writers are beginning to tell our stories, and we are listening intently to the truths of our lives.

Sharon Niederman
Albuquerque, New Mexico
September, 1989

CAROL K. HOWELL

THE TORNADO WATCH COOKBOOK

The sky was yellow when I left Chicago. The hot motionless air seemed to coat my skin, sealing off the pores as though I'd been laminated in plastic. The air conditioner was broken and tepid baths did no good, so I decided to take a long drive with the windows open, the way my father used to ride us around Gothenberg on hot summer nights. I wanted to go north, maybe Canada, but the weatherman predicted storms, so I put a box of clothes in the car—Brent had taken both suitcases, as if he were the only one who traveled—and turned west onto I-80. Instead of cool sunshine, I drove into more sullen heat. The trees along the highway looked painted, fixed to a yellowish canvas. Each time I stopped at a gas station to use the Ladies' Room, my skin would be slick by the time I came out. I squeaked across the vinyl seat.

As soon as I crossed into Iowa the sky got dark. Lightning flared ahead, then wind and rain burst around my car. I had to grip the wheel and turn against the wind to keep from being pushed off the road. In this Wagnerian opera of a thunderstorm, I finally drove into Gothenberg. My mother was watching from the window as I turned up the driveway. She hurried out under a striped umbrella big enough for three people and tried to take my box.

"Come inside!" she shouted, as if I might have other ideas.

The house was a five-bedroom split-level that my father built when we first moved to town. It was more than he could afford and bigger than we needed, but he said he wanted the goyim to know we were here. Inside, I was overpowered by the smell of warm honey and cinnamon. My mother triumphantly withdrew a pan of pecan rolls from the oven, but I shook my head. I was still queasy from the long drive.

"No?" she said. "All right, but tomorrow I'm making strudel."

"Why so much baking? Someone's Bar Mitzvah?"

She hooted. "Bar Mitzvah! Who's left to be a Bar Mitzvah? Soon we won't have a shul at all but a Jewish Home for the Aged. No, Esther, listen.'' She fluffed out her hair and leaned forward. "I'm writing a cookbook!''

The tiny Hadassah had issued an emergency call to all members of the congregation: the shul needed a new roof. It needed a lot of other things besides, primarily new blood, but a roof was easier to find. The Hadassah, well-acquainted with my mother's powers of persuasion, elected her Chief Fund raiser. They probably also wanted to take her mind off my father, who fell dead on the driveway eight months ago while putting his golf clubs into the car. During the week of his funeral, which, strictly speaking, should have been spent sitting motionless in mourning, my mother made one thousand pieces of strudel.

"I can't sit,'' she'd said. "Besides, your father loved my strudel.''

Brent drove in for the funeral and went back the next day. My mother sent strudel home with him, enough to feed the entire cast and crew of the play he was in; she sent strudel home with everybody, but at the end of the week of mourning, she still had six hundred pieces left. These she took to the Good Samaritan Nursing Home, where there were half a dozen Jewish residents. One of these, little half-blind Mrs. Zweig, tasted the strudel and wept. "Like I used to make myself,'' she said. "Nobody makes like this anymore.'' And that, said my mother, gave her a brainstorm: she would write a cookbook that explained traditional recipes in such a modern forthright manner that any Jewish girl, no matter how assimilated, could make a dinner even her grandparents could eat with pleasure.

"I'll donate the royalties to Hadassah,'' she said. "But I think I should keep whatever I make from personal appearances. After all, I'll have expenses. That's fair, don't you think?''

She'd made up her face and put on her diamond earrings. Her eyes snapped and sparkled. I hadn't seen her so excited since the time my father surprised her with a mink coat and she went running up and down the stairs to look at herself in all the mirrors.

"And now that you're here, you can help,'' she said, beaming. "I'll give you a credit in the acknowledgements.''

"I don't know anything about cookbooks,'' I said. "I never use them.''

"You cook out of your head?'' she asked doubtfully.

"I don't cook at all."

"Everybody cooks."

"Not the everybody I know."

"How could you not learn to cook? I've spent half my life in the kitchen!"

"You didn't want me hanging around. I was in the way or something." I shrugged and drank my coffee. "I was never that interested anyway."

"That's not the way I remember it."

The coffee seethed in my stomach. I could feel acid climbing the back of my throat. "You have any saltines in the house?" I asked.

"I make pecan rolls and you want saltines?"

"They're all I can eat."

"I never heard of the driver getting carsick," she muttered as she went to get the crackers.

I hadn't told her about Brent. When I called from the gas station, I just said I wanted to spend a few days at home. My mother, a great believer in intuition, asked no questions but baked my favorite pecan rolls, timing them so they'd be done just as I walked through the door. She was a master of special effects.

"I know one thing about cookbooks," I told her. "If you want it to sell, you need an angle. There are cookbooks these days just for goat cheese or edible centerpieces. I saw one the other day for round foods — everything in it was round."

"I thought you didn't read cookbooks."

"I can't help it if I see the titles in bookstores."

She considered, tapping her eternity ring against her cup. "Well, I don't know if this is an angle, but if there's one thing a girl should be able to cook, it's a real Shabbos dinner." She stopped and looked at me. "I could do a chapter on each course. That would give me lots of room for commentary."

My mother loved commentary as much as any Talmudic scholar. "It would do that."

She beamed again and poured me more coffee. "So when can you start?"

The wind dropped overnight but picked up again at dawn. I slept badly and woke early. My mother spent the morning cooking, watching talk shows, and instructing me. European Jews have made strudel this way for hundreds of years, she said: the secret ingredient is ginger ale.

"They had ginger ale in Europe hundreds of years ago?" I asked.

My mother was not dismayed. "Who knows?" she said. "They probably had something even better."

The dough was a soft powdered ball, a baby's bottom. She covered it with a white dish towel to let it rest.

"My mother used to mix the dough right on the table," she told me. "She'd make a mound of flour, dig a hole in the center, pour in the eggs and oil, and squeeze it together with her hands. I can't do that."

I scribbled notes on a pad. My grandmother came to New York when she was a young woman. I only saw her a few times. One of her front teeth was gold and half of her left ear lobe was torn away. My mother said that someone had done a bad job of piercing it when my grandmother was a baby. She always wore a kerchief on her head, either to honor God or to hide her ragged ear. After my grandfather died, she went to live with Uncle Hersh. When I was sixteen, Uncle Hersh had to put her in a nursing home. My mother flew to New York to find out why. Every night she called us with incredible stories: "Mama doesn't even know me. All she does is shuffle up and down the hallway, making cries like a sea gull." My grandmother tore down pictures and drapes. She knocked on every door she passed. The only thing that gave her any comfort was having something to push up and down the hall. My mother went to F.A.O. Schwartz and bought her a doll buggy to keep her from stealing the laundry carts. "It's Alzheimer's," she told us over the phone. There was so much static I could barely hear her. "The sudden kind. There's a twelve per cent chance it's hereditary."

When my grandmother died, my father flew east alone for the funeral. I stayed home and took my SAT's again, hoping for a higher score. I was determined to go to the University of Chicago and become a lawyer.

While I took notes, my mother chopped apples and nuts in her Cuisinart, then covered the table with a cloth and sprinkled it with flour. She rolled the strudel dough as thin as possible, then thinner still.

"Now we stretch it," she said. "The secret is to flour your knuckles." She whitened her hands with flour and slipped them palms down under the dough, stretching until it looked transparent.

"Why doesn't it tear?" I asked.

"Because," she said with a mysterious smile, "it's torn so many times before."

"That's what I'm supposed to tell the readers?"

"Tell them to flour their knuckles." She gave me a sharp glance and I saw that my tone had offended her. Grimly, she added the filling, rolled the strudel up, and brushed the top with melted butter.

The smell of the butter suddenly made me sick. I backed out of the kitchen and threw up in the guest bathroom, running both faucets so she wouldn't hear. When I came out, I stayed in the living room for awhile. Outside, rain fizzed along the driveway and rattled the leaves. Inside, everything looked cool and neutral: the toffee sofa, the cream rug, the gray easy chair where my father used to sit smoking his pipe and listening to music. Beside the chair was his hifi, polished so hard that it gleamed even in this dull rainy light. I flipped through his records, settling on *H.M.S. Pinafore*. My father loved Gilbert and Sullivan. He knew every word to every song and he could do all the voices. At my ninth birthday party he cracked everyone up by singing "I Am The Captain Of The Pinafore" in Little Buttercup's falsetto. I listened to the overture, then took the record off again.

For lunch I had crackers and ginger ale. My mother predicted constipation and threatened to cook tsimmes with prunes. "When you were a baby, tsimmes was all you would eat," she said. "I had to cook it every week."

"I'm sorry I was so much work." I took a can of ginger ale and pressed it to my forehead.

My mother frowned. "Are you sick? I could call Dr. Loeb."

"I'm all right." I put down the can and picked up my notepad. "You never said how long the strudel bakes."

"I don't like your color, Esther. You're green."

"I'm always green."

"No, you're always sallow. This is green." She tilted my chin toward the light.

I pulled away. "Don't do that. You make me feel like a bug."

"A bug?"

"Something bumpy and ugly and green."

"What are you talking, Esther?"

"You always manage to let me know I'm not quite what you had in mind."

"And what did I have in mind? You know that too?"

"Some midwestern corn maiden who can make a perfect blintz. Yentl the Homecoming Queen."

"So now it's a crime to be ambitious for your children? I wanted you to have the best of both worlds."

"But I could never live up to your ambition! I was never pretty enough or smart enough—"

"Smart! You're smart enough for ten girls, if only you'd apply it. Look at you, the first girl in my family ever to go to college, and for what? So you could spend your life in a fruit store making little piles of tomatoes and lemons? Whatever happened to law school?"

"There are no jobs for lawyers now. The market is flooded."

"A girl with some determination could find a job."

"You just don't know me, do you? You don't know me at all."

She slammed her spoon down on the counter. "Well, if I don't, it's because you never bother to tell me anything!"

"I never tell you anything because you always use it against me. Remember the eye make-up?"

"For heaven's sake, Esther, that was eighth grade!"

"Remember when I had crushes on boys who weren't Jewish? I could have gone sneaking behind your back but I told you, and what did you do? You canceled my social life."

"There were Jewish boys your age."

"There were five! One was obese, one was stupid, and the other three were jerks."

"Well, I wasn't asking you to marry them. And you were too young for make-up. Besides, you wanted to wear green eyeshadow—with that skin!"

"You see?" I said. "A bug. A toad."

My mother sighed, cracking an egg into a bowl. "That's ridiculous. You're a very attractive girl."

"But not attractive enough for ten girls?"

"Was it my fault you inherited the Lipschitz nose? I begged you to get corrective surgery the summer after graduation, remember? You could have gone to college with a new nose and no one would have ever known."

"Is it so hard to understand why I didn't want to have every bone in my nose broken?"

"And the braces? We were *dying* to give you braces—"

"I was not about to do anything which called any more attention to my mouth. Do you know what happens to a name like Lipschitz in grammar school?"

"I don't want to hear."

"It becomes Shit-Lips. Esther Shit-Lips, that's who I was. Why didn't you at least give me a nice first name? Of the three Jewish girls in my class, one was Jody Robb—"

"Robinowitz!" my mother hissed.

"And the other two were both named Cindi."

"You know you were named for my grandmother. Besides, Queen Esther was a great Jewish heroine."

"Well, I'm not."

"No one said you had to be."

"Then why isn't my nose good enough? Or my job?"

For a moment she looked at me, shaking her head. Then she picked up the bowl and began to beat the eggs. "Esther, when you were born my labor started while I was standing in a grocery store picking out salad dressing. All of a sudden—boom! Water everywhere! I was mortified, but, thinking fast, I grabbed a big jar of dill pickles and dropped it on the floor to cover the mess. That must have been my big mistake, because you've been sour ever since."

I couldn't help it; I had to laugh a little. All the energy went out of me and I sank down on a chair.

My mother put down the bowl. "Esther, tell me: you're not sick? You're not in trouble?"

"I'm fine."

"What about your job? And Brent?"

Before I could answer there was a shrill beeping from the TV. A message was moving across the bottom of the screen: *The National Weather Service has issued a tornado watch for the following counties . . .*

"I knew it!" my mother cried. Then she turned back to me. "I don't care what you say. As soon as I put this in the oven, I'm calling Dr. Loeb."

Wearily I picked up my pencil. "How hot an oven?" I said. "How long?"

» «

When the doctor called with the test results, my mother was rolling lumps of margarine in rosemary and lemon to slip under the skin of a capon as large as a small child. I was inhaling lemon peel to keep from smelling the margarine. When the phone rang, I reached it first.

"Well?" said my mother when I hung up.

"Just what I expected. Nothing serious."

"If it's what you're expecting, it's as serious as can be."

"What did you do?" I said. "Talk to Loeb behind my back?"

"I didn't have to," she said proudly. "I come from a tradition of mid-wives. We *know* these things." She reached for a towel and wiped her hands. "So now we have a situation. You're lucky I'm such a progressive thinker. When are you going to tell him?"

I sat down and reached for my lemon peel. "When I get a postcard with a return address."

It took a moment to sink in. Then she sat down too. "You mean he left you?"

"We left each other. He just went further, that's all."

She looked dazed. "But why?"

"He wanted to look for real acting jobs."

"Real actors can't get married?"

"Listen, it's a good thing we never did. Much simpler this way."

"What are you talking, Esther? Nothing's simple now." She tapped her ring on the table till I stared at it so pointedly that she stopped. "He'll write. He'll come to his senses. Meanwhile, thank God, you can stay with me. Maybe after the baby comes you can think about law school again. After all, you'll have me to help with the baby—"

"It's not a baby yet. It looks like an apostrophe."

"What do you mean?" she said sharply. "Esther, you're not thinking about—"

"I'm considering all my options."

"I don't believe it!"

I got up and pointed my finger at her, something I was never permitted to do as a child. "Listen, Mother, it's *my* life—"

"No, you listen!" She pushed back her chair, stood up, then sat down again. "What did you come home for? Why didn't you just go to a clinic in Chicago?" She jabbed a finger at me. "You came home because you want me to talk you out of it, that's why!"

"I told you, I haven't decided."

Tears made her eyes brilliant. "Are you doing this to punish me? At last you have a weapon big enough?"

"You've been watching too many talk shows."

"If it's a boy, we could name him for your father."

I turned and headed for the door.

"Where are you going?" she cried.

"Just for some air. Unless there's an abortion clinic at the end of the driveway, you have nothing to worry about."

"How can you joke?" she said. Then: "There's a tornado watch. Take a sweater."

»«

Now my mother began cooking in earnest. She made tsimmes, three stewpots full. Carrots, sweet potatoes, prunes, and brisket simmered in a honey bath for two days straight. The aroma filled every room in the house. I spent my time sitting on the porch, talking to my mother through the screen door.

"Why are you making so much tsimmes?" I asked.

"For the freezer," she replied as if that were a reason. She was buoyant again, rattling pans, dashing pepper into the pot.

"You don't fool me," I said. "You think you're making baby food. You're going to be stuck with a lot of tsimmes."

"Tsimmes keeps." She opened the screen door and thrust a glass of milk at me. "Here."

"I don't want this."

"You'll need it. Listen, when you were born you drained all the calcium out of my body. I've had teeth problems ever since."

"It wasn't intentional," I said. "Do you have any other ancient grudges you'd like to tell me about?"

But she was fiddling with the TV and didn't hear. Merv Griffin was singing "My Way" through the static of an electrical storm. I poured the milk out over the rosebushes.

"I've been thinking," my mother called. "Maybe we should do a chapter on Jewish history. The kind of thing I used to say during my Good Will presentations, remember?"

Oh, did I remember. When the Hadassah elected my mother Good Will Ambassador, she traveled to clubs and churches and schools throughout the community, explaining Jewish customs and beliefs. She always took a menorah, a Kiddush cup, a Seder plate, and me. I had to cover my head with an embroidered napkin and bless the Sabbath candles. It was excruciating. Everyone knew us. The ladies used to pat my head and say, with unintentional sympathy, that I was the very picture of my father.

My mother was also famous for arranging other people's parties, for her frosted fruit towers trickling with champagne fountains, her heads sculpted from chopped liver, and, especially, for her weddings. She simply took over: the food, the flowers, the tables, the gifts, even the bridesmaids and ushers. Whenever anyone said, "Helene, however do you manage it?" she replied, "I'm practicing for my daughter's wedding. I only have one daughter so I have to get it right."

"Wake up, dreamer." My mother was at the door again, holding out a bag of carrots. "Scrape these for me. They bring good luck."

"Where'd you hear that one?"

"My mother used to say it. And she used to say that unless every-one tasted the Sabbath wine, the family wouldn't have a healthy week."

"Maybe she was neurotic."

"No, it was a tradition. In a way, it's comforting, don't you think? To believe that a sip of wine could ward off the Evil Eye."

"So what's lucky about carrots?"

"In Yiddish they're *mehren*. Multiply. You know: make fertile."

"Oh, that kind of luck." I ripped open the bag and began scraping. "Listen, we are not going to have this conversation again."

"You take everything so personally."

"Besides, fertility is not the issue. My fertility has been adequately demonstrated."

"Because you got pregnant one time?"

"Because the one time I got caught off-guard, it took. Now is that fertile or not?"

"What do you mean, you got caught off-guard?" she said craftily, and I saw that she was looking for something to use as an argument for reconciliation.

"We hadn't been sleeping together for a while. Then one night we got drunk." I shrugged. "You owe the conception of your first grand-child to a gallon of Rossi Red."

My mother put down her knife and came back to the door. "You say first grandchild. You assume there will be others?"

"Why not? There must be some men around who don't mind a big nose and an overbite. At least I have good hair."

"Oh, Esther!" She pushed the door open and squeezed down beside me on the steps. "You have beautiful hair. And nice eyes and smooth skin — I told you, you're a very attractive girl. But that's not the point. Listen, why do you think you never had a brother or sister? Look at all the rooms in this house! We had great plans, your father and I, but we only got lucky once. And then I had that operation when I was still a young woman."

"But what's that got to do with me?"

"Who's to say? You look like your father on the outside — maybe you're like me on the inside. Everybody inherits something."

A gust of wind sent a chilling spray over us and I shivered. My mother stood up and held the door open. "Come inside."

I gathered up the carrots. "You're not making more tsimmes, I hope."

"No, these are for soup. You know, they have scientific proof now that chicken soup makes good medicine. They used to call that a superstition too."

"What else do you believe?"

"Oh, I never say a baby's beautiful. I wash my hands after a trip to the cemetery. And since honey sweetens the fortune of an unborn child, I ate a lot of honeycake while I was carrying you."

"So maybe that's what rotted your teeth," I said, following her into the house.

» «

In the middle of the night I woke up, starving. There was a faint rattle of hail at the window. I decided to try some more crackers and maybe some cottage cheese, but when I got downstairs I found my mother at the kitchen table eating Peppermint Stripe ice cream. Suddenly I could think of no better taste than the bright cool mint.

"Is there any more of that?" I asked.

She turned, and I could see by the distant look in her eyes that she had not been thinking of me. "Sit down," she said and brought me a bowlful of perfect ice-cream-parlor scoops. The first bite was startling, then it all went down in a rush.

"What were you thinking about?" I asked. I couldn't remember ever having asked her that question before.

She tilted up her ice cream bowl as if reading a fortune in the melted pink puddle. "Your father. I used to wait up nights for him when he was working."

"He worked nights at the bank?"

"No, when I was expecting you he had to take a second job, unloading trucks of fruit and vegetables."

"Daddy handled fruits and vegetables?"

"He did it so you wouldn't have to," she said tartly. "Anyway, we used to have a box we hung outside the window to keep things cold. In winter it kept ice cream. When he came back from unloading the trucks, we'd have ice cream, like this, in the middle of the night. It felt very luxurious."

"What flavor did he like?"

"Strawberry." She smiled. "He liked pink."

"Sometimes I go into a drugstore and stand in front of the pipe counter, just to smell the tobacco."

"Would you like to have one of his pipes?"

It hadn't occurred to me that she'd kept them. "Yes, I would."

"You can pick it out tomorrow. They're in the nightstand on his side of the bed." She gave me a sad smile. "His side, my side. No difference anymore. It's so hard to get used to."

"I know. It was so strange to come home and see him lying in that thing. He looked so small. I remember thinking: 'That's not my father!' I thought they'd got the wrong man."

We both stared into our ice cream bowls. After a while, my mother straightened up and went to put the kettle on for tea. Without make-up her skin looked gray and creased like an old paper bag.

"Do you often get up in the middle of the night?" I asked her.

She shrugged. "The older you get, the less you sleep."

"But it's been worse since Daddy died?" The words suddenly made my throat swell shut. Daddy died. They didn't get the wrong man. It was a fact, the one thing I couldn't contradict. There were holes in life that just remain unfilled, huge gaps covered only by thin words like "gone."

My mother slid me a napkin and kept talking. "The nights weren't so bad. All I had to do was lie there and feel it. But when I had to get dressed, do things, answer people, I had to take myself in hand like a small child. I had to say: 'This is the part of your day when you take your shower,' and 'This is the part of your day when you open the mail.' That's how I got myself through." She stirred her tea, though she'd put nothing in it, and squeezed the bag tight against her spoon, wasting not a drop. "It's a hard thing to mourn someone you love. But a harder thing still, I think, to sit shivah for the living."

I felt my face turn to stone. "So how should I feel? He left me."

"That's not what you said before."

"What difference does it make? He's gone. It's over."

"Gone can come back. Over can start again."

"Stop," I said.

"Esther, I spent thirty-five years with your father. You think we never fought? Lucky for all of us a marriage didn't break up so fast in those days. But I used to think every quarrel meant the end. I only wish I'd had a mother to tell me different."

"What do you mean? Your mother was in New York. You could have called her."

She clasped her hands and shook them as if entreating me. "How can I explain? My mother never trusted the telephone — she thought it would give her an electric shock. She cut her hair when she married, she kept two sets of false teeth — one for milk, one for meat. She never looked a man in the eye unless he was a relative. You understand what I'm saying? If I'd told her I was having marital difficulties, she would have said: 'Be a good wife, Lena. Listen to your husband.' " Her eyes filled and she laughed. "You know what she said at the nursing home? She recognized me for a moment and said: 'Nu, Lena, who cooks for your husband and child? You should be ashamed of yourself, leaving your family alone.' "

"Well," I said. "She didn't understand."

My mother sipped her tea, eyeing me. "And is that what you think about me too? I wouldn't understand?" She leaned forward. "You still think I'm going to take away your make-up? Listen, I'll admit it: as a mother I wouldn't win any Peace Prizes. There are things I'd have done differently with a second or third child. I just never got the chance."

I pushed back my chair. "I think it's too late for this."

My mother put her hand on my wrist to keep me at the table. "My mother gave away my dolls when I was twelve, did I ever tell you? It took me years to get over that. I never told her how I felt, because I was afraid of her scorn. I waited all my life for her to ask me about myself, but she never did. That's what 'too late' is. Talk to me."

I put my hand on my belly, which seemed to poke out a little under the nightgown, and tried to imagine my own child sitting here at the table. But all I saw when I closed my eyes was the pale, pudgy, unhappy face from the old photographs upstairs. That gave me a jolt. My mother had lost her dolls at the same age I'd been when she took away my make-up. Now was I going to do the same thing — superimpose myself over the real child, the human apostrophe busily dividing cells within me? We were all of us — my mother and I, the dead and the unborn — caught up in a great chain reaction. Except that my mother was trying to break it: she did not want me to be left with the guilt she'd felt when her own mother died and no real word had passed between them.

I opened my eyes. She was watching me over her teacup with a mixture of exasperation and anxiety. I sat up and forced the muscles in my throat to move.

"When Brent and I talked about getting married — " I began. Her face lit up with hope and I shook my head. "All we did was talk. Mostly about the wedding. He wanted to climb a mountain and have it on the peak. I said if we did that, my parents would have to be lowered by helicopter."

"And you?" she said with interest. "What kind of wedding did you want?"

"City Hall and lunch at the Hyatt," I said. "Sorry."

She waved away the apology. "Go on, go on."

"That's all there is. For him it was just theater, another chance to perform. That was all he cared about. The baby — " I stopped short. My mother nodded encouragingly. "The baby was an accident. A mistake. Brent left because he was tired of me. I don't want to bring him back. You understand now?"

"I understand," she said softly. "You still love him."

"Love?" I said, my voice cracking like a boy's. "I don't know about love."

"How can you not know? I always knew."

"It feels like there's a hole torn out of me. Is that what you mean?"

She knew enough not to put her arms around me, but she came behind my chair and laid a cool hand on my forehead. I leaned back against her, feeling how soft and slack her bosom was beneath her robe. After a moment I got up and took my dish to the sink, bending to peer through the window. The leaves were moving in circles. The whole night seemed to boil with wind. In a great silent wink the sky flashed violet, then white.

"Is the watch still on?" I asked.

"No, now it's a warning. They say a funnel touched down in Glen County." She let out a sigh. "Another reason not to sleep."

"If it touched down in Glen County, it won't touch here."

"Trouble has a mind of its own."

"The Evil Eye?"

"Don't make jokes. Every time they call an All Clear I feel like we've barely escaped disaster. Remember what happened in Turtle Creek? They say you could hear the people screaming a mile away." Then she raised two fingers to her lips and pretended to spit on them. "Shah! Shame on me, frightening a pregnant woman."

"I'm all right."

"*You* are, maybe, but in there —" She pointed. "Who knows the possibilities?"

"I'm sleepy. I'm going up now." I turned to go.

"Esther, listen!" she called after me. "I've been thinking what we should call Volume One."

"Volume One?" I said.

She pointed out the window. "How about *The Tornado Watch Cookbook?* Do you think it would sell?"

"It would in Turtle Creek," I said, already climbing the stairs.

» «

On Friday morning we went to the Good Samaritan nursing home to prepare for the Shabbos dinner we were giving that night to all the residents and staff-members. My mother said she needed the freezer space, but she really just wanted to give a party.

"Like the old days!" she exclaimed when we finished decorating the tables with white cloths and pink net skirtings. At intervals she'd taped pink paper roses and baby's breath, as though this were one of her wedding receptions. We folded napkins into crowns, filled paper cups with grape juice, and arranged flower centerpieces. In the middle of the biggest table she installed the Sabbath candlesticks her mother had brought from Lithuania. "You'll say the blessing, Esther," she said, holding up the embroidered napkin I remembered from so many Kiwanis luncheons.

In the kitchen we made up small plates of gefilte fish trimmed with carrot curls, cherry tomatoes, and radish roses. While I sliced honey-cake and arranged strudel on a platter, my mother tested the piano in the dining hall. She wanted to teach everyone to sing the blessing over the bread. Soon she had an audience of old people, some in wheel-chairs, who had been attracted by the music. My mother sang the blessing for them, then fluffed out her hair and played "Havah Nagi-lah." Then someone asked for "In the Good Old Summertime" and she obliged. The old people sang in thin voices, smiling. Carried away, my mother plunged into "Let Me Call You Sweetheart," bobbing her head in vigorous encouragement, and I wondered if she'd found some-thing here she didn't get when her own mother lay dying and inpene-trable in New York.

As I leaned against the doorway, watching, a small elderly woman shuffled over and introduced herself as Mrs. Zweig. "You're the very image of your mother," she said, clutching my arm and peering through immensely thick glasses. "You must be so proud of each other!"

"Well, if we must," I said, but luckily she was half-deaf as well, and didn't hear.

» «

When everything was ready, we hurried home to bake the challah. It had to be as fresh as possible, my mother said, because it was the most important part of Shabbos dinner. "Bread of the earth," she dictated as I wrote. "Life itself. The secret is adding two spoonfuls of brandy to the dough."

When the dough was high, warm, and fragrant with yeast, we divided it into sections, rolled them between our palms into fat white ropes, and braided them into loaves. When we finished, my mother pulled a bit of dough from one loaf and stuck it on the windowsill.

"What's that for?" I asked.

"To offer the priest."

"Father O'Bannon?"

"No, no. A *cohane*. It's just a symbol."

"But what do you do with it?"

She looked embarrassed. "I bury it. Under the rosebushes."

I put down the notepad. "But Mom, do you really believe this stuff?"

Slowly she brushed egg yolk over the challahs and sprinkled them with poppyseed. "To tell you the truth, I don't know what I really believe or what I partly believe or what I just want to believe. But it's something my mother and grandmother did. It's tradition, it's how I remember, it's what connects me to the past. Jews don't think about heaven—we think about history." Then she added: "We don't just pop into a vacuum, you know."

"I do know," I said.

Just then we heard the rising wail of a siren.

"All Clear," I said.

"For now." She gazed out the window. "Tornado season isn't over yet. We could be swept away still."

"That's true. Better bury that piece of dough."

"Well," said my mother. "It won't hurt the roses."

After cleaning up the kitchen, we sat down to drink tea and smell the bread baking and talk about what to call Volume I. My mother argued passionately for either *The Sabbath Bride Cookbook* or *Heirlooms of the Heart,* but I finally talked her out of both. At last we settled on *The New Jewish Gourmet Traditional Cuisine* because it sounded as if it would sell, and the important thing, after all, was to put a new roof on the shul.

JOANNE GREENBERG

CHILDREN OF JOY

They hadn't changed since I had grown up. The only difference was the one that had always been there: the difference between what they were and the way they appeared in the family stories. My names for them had skipped the generation between. Imah was called "Imah" by my mother and so by me, though she was my grandmother. The other two were my great-aunts, really. Once, impossibly, the aunt across the table had been a flirtatious Hester, dance-mad and party-loving, who had spent a week's wages on ribbons and been beaten for it. She was a large, soft woman now, her hair white and scant.

Next to me, Aunt Ida was sniffing as she tossed a bad nut among the shells on the table. Whenever I saw her, she would enter something new into the catalogue of her illnesses: "conditions." I couldn't see or imagine the girl who had been arrested and jailed for inciting a mob to riot, and that at a time when women, especially immigrant women, did not command attention.

Imah herself must have been other things before she was my grandmother, but in 1890 people must have been different, born old, with only their bodies to age after that.

"I can feel the cold through the walls," Aunt Ida said.

Imah sighed. "I'll go turn up the thermostat."

"Thermostats don't make real heat." But Imah got up and went out of the kitchen and the aunts adjusted dutiful expressions on their faces.

"Enjoying your vacation?" Aunt Hester asked me.

"Yes. Before you came, Imah was telling me about the days in the old country, in Zoromin."

"A waste of time," Aunt Ida said. "Hitler chewed it up, but on its best day, in a good year, it wasn't anything to begin with."

I was shocked. "How can you say that when family life was so much closer, when the air was clean and the rivers and streams were unpolluted, when people ate natural foods and were so much richer spiritually than we are today?''

They looked at each other in what I could have sworn was confusion.

"I don't think they heard about all that in Zoromin," Aunt Hester said. "About the water—well, the women washed clothes in it, the horses drank, the tanner dumped into it. About clean water they didn't hear in Zoromin."

"At least things were what they seemed to be," I said. "You didn't look at everything through a plastic package. People, too. People were what they seemed to be, not packages with an 'image.' You didn't grow food for looks but for nourishment. People remember the old-fashioned cooking and that's why."

"Oh, *that* cooking," Imah said, having come back and seated herself. She grinned and her hand went up to her mouth. Aunt Ida caught her eye and turned away, biting her lip. "Old-fashioned. . . . " And then the three of them began to laugh.

I had gotten up to make more tea. I turned from the stove to look at them, chuckling comfortably above their bosoms.

"What's funny? What's the joke?"

They looked at me and laughed again, Aunt Ida checking the slipping wig she hadn't worn for years.

"You poor girl," Imah said. "You grew up in such a good home, you didn't have time to learn the simplest truths."

"It isn't her fault," and Aunt Ida wiped a crumb from her cheek. I came back to the table and began to clear a place among the nuts and shells. "Listen," Ida went on, and impaled my arm with a forefinger. "First is a family so poor that there is no piece of cloth without a hole. Our father traveled, following the breezes of other men's moving. He sent money in years that ended with two and seven. We saw him coming and going when the road bent that way or when business was bad. Of course, we had our own work, painting the lead soldiers. All of us. I thought you knew about that."

"Yes, but what does it have to do with cooking?"

She shook her head and clucked, then looked at me and shook her head again. "God help us! What has happened to the Jewish mind?

There *was* no cooking, only hunger. We ate potatoes and weak soup, and if you're hungry enough, it's a banquet."

"But Uncle Reuben says—"

"Now there," Aunt Hester said, "walks a sage. To this day, if a thing doesn't give him heartburn, he thinks it wasn't worth eating."

Imah shook her head. "What cook can match herself against hunger and memory?"

Aunt Hester said, "We all carry a dream about Mama's chicken. If they set to music what we feel and remember of that chicken, Beethoven would be a forgotten article altogether."

Ida mused, "I think I know which chicken it was. It was the big one the Nachmansons gave us when they left to come to America."

"Tell me something," Imah asked. "What did it taste like, that chicken?"

"How should I know?" Hester shrugged. "We had to save it for Papa and the boys. By the time they finished, there wasn't anything left."

"I don't think I had any either," Ida said. "You see"—and she turned to me—"the chicken we didn't eat is the one we remember. That chicken is always tender."

"You're both ashamed to tell me." Imah insisted. "People took pieces of that chicken when it was still cooking."

"I didn't touch it," Hester said. "Not a shred."

Imah smiled. "Was I the only one? I thought maybe someone else did too. . . ."

"You little no-good, you! And Mama blamed Izzy!"

"Well, if you ate it, why did you ask what it tasted like?"

"Because I was so frightened, I just pushed it into my mouth and swallowed it and never tasted anything."

Ida asked, "If it was such a big chicken, how come there wasn't enough for us?"

"Wasn't there someone else?" Imah murmured. "I seem to remember—"

"My God, you're right!" Hester cried. "The Saint's children came!" Her eyes sparkled and she sat smiling over this lost moment found among all the million since.

"It was an honor, the Saint's children. We must have invited them to come and eat with us—it wasn't often we could invite someone for Shabbes dinner. That was why there wasn't enough. . . . "

Her eyes were full of warmth. She turned to me. "Our Saint was a wonderful man. We looked up to him, you have no idea; more than a scholar. People used to quote him like Torah. . . . " Then she waved at herself deprecatingly. "Such a man, and look how I forgot him. I wonder where his children are now."

"His name was Simcha," Imah explained to me. "It means joy. People used to call his sons the 'Children of Joy.' "

"What a crew!" Ida said. "They were boils on the backside of Zoromin. I wonder on what backside they are boils now?"

"Ida, how can you say such a thing!" Heads came up, Imah and Hester's mouths widening in unison.

"What, did I spit on something holy, that you should look so stunned? Your Saint was a madman who starved his wife and beggared his children. If it's all the same to you, I won't waste clearing my throat to bless him."

"It isn't right to talk that way," Imah said, motioning toward me. "Your talk is only confusing. It's enough the gentiles have stopped trying to tear down Judaism and left the job to Jews, who do it better."

Ida had her fire up. "Who said anything about Judaism? If that lunatic is Judaism, you can write me off the list—I'll dip myself tomorrow." She sat back, cracking righteously. Shells and nutmeats showered from her hands.

"Aunt Ida thinks he was crazy," I said to Hester, who was sulking. "What makes you think he was a saint?"

"I'll tell you," Aunt Hester said, "and afterwards, Ida can have her say. I'll tell you the facts and you can judge for yourself. Zoromin has nothing to be ashamed of, and neither do the Jewish people. There was, in our town, in Zoromin, a very pious and saintly man—"

"That's facts?" Ida crowed.

"I *said,* a very pious and saintly man. Originally, the family was well off—or as well off as anyone gets in a town like that. Anyway, Simcha was raised with a warm coat in winter and a full belly and good, dry shoes. . . ."

"What a pity his children weren't as well off as he. . . . ' "

"Ida. . . . "

"All right, go on."

"I don't know how it happened, but it was soon after he was married (a beautiful girl from a fine family. How she loved him and looked up to him!). Anyway, out of a clear sky, he came home one day, Godstruck, changed. That day he gave away all his fine things, opened his house to the poor, and declared himself a refuge for anyone who was needy. During the day he walked miles, visiting the sick and hungry. Any penny extra went to the poor. He became even more pious than he had been before, and shamed many people who were more comfortable into being better Jews by his example.

"Well, his wife gave birth, and on each occasion he gave a party — not for the relatives, but for the poor, whose tongues didn't touch a piece of butter cake from one year to the next. His Sabbaths were like the Sabbaths angels must have; his door was never closed.

"I remember most of all, his gentleness. The men in Zoromin worked like animals, sixteen, seventeen hours a day, in little shops, or walking town to town to sell, at the mercy of any robber or policeman on the way. Their lives and spirits became twisted because of it." She made a twisting motion with her old fingers.

"These men weren't gentle with their wives and they had no time to be loving to their children, or to say a pleasant word. What if they whipped a child by mistake and found it out later? They never apologized to that child or admitted the wrong, and if the child . . ."

Suddenly she was that child who had always been waiting for the incident to be found again, the anger and despair fresh although the cause had passed seventy years, and the father and the mistake and the town itself were no more. Weren't the old supposed to have forgiven everything long ago?

It frightened me a little. Maybe it frightened her, too, because she turned from it quickly and hunted her thought again.

"It was no easy place, Zoromin, but there was one man there who would pick up a child who fell in the mud, and brush its clothes off and comfort it. There was one man who would notice if a woman's basket was too heavy and would help her.

"There were women, certain women, Ida, if you remember, who lived outside of town, and our people didn't count them as Jewish women, although we knew one of them was the cobbler's own cousin. These women had no one and nothing and our women spat at them in the streets. Simcha invited these women to his Sabbaths too; and when they were sick, he sent his own wife to nurse them. He used to say, 'The poor should not be denied the blessing of giving,' and he sent money to Jerusalem in their name."

While Hester talked, I looked at Imah and saw her following with an intense look, her lips moving slightly with the words.

"Did you know this Simcha?" I asked her.

"Yes, yes," she said a little vaguely. "I heard of him as a very good man, a very saintly man." She seemed to be listening and answering to something else.

Aunt Ida had been gathering in silence. "Well, don't worry about a place in heaven for that man," she said. "If there is a heaven, he's too good for it altogether; but for the Sages of Zoromin, he was just right. Can you imagine"—and she waved at Aunt Hester—"a grandmother there, and still an innocent. Hester, you don't know any more now than you did when you were ten.

"*He* was the Saint, that Simcha, and his family, who weren't saints, were only cold, hungry and a burden on the town. Watch out for saints, Hester; they eat more than you think. When the Saint decrees that his wealth be given to the poor, somebody has to stand baking all those little bread rolls that are given out of his great love. He says, 'Don't hand the beggar food at the door; ask him in, for he is your brother.' Someone has to clean the cups and the table and the floor after the visit of a hundred brothers. Someone has to fill the house of hungry stomachs with the smell of baking bread. The Saint's clothes are ragged, but he won't get new ones. Which is easier, I ask you—to darn a threadbare coat or to make a new one? Someone has to fix and fix again that saintly garment, and draw the Saint's frown when she curses old cloth that won't hold a needle!

"For heaven's sake, Hester, why do you think the Children of Joy were with us to eat that chicken? Reb Simcha knew he could be rich if he chose; he thought his children had the same choice he did. Those boys could hear a meat bone being dropped into soup half a mile away. If a man brushed a crumb from his beard, there was their knock on his door. . . . And why not? They were starving."

"What are you saying?" Hester looked scornfully at her sister. "That God should run to Zoromin to do the baking? The horror you speak of was that the saintly man drew his wife and children into his sanctity and caused them to do pious things—"

"Without the choice!" Ida cried.

"Aha!" Hester leaped up, her face glowing. Sixty of her years had fallen away, sixty pounds and all the chins and all the knotted veins that contended in her legs, and all the thousand compromises of a lifetime. "Where did that leave them then? Why, with all the rest of Zoromin! Without a choice, hungry and cold, and wondering if the prayer has always to be drowned by the rumbling in the belly. But . . ." (My God, she *had* been beautiful! The old, brown family photographs had missed it all, standing her up dead like an apple in a fruit dish; but she had been dancing with all those bright ribbons, and it was more than the ribbons her father had beaten her for. It had been the headlong, headstrong, passionate eagerness he must have seen in her.)

"With our Simcha, they had a look, Ida, a little minute's venture into the way people should be, the way the holy books tell them to be. Those men, the ordinary men of Zoromin—to them the Torah was only rules, and they never asked why: Wear tefillin, or God will strike you. Don't blow out a candle on the Sabbath or God will cripple you. In that poor place we had a holy man walking, alive, to show the people that a man is not an animal, that there is more than hunger and rules for what is forbidden!"

"And the people saw glory in this one-man Eden, this walking paradise in Zoromin? They did not. They were smarter than you think, Hester. They knew that a poor man gives less charity than a rich one, and that Simcha's children should have been his charity. They weren't exalted, Hester, they laughed at him and despised his wife and children. 'Children of Joy' was a bitter title; as bitter as 'Chosen People' in those days. We were all Children of Joy in Zoromin, singing in the synagogue and starving."

"If the world knew virtue when it saw virtue, wouldn't *men* be Torah? Some didn't laugh at him, Ida. I didn't laugh. Didn't we have hard years after Zoromin? Didn't we need the memory of goodness? He was good, a saint."

"A madman. If Zoromin had been rich enough to build a madhouse, he would have had the master bedroom."

"A saint!"

"A madman!"

"Don't you see?" Imah cried at them as they stood tightfaced, shouting against each other. "He's only mad in English, not in Yiddish. He . . . the *English* makes him mad; in Yiddish he's still a saint!"

Their anger had overflowed their bodies, and suddenly, without reason, it found a home in me. I found myself grinding out words from a source I hadn't known was in me.

"What kind of people are you," I cried. "You had everything my friends and I admire, and you threw it away. You had all the security of the ceremonies and beliefs, lives full of meaning, dignity, and reality. That's what I came to Imah for, to find out how it was lost, the wonderful home life, when parents and children knew how to be loving and peaceful with one another; when there was the simple truth, not like today, all clouded and complicated. And now you've been so perverted by false values and materialism, you can't even remember what the old days were like!" Then, impossibly, "Haven't you any respect for your elders!"

Dead silence. . . . Then a first, small edge of sound from Hester. The edge broke, and then the others came laughing in behind and in the end they conquered me and took me with them, defeated and captive in laughter.

"At least," Ida gasped, "she can still make Jewish jokes." We laughed till tears ran down our faces.

"Zoromin was a poor village," Ida wept. "Maybe they were too poor to afford a real saint."

"After all," Imah wept, "without some saint or other, what would people do?"

"I want saints," I wept, "but I want real ones."

"Who could afford it but Americans?" Hester was gasping. "Listen, when a woman can't have diamonds, she wears rhinestones; and when she can't have rhinestones, she wears glass and holds up her head."

"Is it true—did you mean it when you said that a man can be a saint in Yiddish and a madman in English?"

"If not," Imah said, and got up to get a Kleenex, "wouldn't we all be saints?"

"Then the dream of America was a fantasy—the hope was a lie!"

"American!" Aunt Hester said affectionately, and blew into her handkerchief. "Who would imagine, in so little time, our family would have such Americans?" She gazed at me with deep pride. "Look at her, she doesn't understand a single thing! . . . Oh, my knee aches so, I think I've been sitting in a draft!"

MARSHA LEE BERKMAN

DEEDS OF LOVE
AND RAGE

We are a troubled family. Ephraim left three months ago and Cecilia and I have had to confront each other like enemies who suddenly find themselves at the same party. Yesterday we quarreled and today, dressed in a pair of faded blue denim shorts and a yellow T-shirt that says "Foxy" in flowery iridescent letters, she moves through the house sulking. She is the only thing in motion on this hot sultry day.

My only child. . . . Her dark uncombed hair straggles around a thin face and sad thirteen-year-old eyes swollen from lack of sleep. Last night through the flimsy walls of our apartment, I heard her weeping, and this morning her whole face slumps in sorrow and rage. It is all my fault. I can see it in the frown that bridges her forehead. If only I would make concessions, try harder, her father would come back. And so we are doomed to this summer that continues to stretch endlessly before us, a time that hardly seems to be real at all but just a series of minutes, hours, days to be gotten through and endured together. How we have begun to dislike each other. By the end of summer Ephraim and I shall come to a decision for the sake of the child, but now we are still wavering back and forth. Yes, I can tell from the way her black eyes glow with a fierce fury: She is as tired of me as I am of her.

» «

At the beginning of June Ephraim packed up his bags and took an apartment and a job on the other side of the city. He does not have enough space, he says. How foreign that word sounds on his tongue. We had begun to chip each other into little bits and pieces. Ephraim will not admit it, but sometimes I think it was the strain of the child.

As a baby she was perpetually restless and moody. She came into the world too soon, bounding feet first from the womb. I had nothing prepared. No, not even her name. I had to snatch that also without thought. She cried day and night, refusing any of the usual things, and Ephraim and I would take turns rising from our sleep, moaning with fatigue, too tired to comfort each other for this strange being who had taken over our lives.

Thirteen years and still she remains a puzzle to me, her moods flashing back and forth, a mood for every moment of the day. A look, a remark, or some dark demon within can change her in an instant. I was too old to have her. Yes, I am certain it must be that. But Ephraim is a religious man. He used to say that suffering cleanses the soul, that burdens are to be borne.

"It is a sign," he said then, clasping his heavy hands together, closing and unfolding them nervously, considering it. To Ephraim there is a purpose in the world that escapes me. There are things that we are not supposed to understand. He prefers the difficult to the simple, certain that God is testing him. He was not any easy man to live with.

This morning when Cecilia asks if her father is coming for the Sabbath, which begins at sundown, I tell her that it is hopeless. "Your father is impossible," I blurt out in a weak moment, saying it passionately, throwing up my hands in a gesture of despair. I can hear my voice rising unpleasantly, and as soon as the words are out of my mouth, I am sorry. But it is already too late.

She turns on me. "Bitch," she says without a sound, mouthing the letters with her lips. At first I ignore her. It is far too hot to respond, to become embroiled in another one of these arguments. Anyhow, what would be the use? Let her vent her wrath on me. Let her get it out of her system, think that her father's absence is my fault. What harm can it do? But then she says it again, and this time she whispers it, but loudly enough to hear the ugly sound reverberate in the room.

"Bitch," she says a third time, growing bolder. The word explodes from her mouth, chilling me to the bone although the sun is seeping resolutely through the drapes and the room is sweltering with the heat.

"Bitch," she says again and again, unable to stop, her face contorted with rage. I feel my heart beating faster within the cage of my body, fluttering against the armor of my bones, and rising, I slap her face, so hard that it stings my hand and leaves an ugly red mark on her skin.

She runs to her room and the door slams shut. I can hear the click of her lock snapping closed, then loud sobs as she gasps for breath. I imagine her flung sideways across her bed, her hair falling wildly over the edge, beating the pillow with her tight closed fists and suddenly I am filled with pity for her and shame for myself.

Through the long hours of the morning she remains in retreat and will not come out. Finally I pound on the door and order her to open it, but the only sound is the steady whirring of a fan. Frightened that she has done something rash, racked with guilt that I have lost control, I take a hanger and, bending it, work diligently at the keyhole until at last I swing open the door.

She has stopped crying but her face is splotched with red and there is still an angry imprint where my hand crossed her cheek. She is pouting on the bed, her eyes puffy, her lower lip thrust forward. She will not even look at me. The curtains are drawn against the heat and in the dim shadowed light of the room I see that she has strewn candy wrappers over the floor. An empty Coke bottle sprawls on its side against the dresser. A lonely sock protrudes beneath the bed. A trail of dirty clothes trace a path through the room and end in a corner next to stacks of *True Confession* magazines littering the rug.

"Come out," I say as calmly as I am able, swallowing hard for what we have done to each other, what we continue to do. "We'll make up. Everything will be all right." I try to appear more confident than I really am. "You're only hurting yourself, you know." The words sound as hollow and meaningless as when my own mother uttered them, and I am aware that this sort of logic will never reach her.

"Look," I say, trying to keep my voice steady. "It has nothing to do with you." I keep my eyes fixed firmly on her face although she continues to stare stubbornly at the floor. "It's between your father and me."

At last she lifts heavy lids to look up defiantly. A difficult age, I think, and she is more difficult than most. Beneath that yellow T-shirt with the ludicrous letters, her breasts rise as supple as ripe fruit. Under her arms I see black prickly hair sprouting like desert scrub. She will not let me see her naked anymore. Once I came into the room, catching her by surprise, and saw with a shock that triangle of womanly hair on her body. Now we stare at each other without speaking.

Suddenly overcome with remorse, I long to tell her that I am sorry but the moment passes and instead I say nothing. I retreat and she rises mournfully to take a shower.

» «

When I hear the water running full force, I decide to call Ephraim. He is an engineer, capable of correcting the errors of vast machinery. Perhaps it is still possible for him to correct the errors of our lives. I dial his number at work and he answers the phone himself, startling me, as though he has been standing there all along, arms crossed over his chest in a familiar posture, waiting for me to call.

"Ephraim," I begin, without bothering to ask how he is, "come home tonight. We are eating each other alive."

"On Sunday," he says wearily, for we have been through this before. Ephraim refuses to come on Friday for Shabbes. It is too far he says. He is afraid that something will happen before he gets here and he will have to travel after sundown when it is forbidden. A thousand and one disasters pass through his mind. The car will stall and leave him stranded. A train could have an accident, God forbid. A bus could be hijacked on the highway (he has read of it happening), and he will be caught as night falls and the Sabbath descends without a prayer to stand on.

"Too late," I say. "By Sunday we'll both be dead."

"Don't worry," he answers solemnly as though he hasn't even heard me. "I will pray for us." Suddenly I can see him standing in the fading light, his prayer shawl draped over his shoulders, a skullcap on his balding dome—at dawn, at dusk, in heat or cold, swaying and rocking on the balls of his feet, summoning the God of Israel, communing with his Maker. He is in the wrong century, I think, the wrong life. He should have been Abraham journeying beneath a starry sky, Moses adrift in the wilderness, Jeremiah making his lonely vigil through the desolate city of Jerusalem.

"Ephraim, Ephraim," I plead, desperation overtaking my voice. "Live a little! Take a chance. What harm can it do?" But he is older, more set in his ways. I can hear him sighing and struggling with himself.

"Yes, I'll pray," he repeats again, but he sounds exhausted, as though what is happening to us is all too much for him.

"What good will your prayers do? What good is your God?" I cry, aware that I am beginning to descend over the edge. Then I decide on another tactic and this time my voice is softer, cajoling, "Come home, Ephraim," I say, "I need you. I want you."

I can almost hear the catch in his voice, the hesitation as he thinks it through.

"For the child, Ephraim," I persist.

"It is too difficult," he murmurs at last.

"Ah, Ephraim," I say, "*life* is difficult," but he has made up his mind. He is firm, refusing to commit himself. "For shame," I cry, and slam down the phone.

Tonight, tomorrow he will not even answer it. Once I let the phone ring a hundred times just to test him, knowing that he was there, swaying silently in the dark. Cecilia calls him late at night when she thinks I am asleep. I can hear her whispering about me, telling him how hard it is for us to get along, how she wishes he would come back. Now, hearing footsteps, I wonder if she has been standing there all along. I turn on the tap and quickly splash my burning face with cold water. But even so I can feel myself flushing as though she has caught me in a disreputable act. Her eyes are red and rimmed with fatigue but she has changed her clothes, and clipped her wet hair back from her forehead. Yet the place where I struck her continues to stain her cheek, forming a barrier between us. She says nothing, her face an impassive mask. Perhaps she has not heard anything after all and it is only my imagination which tortures me.

"Come," I say, trying to make the best of a bad day. "It's time to get ready for Shabbes." Before the sun sets we must clean the house, polish the silver, cook the dinner and bake the bread. In these matters Ephraim has trained her well. She obeys me silently, without a word of complaint. I uncover the dough that we prepared earlier, and we take out the bread tray and the silver candlesticks that need polishing. On the shelf next to them a sad solitary imprint marks the spot where Ephraim's wine cup stood.

She places a board on the kitchen table and her fingers move deftly

over the dough, pounding and kneading it into shape, her face color-
ing with the heat, her eyes intent on her task. At last she twists it into
thick braids to slip into the oven, pinching off a piece which she burns
in an ancient ritual, closing her eyes and moving her lips in silent
supplication as she has seen me do. What does she yearn for behind
those sorrowful eyes? What thoughts does she think? For the past year
she has suffered with nightmares that wake her up screaming in the
middle of the night, as though striving to be released from some dread
torment that will not leave her alone. In the morning when I come into
her room I see her sheets twisted into knots, as though demons have
tied them during the night.

"A stage," the doctor says, but I know better. She has always been
this way. Now just more so. Sometimes I think that when I am old and
defenseless, unable to take care of myself, I will have to live with her
and then she will vent her stored-up rage upon my helpless body like
that dough beneath her hands.

I want to say, "Tell me what you're thinking, Cecilia," but she is far
away, her gaze focusing on something else, caught in a web of her own
thoughts.

Yesterday to calm us both I prepared a picnic supper to take to the
park. Other families were there, too, and we spread a blanket on the
grass and had cold slices of roast beef and potato salad. When the ice
cream man came around we bought cherry popsicles and sat at the
edge of the playground to eat them. Children were swinging, and
watching them, Cecilia decided to pump her own skinny legs high
over the sand boxes, soaring higher and higher until her face was filled
with a strange gentle joy. Afterward, she sat very close to me and laid
her her head upon my shoulder, her eyes tranquil, her expression
subdued. But by evening it was obvious that she was brooding. We
quarreled, and later I heard her crying until I finally turned over and
fell asleep.

She is still working soundlessly as the heat builds to a peak of
intensity and I pause to step outside on our small balcony,where we
have some hanging plants that are rapidly wilting, and two old porch
chairs that Ephraim keeps meaning to paint. We are on a quiet street
at the very end of a cul-de-sac, and an occasional car, coming down
here by mistake, will turn around beneath our porch. But now there is

not a sign of life. Across the street windows are sleepy lids, blinds and drapes closed against the broiling sun. The heat is suffocating. From next door I hear the blast of a TV, then a muffled sound as it is quickly turned down. But it is not only the heat which suffocates me. It is the knowledge of what has become of the three of us, of what we are doing to each other.

When I go back into the house Cecilia is still intent on her tasks. She raises her head and looks at me suspiciously without saying anything. The kitchen has become unbearably hot, the sun pouring through the curtains onto the linoleum floor, the futile beating of a fan on top of the refrigerator the only noise that breaks the silence. I join her and we work side by side without uttering a word. Beads of perspiration gather on her forehead and above her upper lip, and I wonder again what she is thinking behind those inscrutable eyes.

"Cecilia," I long to say. "Let's make up, let's not fight," but something holds me back. Her mouth is pursed tightly together, her jaw clenched, and I decide not to say anything.

Instead, I open the oven and take out the bread, setting it on the counter to cool. It is dark brown, the top of the braids blackened slightly at the tips, and she glances approvingly at it. For a moment she seems about to speak, but then stops as though pride still prevents her. I season the chicken and put it in to roast. The sun continues to splash across the kitchen in waves of heat. I stop to take a bath and nap before dinner, and still we have not spoken since morning.

　　»«

When I appear an hour later I see that she has spread a white cloth upon the table and set out the best dishes and silver, placing the candlesticks in the center. Over the mound of fragrant bread is a green and gold embroidered cover Cecilia made one summer at camp with the word Sabbath in Hebrew. She has changed again, this time into a clean white blouse and white shorts, and her hair is tied back with a light blue ribbon. I am wearing a long print skirt and a colorful top I bought one year in Mexico, and my hair, which is beginning to thread with gray at the sides, is pinned on top of my head with a large tortoise-shell clip.

I turn off the fan and open the windows, drawing back the curtains. For the first time in days the heat has begun to break. A cool breeze stirs the material and they flutter lightly against the screens. Before the sun is ready to disappear behind the tops of the houses like an angry red eye, I light the candles and stand before them, arms upraised to say the blessing that ushers in the day of rest. Cecilia takes her place next to me and even though my eyes are closed I can feel her hands circling the air next to mine, drawing the Sabbath closer.

"A good Shabbes," I say, forcing myself to reach out and put my arms around her shoulders, but her spine stiffens at my touch. Her body remains rigid and she averts her somber pupils from mine, her front teeth biting down hard on the middle of her lower lip.

I set the dinner on the table and then we both sit down, neither of us wanting to acknowledge Ephraim's empty place at the head of the table. Memory recalls his strong blunt hands above Cecilia's bowed head, intoning the patriarchal blessing that always brings such a strange quiet joy to her face.

In his absence I say a prayer of thanksgiving over the bread, breaking it apart with my hands, and then we eat it in thick chunks, greedily, suddenly ravenous.

"It's good," I say. "*Very* good," and she blushes with the praise, her tan cheeks turning rosy beneath the surface.

"Do you really think so?" she asks, and her expression changes as she speaks to me for the first time since morning. "You're not just saying that?"

"No. Really. It's good," I say again and I can see that she is pleased. A slight smile passes over her lips and like soldiers on a battlefield it is clear that we have decided to call a truce for the holiday.

But then, in spite of myself, I remark bitterly, "It's a pity your father couldn't be here to taste it."

For the second time that day I am sorry as soon as the words are out of my mouth. A look of pain crosses her face and her eyes linger longingly on the candles. "But he's coming Sunday, isn't he?" she asks intensely.

"Yes," I say. "Of course. On Sunday." I say it calmly this time to reassure her and perhaps myself as well. It seems to sustain the two of us, and we relax and begin to eat with relish. Gradually a strong breeze gathers outside and blows through the room, releasing us, and it appears that the weight of thirteen years does not rest as heavily on her shoulders. The muted light of the candles catches her features in an unexpected expression, and I am startled to see that it is Ephraim's face before me.

As we eat, lengthening shadows fall over the walls in ghostly shapes. Darkness enfolds us, broken only by the bright headlights flooding the living room when they come to the dead end of our apartment.

Cecilia's brow is furrowed in concentration above the slender bridge of her nose. We make desultory talk and I think how far away we are from each other. At last I set out two melons for dessert and crushed grape ices that we spoon into the hollowed centers of the fruit.

We linger for a while longer, still not speaking, and then I clear off the table while she rises to help, thrusting her arms into the soapy dishwater.

She hands me the dishes and I dry them, placing them one by one on the white counter as we work silently, the light of the candles finally sputtering to a close. The smell of burnt wax fills the air. A full moon illuminates Cecilia's slight figure and I see that the red mark on her cheek is nearly gone.

When we finish I hang up the towel to dry and our glances meet as she turns to go. How fragile she looks, how young, I think, so that I yearn to cry out to her as she disappears into the hushed darkness of the hallway. I am filled with a rush of love for her. Flesh of my flesh. Bones of my bone. Then, as though she has read my mind, suddenly she returns and standing on her tiptoes, kisses me goodnight. "Mother, I'm sorry," she says, and then just as quickly she is gone.

On Sunday Ephraim will come and perhaps things will work out after all. Who knows? But for a while at least in the stillness of this moment there is peace. At last there is peace. And tomorrow or the next day anything seems possible now, anything at all.

LAURIE COLWIN

A BIG STORM
KNOCKED IT OVER

Jane Louise Parker sat at her drawing board in her office on a summer day. Everyone was out at lunch and the telephones were quiet. She had been fiddling with a calendar and a pencil trying to figure out exactly when she would give birth to the baby she had learned she was pregnant with just that morning. She and her husband, Teddy, had gone to the doctor who had confirmed their suspicions. According to the doctor, her due date was February 20. According to Jane Louise's private calculations, it was February 10, or perhaps March 6. Each time she added, it came out different. Was it February or March, forty weeks, nine months, or what?

The idea of a baby was at the moment as remote as Saturn. Jane Louise looked entirely unchanged—a tall, skinny person, she did not seem five minutes pregnant although she was in fact six weeks gone. Her doctor had showed her a color picture of a translucent little salamander. That was what had taken up residence inside her.

She and Teddy had gone from the doctor's to an early lunch, where they had decided not to tell anyone. They were going away in August and wanted their secret to themselves. By the time they came back from vacation, this pregnancy would be quite apparent. Then Jane Louise would have to start thinking of the ten million things associated with babies— maternity leave, layettes, baby-sitters and so forth. For now, she simply wanted to be pregnant, which seemed to her a state like suspended animation. When she passed a mirror she realized she was wearing a strange grin—a kind of an involuntary smile.

She and Teddy were a study in opposites. He was a scientist, a chemist. She was an artist, a book designer at a publishing house and an illustrator. She was dark. Teddy was fair. He had been brought up in the Anglican communion, and his mother, a demon gardener, often did the flower arrangements at her church. Jane Louise was an assimilated Jewess. The truth was, she did not know how to *be* a Jew, although she knew how to feel like one. Teddy would be able to take their child to church and sing his way through the service. What would Jane Louise do? Cringe in the back of the synagogue, ashamed that she had never learned Hebrew?

She looked up. There in the hallway, talking on one of the secretaries' phones, was her boss, the art director, Sven Michaelson. Although Jane Louise could not bring herself to approve of him, he had undeniable magnetism. He was built on the principle of the conservation of energy, like a good canoe: trim, lean, compact. He had sandy hair, pale, cold eyes and beautiful clothes. According to him, he had been the hero of a number of novels by good-looking female writers. The streets of New York, it was said, were littered with his conquests. He was the result of the union of a Jewish father and a Danish mother. He himself was on his third marriage and had children from each wife. "A family for every decade is my motto," Sven liked to say.

Several weeks after Jane Louise had been hired, after Sven had time to size her up, he took her out to lunch.

"I wonder what it will be like when we wake up together," he had said. His caressing voice seemed to have curled up in her ear.

Jane Louise knew then what she ought to have said: "You mean when we fall asleep on the bus coming back from the sales conference?" But she did not. Jane Louise was neither in the bloom of youth nor in the exhaustion of age. Lots and lots of lyrical and ridiculous things had been said to her by men. She knew that Sven did not like to leave a stone unturned and that she was another stone. He would wear her down like water over rock until she gave in. If she ever slept with him he would behave the next day as if nothing had happened, as if she were insane and had made the whole thing up.

Despite this, she realized as she watched him on the telephone that she was admiring the line of his leg. Now that she was a pregnant woman, she felt she ought to stop having impure thoughts.

Until she met Teddy, Jane Louise had always thought of herself as somewhat boy-crazy, although she tried as hard as possible to behave herself. Nevertheless, she had had every possible kind of romance: the kind in which you love them better than they love you; in which they love you better than you love them; in which you love them madly and can't stand to be in the same room with them. Then she met Teddy—

the light at the end of the tunnel—and saw that you could love someone *and* marry him.

Teddy was heaven. He had about him a kind of inspired simplicity. The only complication in his life had been his parents' divorce, but that had happened when he was twenty-one, and his lovely character had already been formed. He liked to get right down to the heart of things and he did not believe that information caused pain or trouble. He was an industrial chemist working for a firm that manufactured and invented nontoxic alternatives to household products such as paint, varnish and furniture polish.

He did not have identity problems or spiritual difficulties; often he hardly seemed like a modern person. He certainly did *not* have impure thoughts about louche types he worked with, but then where he worked there were no louche types.

» «

This summer, Jane Louise was in the midst of designing a number of books, and one of them was a big problem. It was an enormous anthology entitled *The Literature of Nature*, with illustrations. The anthologist was a sweet-looking person named Martin Barlow (whose wife, Nicolette, had done the woodcuts). Martin Barlow was also under contract for three novels about country life: *A Big Storm Knocked It Over*, *Marauding Dogs Will Eat It* and *Snow Makes Everything White*. He was considered a hot literary ticket, and the house had high hopes for him. Jane Louise had already chosen the type for *A Big Storm Knocked It Over*, on the first page of which, a girl says to a boy, "I'd like to bite into you like a grape."

Martin Barlow's colossal anthology was divided by landscape categories: fen, heath, moor, meadow, field, bog, swamp, dale and so on. Since the integrity of the book was of great importance to him, he would not accept so much as a sentence cut without the designer.

The Monday after Jane Louise discovered she was pregnant, Martin Barlow sat in her office giving her a hard time.

"Do we need all these pages on marl?" Jane Louise had asked, thinking that the editorial director, Erna Hendershot, should have taken care of this. Erna, however, had said, "He'll let me edit his *novels,* but he says this is a design problem," and left for France with her large family.

"It isn't just marl," Martin Barlow was saying. "It's also morain, and there isn't very much in literature about either of them."

"Well, can't we cut a little of the desert? There's an awful lot about that."

"It's very obscure, terrific stuff," Martin Barlow said rather petulantly. "This isn't your ordinary E.T. Lawrence. This is *art.* Besides, I don't want the balance disturbed."

Jane Louise could understand why you would want to bite into somebody like a grape. In Martin Barlow's case, however, she thought a good nip, like that of an angry terrier, would be more appropriate.

After he left, Jane Louise was exhausted. She slumped over her desk waiting for the delicatessen to deliver her lemonade.

"How'd it go?" Sven asked, appearing in her doorway. He was wearing her jacket.

"He's a mule," Jane Louise said.

"Your shirt's unbuttoned. Is that how you got him to agree to cuts? Nice underwear, though. Coral. I must get some for Edwina."

Edwina was his third wife, mother of little Piers.

"Is this your jacket or your hub's?" Sven asked. He disentangled himself from the jacket and hung it carefully over her chair. Jane Louise realized what a mistake it had been to tell Sven that she and Teddy shared clothes. Now Sven often remarked that he and Jane Louise wore the same size. "I borrowed it to go to a meeting," he said.

"It's mine," Jane Louise answered.

"It's nice," Sven said. "Sort of like wearing *you.*"

Sven also liked to drink out of her coffee cup. This form of sharing was the deprived man's substitute for other forms of contact, he often said.

» «

Every lunchtime Sven disappeared for about two hours. For a year Jane Louise had assumed it was his analytic session. Adele, his secretary, had other thoughts.

"Sometimes he has a business lunch," she said. "But mostly I think he meets girls. You know what I mean?"

"Do I know what you mean?" Jane Louise echoed.

"Yes, you do," Adele said. "He likes it with two girls."

"Really!" Jane Louise said. "How ever do you know that?"

"I heard him on the phone telling this girl to bring a friend."

"Maybe he meant a friend for a friend of his," Jane Louise said.

"Sven doesn't have friends," Adele said. "Maybe he plays poker with some guys. You see how he is in meetings with Al and Dave. They sort of don't exist for him."

"They seem to like Sven."

"They don't even notice," Adele said.

» «

July crawled by. Each day Jane Louise thought she was getting a little more pregnant. The little salamander had not made his or her presence felt in the slightest, except for a slight queasiness in the early morning. It was hard to believe that sometime before the spring sales conference, she would have a real, live baby with fingernails and a personality.

She took Adele aside one day, swore her to secrecy and told her that she was going to have a baby. Adele was engaged to a person named Phil. Marriage, birth and Sven were her three topics.

"Sven'll swoon when he finds out," Adele said. "Or maybe you haven't heard him on the subject of pregnant women."

Jane Louise felt as if she were in a speeding elevator.

"What *are* his thoughts about pregnant women?" she asked. "He hasn't shared them with me."

"Oh, he respects you. To me he says any old thing," Adele said. "He once told me, 'My fantasy is to enter a room full of women, all of whom are pregnant with my child.'"

"Hmm."

"So watch it," Adele said. "He goes for your type."

"What does that mean about Edwina?" Jane Louise said. Edwina was large and blonde.

"He marries out of type," Adele said. "I've seen him on the street with girls. They're always dark and skinny, like you."

Jane Louise wished this information did not cause an inward lurch, but it did. When Adele was married and pregnant, would she ever feel an inward lurch? Jane Louise doubted this. Phil was Adele's high-school sweetie. On the days she didn't have lunch with him, she sat at her desk polishing her nails and reading *Today's Bride*.

This made Jane Louise think of Erna Hendershot, a large, florid, handsome woman with five children. She was married to Alfred Hendershot, the political adviser, and was an almost perfect person. She gave elaborate dinner parties and belonged to the Royal Guild of Needleworkers — she did fine embroidery in her two minutes of spare time. She made very fancy cakes for the bake sales at her children's school, and she took them all ice-skating every Saturday.

She also had, in Jane Louise's opinion, a major crush on Sven. She could hardly leave him alone. She ranted at Sven. They had equal power — Erna over editorial, and Sven over design and production — but Sven could make life miserable for Erna by holding up a jacket or page proofs. Needless to say, they clashed often, or rather, Erna ranted at Sven and Sven sat impassive in his chair. Erna left these meetings looking as if she were a teenager after a necking session. The amazing thing was, Erna had no idea what she was feeling. She spoke of Sven as if he were a household pest.

"She's like a ten-year-old," Adele said. "She'd like to get her hands on him, but she doesn't really know what to do. She'd hit him if she could."

Jane Louise thought Adele was a sort of genius. She especially relished "He marries out of type." When she recounted these things to Teddy over dinner one night, he said, "Her problem is that she's a genius in a very limited field. She's only brilliant on the subject of Sven."

» «

According to her birth book, with each day Jane Louise's salamander began to look more and more like the beginning of a human creature. The fact that this process was happening inside her was often so startling to Jane Louise that it caused her to lose breath. Every morning on the bus and in the street she saw flocks of pregnant women carrying on as if nothing special at all were happening to them. Why, this even happened to Sven's wives! And Sven himself was a father!

Jane Louise and Sven both took their vacations in August, a notoriously moribund month in the publishing industry. Sven and Edwina went to Martha's Vineyard with little Piers and the children of Sven's previous unions: Aneek, eighteen, who lived in Paris, and the fifteen-year-old twins, Allard and Desdemona, who lived in San Francisco. Aneek was beautiful. Her mother had been a famous beauty; she now lived with a French Marxist aristocrat.

"Her stepfather's a count, and her father's a Jew prole," Sven said.

Jane Louise said she did not think there was anything very Jewish or very proletarian about Sven.

Aneek was a very sensible girl who treated her father as if he were lovable but totally beside the point. Jane Louise was never startled to see Sven appraising his own daughter: It was a reflex. Besides, he was much too interested in the complicated spin paternity put on his personality to investigate anything as tacky as incest. This summer, that look in Sven's eyes caused Jane Louise to feel the grip of a low-level depression. Sven was unrelenting. There was nothing to be done about him. Or perhaps he was irresistible, and Jane Louise knew she couldn't stop him.

Every August Jane Louise and Teddy house-sat for Teddy's mother while she traveled about Britain with a childhood pal. Teddy's father hated driving, and he also hated the British Isles and gardening, which were her passions. As soon as they were divorced, Teddy's father moved to Arizona and Teddy's mother bought a house in the country and took two or three trips a year to England to see famous gardens and to go to the Chelsea Flower Show.

As was their custom, Jane Louise and Sven always had lunch together before they went away. They would discuss the upcoming fall list, like good colleagues. Jane Louise never thought of these lunches without a kind of compelling dread. It would be bad news if Sven ever decided to really focus on her. On the day of the lunch, Jane Louise, in need of moral support, went to find Adele, but Adele had gone out to lunch — doubtless shopping for sheets and towels with Phil, leaving behind on her desk a magazine called *Modern Engagements*.

Sven sauntered out of his office wearing a white linen jacket. He poked at the magazine as if it were a dead mouse. The fact that Adele was getting married meant nothing to him, but it was hard to figure him on the subject of marriage. On the one hand, he had been married three times. On the other, three times was a lot of times. Adele said that Sven married because it made him feel more guilty. It was not Jane Louise's opinion that guilt was anything felt by Sven. If he ever felt the merest twinge of remorse it was as if it were a cologne he dabbed behind his ears.

"Adultery means a lot to him," Adele said.

They went to Sven's hangout — a bar around the corner known for excellent food.

"So," said Sven as he surveyed the menu. "You and Teddy. Same as usual this summer?"

This caused Jane Louise to blush. This summer would not be quite the same as usual.

"The same," Jane Louise said brightly. "We're going to visit Martin Barlow and his wife. They live half an hour from Teddy's mother, it turns out."

"You watch him," Sven said. "Those nature boys are like octopuses. All hands."

"He's a sweet, harmless kid," said Jane Louise, who did not believe it for a moment.

"Mark my words," Sven said. "He probably hasn't recovered from the sight of your coral-colored underwear."

An integrated person — someone like Adele or Erna Hendershot — would have been immune to Sven, especially while pregnant. Jane Louise surveyed the menu.

"And your vacation?" she said.

"Oh, ever the cheerful father and husband," Sven said. "All as smooth as cream of wheat. Aneek and Desdemona work on their tans and get invited to parties. Piers digs in the sand with his little friends. We all watch the meteor showers with Allard because he's the family astronomer."

"I've never actually seen a shooting star," Jane Louise said. "Teddy says they're very cheering."

"That's the difference between us and them," Sven said. "Gentiles are on such chummy terms with the unknown. I find star showers intimidating."

"I never think of you as finding anything intimidating," Jane Louise said.

"Only the void," Sven said. "Let's order."

When the waiter departed, silence fell. Sven sipped his gin and tonic.

"I like a meteor shower," he said. "I like that time of year. I like those nights that are hot and cold—you know what I mean. Clammy and sticky. People kind of stick together or get all nice and slippery."

"Uh-huh," said Jane Louise. A club sandwich was placed in front of her. It looked somehow sinister, with nasty pieces of bacon poking out and mayonnaise dripping down its toasted sides. Surely this was an effect of early pregnancy.

"It's a good thing we're both going away," Sven said, as if to a passing waiter. "I've been dreaming about you a lot."

Jane Louise felt like a block of wood.

"I dreamed about Teddy, too." Sven said. "In my dream, he was . . . oh, never mind what he was. Like should never get together with like. Men should marry women. Jews should marry gentiles. Americans and Europeans. Blacks and whites. People are *against* each other. That's what sex is about—the great bridge across."

Jane Louise stared straight ahead. She was extremely tired. At the end of this lunch, how was she going to put one foot in front of the other? If there was an Us and a Them, she wanted to be on the same side as Teddy, but of course she was on the same side as Sven—the side of complication.

She felt Sven's warm hand on her neck. She heard his voice in her ear.

"Snap out of it!" he said. "I've been talking to you for five minutes. Don't fall asleep on me, Janey. Hey! Waiter! Bring me the check."

Jane Louise felt she might burst into tears. Instead she picked up Sven's glass and drank the dregs of his gin and tonic. There wasn't much left and most of it was water. Therefore she would not have to worry about fetal alcohol syndrome.

"There's something essentially loathsome about you," she said.

"That's my girl," Sven said.

» «

Jane Louise loved staying at Teddy's mother's house. It was so unlike her childhood home. Jane Louise's mother was a kitchen fascist. She believed in order at any cost. Everything had its place within a glass jar. Crackers and biscuits were taken from their boxes and bags and put into tins. Cookies lived in the cookie jar. Her refrigerator, as many of Jane Louise's friends had noticed, was a work of art: parsley in a white pot, leftovers in English crockery.

Teddy's mother was a traveler. Her tiny library, a former pantry, was filled with travel books. Her kitchen was not messy but minimal. In the cupboards were the remains of her food crazes — things usually sent to her from New York by Jane Louise: musty bags of now unlabeled spices from the Indian store; a jar of strange, brown pellets from a Chinese grocery. Teddy's mother's dining-room table was an old farm table whose surface was charmingly flawed with knife cuts. She had bought it at an auction. A farm table would have been an aberration to Jane Louise's mother, who had inherited an enormous mahogany table from *her* mother. Jane Louise had a love-hate relationship with this massive piece of furniture and alternately shuddered or was exalted to think that it would someday be hers.

It was at Teddy's mother's that Jane Louise had met her future husband. She was staying with friends in the country, and Teddy, who had just broken up with some girl or other, was house-sitting for his mother. Jane Louise's host and hostess felt that Teddy and Jane Louise should meet.

It had been a hot day in August, in the haying season. The house, which bordered on a meadow, smelled of fresh-cut grass. Teddy showed Jane Louise around. In the guest bedroom was an old carved bedstead with a bas-relief of grapes and cupids.

"Oh, what a wonderful bed!" Jane Louise said. She closed her eyes against a vision she was having of herself and Teddy in it.

Two days later she walked right over to Teddy's mother's house without so much as an excuse or a second thought. She felt propelled. She did not even care if Teddy misinterpreted her. The air smelled of clover, and the sun, blocked by a rose of Sharon tree, made spots on the guest-room carpet. In that sunlight, she and Teddy were as speckled as a pair of leopards. A year later they were married.

Jane Louise had always thought of this as a very sweet story. In fact, she had once found herself telling a watered-down version of it to Sven. It had registered completely with him, making Jane Louise realize that she had done the wrong thing. He had never forgotten it. Now as she set off on vacation, he said: "I bet Martin Barlow has a pretty fancy bed in his guest room."

» «

Jane Louise had cause to ponder this when she and Teddy went to visit the Barlows for lunch. They lived in a restored farmhouse near a historic town. In the back of the house was a large, dead tree.

"We keep it for the woodpeckers," Martin explained.

"What happened to it?" Teddy asked.

"It was struck by lightning," Martin said, and Jane Louise felt sure that she had just heard the titles of his next two books.

The Barlows had a baby called Lucy who was fourteen months old. Jane Louise tried not to show too much interest in this creature — it was none of Martin Barlow's business for the moment that she was pregnant — but her attention wandered constantly toward the baby, who during lunch sat on the floor playing with a family of red rubber pigs.

After lunch it was arranged that Nicolette and Teddy would walk Lucy down the road to the neighboring sheep farm while Jane Louise and Martin went over the final proofs of *The Literature of Nature*. By the time they came back, Martin and Jane Louise would have finished their work, and Lucy would be ready for her nap.

» «

Martin Barlow's study was so flooded with light, it was almost impossible to see him. Jane Louise wondered how he got any work done between twelve and two in the afternoon.

Jane Louise was wearing a yellow sundress and green espadrilles. As she had put her dress on that morning she had realized that in a few weeks it would no longer fit her and also that she would doubtless feel Martin Barlow's bare hands on her bare back.

As she squinted over his proofs, what she had known would happen happened. She was spun around. Martin Barlow pressed his hands against her back and kissed her.

"Go away, Martin," she said as if to an annoying dog, although she felt she could have stood kissing him in that hot room all afternoon. What did this mean? After all, she had spent half the morning kissing her own husband. "Go away," she said giving him a little shove.

He did go away. He retreated to the one dark corner of his room like a punished child.

"I'm horribly sorry," he said. "Really I am. I was just dying to kiss you."

"I was dying to kiss you too," Jane Louise said before she stopped herself.

"Really?" Martin said. "You don't suppose . . . "

"I only said that to make you feel better," Jane Louise lied.

From downstairs came the sound of a slamming door.

"Martin! Martin!" Nicolette called up. "Lucy can say 'sheep'!"

"I can't say what I feel," Martin whispered hoarsely. He grabbed Jane Louise's hand and kissed it. "Thank you," he murmured.

"And thank you," said Jane Louise.

> »«

On the night of the meteor shower, Jane Louise was apprehensive. She was not keen to peer into the void, and she had gotten a postcard from Sven — it was their custom to exchange postcards during vacation. Hers to him said, "The weather is perfect and the Barlows are as adorable as mice. I am happy to say that I have done next to nothing since we arrived."

His to her said, "Don't forget to contemplate the Almighty as you watch the stars fall down. Very scary. It's hot up here — good for one's dream life.''

Teddy was more than happy to be his wife's guide to the heavens. He spent the day looking skyward for any weather fronts that might obscure his view.

Teddy was enraptured at the thought of fatherhood. It held no terrors for him. He was a truly level person, perhaps a result of early progressive education, and he took things as they came. When Jane Louise took her afternoon nap, he lay down beside her and read her birth books. He learned that in a matter of a few months the creature would begin to move and Jane Louise would be able to feel it. As it got bigger, he would feel it too. This filled him with joy. The way toward fatherhood looked as clean as a swept path to him. The thought of motherhood, though, was not similarly unmixed to Jane Louise.

How would this child be brought up? Would Jane Loiuse find herself reduced to asking Sven advice about how to get some Jewish consciousness into the child of a mixed marriage? And what sort of person was she to allow people like Martin Barlow to hit on her? Or to put herself in the path of Sven, who hid under rocks like a lizard waiting to make a move? What sort of mother would such a woman make? Jane Louise wondered.

At eleven o'clock that night, Teddy set out a deck chair. He carefully read the bottle of insect repellent to see if it was safe for use on pregnant women before painting Jane Louise's arms with it. Then he went downstairs to make a pot of mint tea.

"Don't let anything start till I get back," he said. He returned with two mugs of tea and a blanket. Then he wedged himself behind Jane Louise, performing the service of a backrest, and he covered her legs with the blanket. He put his arms around her waist.

"Look!" he said. "Over there!" Jane Louise leaned back against his chest to see a star — or something like a star — blaze across the sky, and then another and another. At the corner of the horizon, lights flashed. There was not a sound. Above her the sky was as smooth as black velvet, sprinkled with rhinestones. It covered the whole planet. It was everywhere. *So this is the universe!* Jane Louise thought with a shudder.

The night sky, like the God of Moses, was unending, incomprehensible, full of enormous, indecipherable messages. Who wouldn't be anxious in the face of this?

Teddy breathed happily. It was all science to him. Teddy knew what he believed and therefore the incomprehensible did not throw him into a swivet. Jane Louise squirmed in his arms.

"These mosquitoes are treating me like French toast," she said. "Anyplace there's no repellent, they're having a picnic."

"Look!" Teddy said. "There's more."

Jane Louise lifted her face from his shoulder. She realized she had turned in her seat and was clinging to him. This really was some big deal. Above her was the amazingness of outer space, and meanwhile she was a container for the miracle of inner space. The enormity of it made her tremble.

The sky flashed. The comets blazed.

"Martin Barlow made a pass at me in his study," Jane Louise said.

"I hope you made him cringe like a dog," Teddy said.

"I did, actually," Jane Louise said. "I think I've had enough of these Perseids."

"Okay. Let's go inside and give little Heathcliff or little Catherine a rest," Teddy said.

How simple it could be! The answer to the problem of being anything was *being* it. Maybe people like Erna and Adele simply settled on what they were going to be and denied everything else. Maybe pregnancy would make her immune. She would have a baby and become all of a piece. She would find her place in the celestial order, tell Sven to go to hell and light the Sabbath candles. Little Heathcliff or Catherine could go to church with their daddy on Sunday and synagogue with their mommy on Friday night.

"I'm freezing," Jane Louise said.

"I'll warm you up," Teddy said.

Jane Louise put her arm around him. He opened the screen door and they walked dreamily to the guest bedroom where everything between them had happened with such apparent simplicity so long ago.

GRACE PALEY

ZAGROWSKY TELLS

I was standing in the park under that tree. They call it the Hanging Elm. Once upon a time it made a big improvement on all kinds of hooligans. Nowadays if, once in a while. . . . No. So this woman comes up to me, a woman minus a smile. I said to my grandson, Uh oh, Emanuel. Here comes a lady, she was once a beautiful customer of mine in the pharmacy I showed you.

Emanuel says, Grandpa, who?

She looks okay now, but not so hot. Well, what can you do, time takes a terrible toll off the ladies.

This is her idea of a hello: Iz, what are you doing with that black child? Then she says, Who is he? Why are you holding on to him like that? She gives me a look like God in judgment. You could see it in famous paintings. Then she says, Why are you yelling at that poor kid?

What yelling? A history lesson about the park. This is a tree in guide books. How are you by the way, Miss . . . Miss . . . I was embarrassed. I forgot her name absolutely.

Well, who is he? You got him pretty scared.

Me? Don't be ridiculous. It's my grandson. Say hello, Emanuel, don't put on an act.

Emanuel shoves his hand in my pocket to be a little more glued to me. Are you going to open your mouth sonny, yes or no?

She says, Your grandson? Really, Iz, your grandson? What do you mean, your grandson?

Emanuel closes his eyes tight. Did you ever notice children get all mixed up? They don't want to hear about something, they squinch up their eyes. Many children do this.

Now listen Emanuel, I want you to tell this lady who is the smartest boy in kindergarten.

Not a word.

Goddamnit, open your eyes. It's something new with him. Tell her who is the smartest boy — he was just five, he can already read a whole book by himself.

He stands still. He's thinking. I know his little cute mind. Then he jumps up and down yelling, Me me me. He makes a little dance. His grandma calls it his smartness dance. My other ones (three children grown up for some time already) were also very smart, but they don't hold a candle to this character. Soon as I get a chance, I'm gonna bring him to the city to Hunter for gifted children; he should get a test.

But this Miss . . . Miss . . . she's not finished with us yet. She's worried. Whose kid is he? You adopt him?

Adopt? At my age? It's Cissy's kid. You know my Cissy? I see she knows something. Why not, I had a public business. No surprise.

Of course I remember Cissy. She says this, her face is a little more ironed out.

So, my Cissy, if you remember, she was a nervous girl.

I'll *bet* she was.

Is that a nice way to answer? Cissy *was* nervous . . . the nervousness, to be truthful, ran in Mrs. Z.'s family. Ran? Galloped . . . tarum tarum tarum.

When we were young I used to go over there to visit, and while me and her brother and uncles played pinochle, in the kitchen the three aunts would sit drinking tea. Everything was Oi! Oi! Oi! What for? Nothing to oi about. They got husbands . . . perfectly fine gentlemen. One in business, two of them real professionals. They just got in the habit somehow. So I said to Mrs. Z., one oi out of you and it's divorce.

I remember your wife very well, this lady says. *Very* well. She puts on the same face like before; her mouth gets small. Your wife *is* a beautiful woman.

So . . . would I marry a mutt?

But she was right. My Nettie when she was young, she was very fair, like some Polish Jews you see once in a while. Like for instance maybe some big blond peasant made a pogrom on her great-grandma.

So I answered her, Oh yes, very nice looking; even now she's not so bad, but a little bit on the grouchy side.

Okay, she makes a big sigh like I'm a hopeless case. What did happen to Cissy?

Emanuel, go over there and play with those kids. No? No.

Well, I'll tell you, it's the genes. The genes are the most important.

Environment is okay. But the genes . . . that's where the whole
story is written down. I think the school had something to do with it
also. She's more an artist like your husband. Am I thinking of the right
guy? When she was a kid you should of seen her. She's a nice-looking
girl now, even when she has an attack. But then she was something.
The family used to go to the mountains in the summer. We went
dancing, her and me. What a dancer. People were surprised. Sometimes we danced until 2 a.m.

I don't think that was good, she says. I wouldn't dance with my son
all night. . . .

Naturally, you're a mother. But "good," who knows what's good?
Maybe a doctor. I could have been a doctor, by the way. Her brothe-
r-in-law in business would of backed me. But then what? You don't
have the time. People call you day and night. I cured more people in a
day than a doctor in a week. Many an M.D. called me, said, Zagrowsky,
does it work . . . that Parke-Davis medication they put out last
month, or it's a fake? I got immediate experience and I'm not too stuck
up to tell.

Oh, Iz, you are, she said. She says this like she means it but it makes
her sad. How do I know this? Years in a store. You observe. You watch.
The customer is always right, but plenty of times you know he's wrong
and also a goddamn fool.

All of a sudden I put her in a certain place. Then I said to myself, Iz,
why are you standing here with this woman? I looked her straight in
the face and I said, Faith? Right? Listen to me. Now you listen, because
I got a question. Is it true, no matter what time you called, even if I was
closing up, I came to your house with the penicillin or the tetracycline
later? You lived in the fourth-floor walk-up. Your friend what's-her-
name, Susan, with the three girls next door? I can see it very clear.
Your face is all smeared up with crying, your kid got 105°, maybe
more, burning up, you didn't want to leave him in the crib screaming,
you're standing in the hall, it's dark. You were living alone, am I right?
So young. Also your husband, he comes to my mind, very jumpy
fellow, in and out, walking around all night. He drank? I betcha. Irish?
Imagine you didn't get along so you got a divorce. Very simple. You
kids knew how to live.

She doesn't even answer me. She says . . . you want to know

what she says? She says, Oh shit! Then she says, Of course I remember. God, my Richie was sick! Thanks, she says, thanks, god-almighty thanks.

I was already thinking something else: The mind makes its own business. When she first came up to me, I couldn't remember. I knew her well, but where? Then out of no place, a word, her bossy face maybe, exceptionally round, which is not usual, her dark apartment, the four flights, the other girls—all once lively, young . . . you could see them walking around on a sunny day, dragging a couple kids, a carriage, a bike, beautiful girls, but tired from all day, mostly divorced, going home alone? Boyfriends? Who knows how that type lives? I had a big appreciation for them. Sometimes, five o'clock I stood in the door to see them. They were mostly the way models *should* be. I mean not skinny—round, like they were made of little cushions and bigger cushions, depending where you looked; young mothers. I hollered a few words to them, they hollered back. Especially I remember her friend Ruthy—she had two little girls with long black braids, down to here. I told her, In a couple of years, Ruthy, you'll have some beauties on your hands. You better keep an eye on them. In those days the women always answered you in a pleasant way, not afraid to smile. Like this: They said, You really think so? Thanks, Iz.

But this is all used-to-be and in that place there is not only good but bad and the main fact in regard to *this* particular lady: I did her good but to me she didn't always do so much good.

So we stood around a little. Emanuel says, Grandpa, let's go to the swings. Go yourself—It's not so far, there's kids, I see them. No, he says, and stuffs his hand in my pocket again. So don't go. Ach, what a day, I said. Buds and everything. She says, That's a catalpa tree over there. No kidding! I say. What do you call that one, doesn't have a single leaf? Locust, she says. Two locusts, I say.

Then I take a deep breath: Okay—you still listening? Let me ask you, if I did you so much good including I saved your baby's life, how come you did *that?* You know what I'm talking about. A perfectly nice day. I look out the window of the pharmacy and I see four customers, that I seen at least two in their bathrobes crying to me in the middle of the night, Help help! They're out there with signs. ZAGROWSKY IS A

RACIST. YEARS AFTER ROSA PARKS, ZAGROWSKY REFUSES TO SERVE BLACKS. It's like an etching right *here*. I point out to her my heart. I know exactly where it is.

She's naturally very uncomfortable when I tell her. Listen, she says, we were right.

I grab on to Emanuel. You?

Yes, we wrote a letter first, did you answer it? We said, Zagrowsky, come to your senses. Ruthy wrote it. We said we would like to talk to you. We tested you. At least four times, you kept Mrs. Green and Josie, our friend Josie, who was kind of Spanish black . . . she lived on the first floor in our house . . . you kept them waiting a long time till everyone else was taken care of. Then you were very rude, I mean nasty, you can be extremely nasty, Iz. And then Josie left the store, she called you some pretty bad names. You remember?

No, I happen not to remember. There was plenty of yelling in the store. People *really* suffering; come in yelling for codeine or what to do their mother was dying. That's what I remember, not some crazy Spanish lady hollering.

But listen, she says—like all this is not in front of my eyes, like the past is only a piece of paper in the yard—you didn't finish with Cissy.

Finish? *You* almost finished my business and don't think that Cissy didn't hold it up to me. Later when she was so sick.

Then I thought, Why should I talk to this woman. I see myself: how I was standing that day how many years ago?—like an idiot behind the counter waiting for customers. Everybody is peeking in past the picket line. It's the kind of neighborhood, if they see a picket line, half don't come in. The cops say they have a right. To destroy a person's business. I was disgusted but I went into the street. After all, I knew the ladies. I tried to explain, Faith, Ruthy, Mrs. Kratt—a stranger comes into the store, naturally you have to serve the old customers first. Anyone would do the same. Also, they sent in black people, brown people, all colors, and to tell the truth I didn't like the idea my pharmacy should get the reputation of being a cut-rate place for them. They move into a neighborhood . . . I did what everyone did. Not to insult people too much, but to discourage them a little, they shouldn't feel so welcome. They could just move in because it's a nice area.

All right. A person looks at my Emanuel and says, Hey! He's not altogether from the white race, what's going on? I'll tell you what: Life is going on. You have an opinion. I have an opinion. Life don't have no opinion.

I moved away from this Faith lady. I didn't like to be near her. I sat down on the bench. I'm no spring chicken. Cock-a-doodle-do, I only holler once in a while. I'm tired, I'm mostly the one in charge of our Emanuel. Mrs. Z. stays home, her legs swell up. It's a shame.

In the subway once she couldn't get off at the right stop. The door opens, she can't get up. She tried (she's a little overweight). She says to a big guy with a notebook, a big colored fellow, Please help me get up. He says to her, You kept me down three hundred years, you can stay down another ten minutes. I asked her, Nettie, didn't you tell him we're raising a little boy brown like a coffee bean? But he's right, says Nettie, we done that. We kept them down.

We? We? My two sisters and my father were being fried up for Hitler's supper in 1944 and you say we?

Nettie sits down. Please bring me some tea. Yes, Iz, she says: We.

I can't even put up the water I'm so mad. You know, my Mrs., you are crazy like your three aunts, crazy like our Cissy. Your whole family put in the genes to make it for sure that she wouldn't have a chance. Nettie looks at me. She says, Ai ai. She doesn't say oi anymore. She got herself assimilated into ai . . . that's how come she also says "we" done it. Don't think this will make you an American, I said to her, that you included yourself in with Robert E. Lee. Naturally it was a joke, only what is there to laugh?

I'm tired right now. This Faith could even see I'm a little shaky. What should she do, she's thinking. But she decides the discussion ain't over so she sits down sideways. The bench is damp. It's only April.

What about Cissy? Is she all right?

It ain't your business how she is.

Okay. She starts to go.

Wait wait! Since I seen you in your nightgown a couple of times when you were a handsome young woman . . . She really gets up this time. I think she must be a woman's libber, they don't like remarks about nightgowns. Bathrobes, she didn't mind. Let her go!

The hell with her . . . but she comes back. She says, Once and for all, cut it out, Iz. I really *want* to know. Is Cissy all right?

You want. She's fine. She lives with me and Nettie. She's in charge of the plants. It's an all-day job.

But why should I leave her off the hook. Oh boy, Faith, I got to say it, what you people put on me! And you want to know how Cissy is. *You!* Why? Sure. You remember you finished with the picket lines after a week or two. I don't know why. Tired? Summer maybe, you got to go away, make trouble at the beach. But I'm stuck there. Did I have air-conditioning yet? All of a sudden I see Cissy outside. She has a sign also, She must've got the idea from you women. A big sandwich board, she walks up and down. If someone talks to her, she presses her mouth together.

I don't remember that, Faith says.

Of course, you were already on Long Island or Cape Cod or someplace — the Jersey shore.

No, she says, I was not. I was not. (I see this is a big insult to her that she should go away for the summer.)

Then I thought, Calm down, Zagrowsky. Because for a fact I didn't want her to leave, because, since I already began to tell, I have to tell the whole story. I'm not a person who keeps things in. Tell! That opens up the congestion a little — the lungs are for breathing, not secrets. My wife never tells, she coughs, coughs. All night. Wakes up. Ai, Iz, open up the window, there's no air. You poor woman, if you want to breathe, you got to tell.

So I said to this Faith, I'll tell you how Cissy is but you got to hear the whole story how we suffered. I thought, okay. Who cares! Let her get on the phone later with the other girls. They should know what they started.

How we took our own Cissy from here to there to the biggest doctor — I had good contacts from the pharmacy. Dr. Francis O'Connell, the heavy Irishman over at the hospital, sat with me and Mrs. Z. for two hours, a busy man. He explained that it was one of the most great mysteries. They were ignoramuses, the most brilliant doctors were dummies in this field. But still, in my place, I heard of this cure and that one. So we got her massaged fifty times from head to toe, whatever someone suggested. We stuffed her with vitamins and minerals — there was a real doctor in charge of this idea.

If she would take the vitamins — sometimes she shut her mouth. To her mother she said dirty words. We weren't used to it. Meanwhile, in front of my place every morning, she walks up and down. She could of got minimum wage, she was so regular. Her afternoon job is to follow my wife from corner to corner to tell what my wife done wrong to her when she was a kid. Then after a couple months, all of a sudden she starts to sing. She has a beautiful voice. She took lessons from a well-known person. On Christmas week, in front of the pharmacy she sings half the *Messiah* by Handel. You know it? So that's nice, you think. Oh, that's beautiful. But where were you you didn't notice that she don't have on a coat. You didn't see she walks up and down, her socks are falling off? Her face and hands are like she's the super in the cellar. She sings! She sings! Two songs she sings the most: One is about the gentiles will see the light and the other is, Look! a virgin will conceive a son. My wife says, Sure, naturally, she wishes she was a married woman just like anyone. Baloney. She could of. She had plenty of dates. Plenty. She sings, the idiots applaud, some skunk yells, Go, Cissy, Go. What? Go where? Some days she just hollers.

Hollers what?

Oh, I forgot about you. Hollers anything. Hollers, Racist! Hollers, He sells poison chemicals! Hollers, He's a terrible dancer, he got three left legs! (Which isn't true, just to insult me publicly, plain silly.) The people laugh. What'd she say? Some didn't hear so well; hollers, He goes to whores. Also not true. She met me once with a woman actually a distant relative from Israel. Everything is in her head. It's a garbage pail.

One day her mother says to her, Cissile, comb your hair, for godsakes, darling. For this remark, she gives her mother a sock in the face. I come home I see a woman not at all young with two black eyes and a bloody nose. The doctor said, Before it's better with your girl, it's got to be worse. That much he knew. He sent us to a beautiful place, a hospital right at the city line — I'm not sure if it's Westchester or the Bronx, but thank God, you could use the subway. That's how I found out what I was saving up my money for. I thought for retiring in Florida to walk around under the palm trees in the middle of the week. Wrong. It was for my beautiful Cissy, she should have a nice home with other crazy people.

So little by little, she calms down. We can visit her. She shows us the candy store, we give her a couple of dollars; soon our life is this way. Three times a week my wife goes, gets on the subway with delicious foods (no sugar, they're against sugar); she brings something nice, a blouse or a kerchief—a present, you understand, to show love; and once a week I go, but she don't want to look at me. So close we were, like sweethearts—you can imagine how I feel. Well, you have children so you know: little children little troubles, big children big troubles—it's a saying in Yiddish. Maybe the Chinese said it too.

Oh, Iz. How could it happen like that? All of a sudden. No signs?

What's with this Faith? Her eyes are full of tears. Sensitive I suppose. I see what she's thinking. Her kids are teenagers. So far they look okay but what will happen? People think of themselves. Human nature. At least she doesn't tell me it's my wife's fault or mine. I did something terrible! I loved my child. I know what's on people's minds. I know psychology *very* well. Since this happened to us, I read up on the whole business.

Oh, Iz. . . .

She puts her hand on my knee. I look at her. Maybe she's just a nut. Maybe she thinks I'm plain old (I almost am). Well, I said it before. Thank God for the head. Inside the head is the only place you got to be young when the usual place gets used up. For some reason she gives me a kiss on the cheek. A peculiar person.

Faith, I still can't figure it out why you girls were so rotten to me.

But we were right.

Then this lady Queen of Right makes a small lecture. She don't remember my Cissy walking up and down screaming bad language but she remembers: After Mrs. Kendrick's big fat snotty maid walked out with Kendrick's allergy order, I made a face and said, Ho ho! The great lady! That's terrible? She says whenever I saw a couple walk past on the block, a black-and-white couple, I said, Ugh—disgusting! It shouldn't be allowed! She heard this remark from me a few times. So? It's a matter of taste. Then she tells me about this Josie, probably

Puerto Rican, once more — the one I didn't serve in time. Then she says, Yeah, and really, Iz, what about Emanuel?

Don't you look at Emanuel, I said. Don't you dare. He has nothing to do with it.

She rolls her eyes around and around a couple of times. She got more to say. She also doesn't like how I talk to women. She says I called Mrs. Z. a grizzly bear a few times. It's my wife, no? That I was winking and blinking at the girls, a few pinches. A lie . . . maybe I patted, but I never pinched. Besides, I know for a fact a couple of them loved it. She says, No. None of them liked it. Not one. They only put up with it because it wasn't time yet in history to holler. (An American-born girl has some nerve to mention history.)

But, she says, Iz, forget all that. I'm sorry you have so much trouble now. She really is sorry. But in a second she changes her mind. She's not so sorry. She takes her hand back. Her mouth makes a little O.

Emanuel climbs up on my lap. He pats my face. Don't be sad, Grandpa, he says. He can't stand if he sees a tear on a person's face. Even a stranger. If his mama gets a black look, he's smart, he doesn't go to her anymore. He comes to my wife. Grandma, he says, my poor mama is very sad. My wife jumps up and runs in. Worried. Scared. Did Cissy take her pills? What's going on? Once, he went to Cissy and said, Mama, why are you crying? So this is her answer to a little boy: she stands up straight and starts to bang her head on the wall. Hard.

My mama! he screams. Lucky I was home. Since then he goes straight to his grandma for his troubles. What will happen? We're not so young. My oldest son is doing extremely well — only he lives in a very exclusive neighborhood in Rockland County. Our other boy — well, he's in his own life, he's from that generation. He went away.

She looks at me, this Faith. She can't say a word. She sits there. She opens her mouth almost. I know what she wants to know. How did Emanuel come into the story. When?

Then she says to me exactly those words. Well, where does Emanuel fit in?

He fits, he fits. Like a golden present from Nasser.

Nasser?

Okay, Egypt, not Nasser — he's from Isaac's other son, get it? A close relation. I was sitting one day thinking. Why? Why? The answer: to remind us. That's the purpose of most things.

It was Abraham, she interrupts me. He had two sons, Isaac and Ishmael. God promised him he would be the father of generations; he was. But you know, she says, he wasn't such a good father to those two little boys. Not so unusual, she has to add on.

You see! That's what they make of the Bible, those women; because they got it in for men. Of *course* I meant Abraham. Abraham. Did I say Isaac? Once in a while I got to admit it, she says something true. You remember one son he sent out of the house altogether, the other he was ready to chop up if he only heard a noise in his head saying, Go! Chop!

But the question is, Where did Emanuel fit. I didn't mind telling. I wanted to tell, I explained that already.

So it begins. One day my wife goes to the administration of Cissy's hospital and she says. What kind of a place you're running here. I have just looked at my daughter. A blind person could almost see it. My daughter is pregnant. What goes on here at night? Who's the supervisor? Where is she this minute?

Pregnant? they say like they never heard of it. And they run around and the regular doctor comes and says, Yes, pregnant. Sure. You got more news? my wife says. And then: meetings with the weekly psychiatrist, the day-by-day psychologist, the nerve doctor, the social worker, the supervising nurse, the nurse's aide. My wife says, Cissy knows. She's not an idiot, only mixed up and depressed. She *knows* she has a child in her womb inside of her like a normal woman. She likes it, my wife said. She even said to her, Mama, I'm having a baby, and she gave my wife a kiss. The first kiss in a couple of years. How do you like that?

Meanwhile, they investigated thoroughly. It turns out the man is a colored fellow. One of the gardeners. But he left a couple months ago for the Coast. I could imagine what happened. Cissy always loved flowers. When she was a little girl she was planting seeds every minute and sitting all day in front of the flower pot to see the little flower cracking up the seed. So she must of watched him and watched him. He dug up the earth. He put in the seeds. She watches.

The office apologized. Apologized? An accident. The supervisor was on vacation that week. I could sue them for a million dollars. Don't think I didn't talk to a lawyer. That time, then, when I heard, I called a detective agency to find him. My plan was to kill him. I would tear him limb from limb. What to do next. They called them all in again. The psychiatrist, the psychologist, they only left out the nurse's aide.

The only hope she could live a half-normal life — not in the institutions: she must have this baby, she could carry it full term. No, I said, I can't stand it. I refuse. Out of my Cissy, who looked like a piece of gold, would come a black child. Then the psychologist says, Don't be so bigoted. What nerve! Little by little my wife figured out a good idea. Okay, well, we'll put it out for adoption. Cissy doesn't even have to see it in person.

You are laboring under a misapprehension, says the boss of the place. They talk like that. What he meant, he meant we got to take that child home with us and if we really loved Cissy. . . . Then he gave us a big lecture on this baby: it's Cissy's connection to life; also, it happens she was crazy about this gardener, this son of a bitch, a black man with a green thumb.

You see I can crack a little joke because look at this pleasure. I got a little best friend here. Where I go, he goes, even when I go down to the Italian side of the park to play a little bocce with the old goats over there. They invite me if they see me in the supermarket: Hey, Iz! Tony's sick. You come on an' play, O.K.? My wife says, Take Emanuel, he should see how men play games. I take him, those old guys they also seen plenty in their day. They think I'm some kind of a do-gooder. Also, a lot of those people are ignorant. They think the Jews are a little bit colored anyways, so they don't look at him too long. He goes to the swings and they make believe they never even seen him.

I didn't mean to get off the subject. What is the subject? The subject is how we took the baby. My wife, Mrs. Z., Nettie, she plain forced me. She said, We got to take this child on us. I will move out of here into the project with Cissy and be on welfare. Iz, you better make up your mind. Her brother, a top social worker, he encouraged her, I think he's a Communist also, the way he talks the last twenty, thirty years. . . .

He says: You'll live, Iz. It's a baby, after all. It's got your blood in it. Unless of course you want Cissy to rot away in that place till you're so poor they don't keep her anymore. Then they'll stuff her into Bellevue or Central Islip or something. First she's a zombie, then she's a vegetable. That's what you want, Iz?

After this conversation I get sick. I can't go to work. Meanwhile, every night Nettie cries. She don't get dressed in the morning. She walks around with a broom. Doesn't sweep up. Starts to sweep, bursts into tears. Puts a pot of soup on the stove, runs into the bedroom, lies down. Soon I think I'll have to put her away too.

I give in.

My listener says to me, Right, Iz, you did the right thing. What else could you do?

I feel like smacking her. I'm not a violent person, just very excitable, but who asked her? Right, Iz. She sits there looking at me, nodding her head from rightness. Emanuel is finally in the playground. I see him swinging and swinging. He would swing for two hours. He likes that. He's a regular swinger.

Well, the bad part of the story is over. Now is the good part. Naming the baby. What should we name him? Little brown baby. An intermediate color. A perfect stranger.

In the maternity ward, you know where the mothers lie, with the new babies, Nettie is saying, Cissy, Cissile darling, my sweetest heart (this is how my wife talked to her, like she was made of gold — or eggshells), my darling girl, what should we name this little child?

Cissy is nursing. On her white flesh is this little black curly head. Cissy says right away: Emanuel. Immediately. When I hear this, I say, Ridiculous. Ridiculous, such a long Jewish name on a little baby. I got old uncles with such names. Then they all get called Manny. Uncle Manny. Again she says — Emanuel!

David is nice, I suggest in a kind voice. It's your grandpa's, he should rest in peace. Michael is nice too, my wife says. Joshua is beautiful. Many children have these beautiful names nowadays. They're nice modern names. People like to say them.

No, she says, Emanuel. Then she starts screaming, Emanuel Emanuel. We almost had to give her extra pills. But we were careful on account of the milk. The milk could get affected.

Okay, everyone hollered. Okay. Calm yourself, Cissy. Okay. Emanuel. Bring the birth certificate. Write it down. Put it down. Let her see it: Emanuel.

In a few days, the rabbi came. He raised up his eyebrows a couple times. Then he did his job, which is to make the bris. In other words, a circumcision. This is done so the child will be a man in Israel. That's the expression they use. He isn't the first colored child. They tell me long ago we were mostly dark. Also, now I think of it, I wouldn't mind going over there to Israel. They say there are plenty black Jews. It's not unusual over there at all. They ought to put out more publicity on it. Because I have to think where he should live. Maybe it won't be so good for him here. Because my son, his fancy ideas . . . ach, forget it.

What about the building, your neighborhood, I mean where you live now? Are there other black people in the community?

Oh yeah, but they're very snobbish. Don't ask what they got to be so snobbish.

Because, she says, he should have friends his own color, he shouldn't have the burden of being the only one in school.

Listen, it's New York, it's not Oshkosh, Wisconsin. But she gets going, you can't stop her.

After all, she says, he should eventually know his own people. It's their life he'll have to share. I know it's a problem to you, Iz, I know, but that's the way it is. A friend of mine with the same situation moved to a more integrated neighborhood.

Is that a fact? I say, Where's that?

Oh, there are . . .

I start to tell her, Wait a minute, we live thirty-five years in this apartment. But I can't talk. I sit very quietly for a while, I think and think. I say to myself, Be like a Hindu, Iz, calm like a cucumber. But it's too much. Listen, Miss, Miss Faith—do me a favor, don't teach me.

I'm not teaching you, Iz, it's just . . .

Don't answer me every time I say something. Talking talking. It's true. What for? To whom? Why? Nettie's right. It's our business. She's telling me Emanuel's life.

You don't know nothing about it, I yell at her. Go make a picket line. Don't teach me.

She gets up and looks at me kind of scared. Take it easy, Iz.

Emanuel is coming. He hears me. He got his little worried face. She sticks out a hand to pat him, his grandpa is hollering so loud.

But I can't put up with it. Hands off, I yell. It ain't your kid. Don't lay a hand on him. And I grab his shoulder and push him through the park, past the playground and the big famous arch. She runs after me a minute. Then she sees a couple friends. Now she has what to talk about. Three, four women. They make a little bunch. They talk. They turn around, they look. One waves. Hiya, Iz.

This park is full of noise. Everybody got something to say to the next guy. Playing this music, standing on their heads, juggling — someone even brought a piano, can you believe it, some job.

I sold the store four years ago. I couldn't put in the work no more. But I wanted to show Emanuel my pharmacy, what a beautiful place it was, how it sent three children to college, saved a couple lives — imagine: one store!

I tried to be quiet for the boy. You want ice cream, Emanuel? Here's a dollar, sonny. Buy yourself a Good Humor. The man's over there. Don't forget to ask for the change. I bend down to give him a kiss. I don't like that he heard me yell at a woman and my hand is still shaking. He runs a few steps, he looks back to make sure I didn't move an inch.

I got my eye on him too. He waves a chocolate popsicle. It's a little darker than him. Out of that crazy mob a young fellow comes up to me. He has a baby strapped on his back. That's the style now. He points to Emanuel, asks like it's an ordinary friendly question. Gosh what a cute kid. Whose is he? I don't answer. He says it again. Really some cute kid.

I just look in his face. What does he want? I should tell him the story of my life? I don't need to tell. I already told and told. So I said very loud — no one else should bother me — how come it's your business, mister? Whose do you think he is? By the way, whose kid you got on *your* back? It don't look like you.

He says, Hey there buddy, be cool be cool. I didn't mean anything. (You met anyone lately who meant something when he opened his mouth?) While I'm hollering at him, he starts to back away. The women are gabbing in a little clutch by the statue. It's a considerable distance, lucky they got radar. They turn around sharp like birds and fly over to the man. They talk very soft. Why are you bothering this old man, he got enough trouble? Why don't you leave him alone?

The fellow says, I wasn't bothering him. I just asked him something.

Well, he thinks you're bothering him, Faith says.

Then her friend, a women maybe forty, very angry, starts to holler, How come you don't take care of your own kid? She's crying. Are you deaf? Naturally the third woman makes a remark, doesn't want to be left out. She taps him on his jacket: I seen you around here before, buster, you better watch out. He walks away from them backwards. They start in shaking hands.

Then this Faith comes back to me with a big smile. She says, Honestly, some people are a pain, aren't they, Iz? We sure let him have it, didn't we? And she gives me one of her kisses. Say hello to Cissy, okay? She puts her arms around her pals. They say a few words back and forth, like cranking up a motor. Then they bust out laughing. They wave goodbye to Emanuel. Laughing. Laughing. So long, Iz . . . see you. . . .

So I say, What is going on, Emanuel; could you explain to me what just happened? Did you notice anywhere a joke? This is the first time he doesn't answer me. He's writing his name on the sidewalk. EMAN-UEL. Emanuel in big capital letters.

And the women walk away from us. Talking. Talking.

LYNN FREED

·

 FOREIGN STUDENT

I was once told by a displaced Rumanian, fellow Jew, in a variation on the old adage, that each country gets the Jews that it deserves. What was I to make, in the light of this, of my first day in Far Rockaway, New York, with the family Grossman? I knew already that all Jews were not the same. But what, I wondered, did America do to deserve this?

In the end I was probably more of a shock to them. I at least had had a hint of the world into which I was being exchanged for a year. I'd seen American movies and listened to records of American Jewish humor. I knew a gunnif from a mensch. But nothing had prepared them for the goyish Jewish foreign student to whom they were opening their home and themselves. No one had given them to understand that I'd feel anything other than right at home, flesh of their people's flesh, blood of their people's blood.

It was July, 1963. I stood with my luggage on the sidewalk of East 43rd Street. Even in the subtropics from which I'd come, nothing was comparable to this heat. It was tangible, sitting like an incubus on the cement earth, unmoving. No breeze, no natural force to displace air with air. It burned through the soles of my shoes. It melted my hairspray. People skulked along in the shade of buildings. Air-conditioners buzzed and dripped. No one stood aimlessly as I did, waiting in the heat, looking up and down the street for the silver Cadillac convertible that finally slipped around the corner.

Goldie Grossman and her daughter Marsha leapt out of the car and pressed cool faces against my wet skin. They held me at arm's length. They filled the street with whoops of pleasure. "Let's go!" they shouted, and I slid into the front seat next to Marsha, looked back as we moved off down the street, cool and comfortable.

"Put the top down Ma!" Marsha ordered. Down, back it went, exposing us directly to the hot and acrid fumes of New York. It is odd now that, returning to New York, I can smell those smells and experience something akin to nostalgia for the place. At the time I was sure that I was being irretrievably poisoned and for weeks afterwards tried shallow breathing.

They took me across a bridge, onto a freeway, off a freeway. When I wasn't concentrating on my breathing I looked about me. I saw the streets of Long Island with rising panic. Panic stuck in my throat and made me mute. I nodded and smiled at the information I was receiving—the fashionable exits, the outings planned, etc.—but I could not utter more than three words in a row without swallowing. I cupped my hand over my nose to filter out the heavier pollutants, pretending to be deep in admiration.

Marsha stared at me unconvinced. "Don't ever get a nose job," she said. "Even if you could die for one. Look what they did to me."

I uncovered my nose, startled, and looked at hers.

"Had mine done six weeks ago," she said. "They took off too much. Now I have to go back in to have some put on again."

I couldn't have come at a better time.

» «

We turned a corner and drew up beside a drab, gray, two-storey house.

"Here we are!" Marsha shouted.

"Home sweet home," said Goldie.

The house stood on a corner at the end of a long row of equally modest siblings. All were covered in gray or brown asbestos shingle and had coordinated metal awnings, screens, and porches. Some had tricycles in front, or basketball hoops tacked over garage doors. Children climbed over and around parked cars. And over all hung the heavy haze of New York misdsummer.

A woman with her head covered in curlers and a scarf waved from the next door porch.

"Hey, Ethel!" Goldie shouted. She tugged at my sleeve. "This is the one! Our foreign student!"

Ethel hung her folded arms and huge breasts over the porch railing. "She's *darling*!" she said. "Welcome!"

» «

Inside, the house was unlike any I'd ever seen. It was unhouselike. Closed in, closed off. I stood in the cool front hall trying to adjust my eyes to the dim light. My voice had faded and dried up. I couldn't bring it back. But Marsha and Goldie took my silence for approval and flew around touching things and talking about them, shepherding me from room to room.

In all the rooms, shades were drawn over the windows to keep out the heat. Air-conditioners buzzed in those rooms which were in use. In others, such as the living room, doors remained closed throughout summer and winter, and temperature controls were used only for guests. They switched on a lamp for me to see by. But before I could see, I smelt the strange odor of synthetic fibers long out of touch with fresh air. Lots of the things in the house seemed beyond touch. All moveable objects were covered in specially fitted clear plastic wrappers — lampshades, sofas, telephone books, table tops. Brocade and gold leafing shone through, pristine and inaccessible. Plastic runners criss-crossed wildly over royal blue carpeting. Glass covered the oil paintings — landscapes and seascapes. Gilded cornucopias camouflaged the light switches.

Strangest of all was the music. Over all the incidental noise of the household — the Grossmans' shouting, the air-conditioning, the traffic outside — there was music. The whole house was ingeniously wired up for it, even the toilet. Mantovani was the favorite, but close behind came Ray Conniff, Arthur Fiedler, and some group playing American Jewish folk songs. We slipped smoothly from "Lady of Spain" to "Hava Nagila" and then back to "Pomp and Circumstance." Goldie sang and hummed constantly, occasionally picking out the tunes as accompaniment on an electric organ.

Throughout the house Goldie had surrounded herself with strange wisdom. A "Recipe for Happiness" hung on one kitchen wall. "Smile, you may never see tomorrow," sang the bathroom mirror. All sorts of injunctions in bronze on loving and helping and cooperating mingled on the surfaces of dressers and mantle pieces with bowling trophies and plaques of appreciation.

I watched Goldie with wonder. She was completely different from the women I knew at home. Wearing bermuda shorts and sneakers and short streaked hair, chewing gum with her mouth open, she seemed wrong in the role of adult. No dignity removed her from Marsha and me. She slopped into a chair and complained loudly about menstruation. She reached for a pair of my shoes and squashed her feet into them. "Nice," she said. "Can I wear them some time?"

After I'd unpacked she led me to what looked like a hidden panel in the wainscotting of the front hall. "Sam's office," she explained. "He's waiting for us."

She rapped quickly on the panel and a door was unlocked from the other side, opening into a large waiting room. On benches around the wall sat ten or twelve obese women puffing and fanning themselves against the heat.

Goldie saw me staring. "He's a diet doctor," she whispered. "They come to him from miles around. Every borough of the city."

I wondered if the women on the benches were all new patients.

"Come," she said, "Sam's time is money."

"Aha!" Sam Grossman pulled himself out of a black swivel chair. He breathed in deeply, a small fat man trying to be tall and thin. He seemed to be smiling, but his mouth was lost in the shadow of an enormous pink nose that governed his face. Tiny black eyes, too close to each other, watched the way I folded my hands behind me. "Come here sweetheart," he said. "Let's have a look at you."

"Isn't she *beautiful,* Sam! Just wait'll you hear her *talk!*"

"So talk!" He held out his hands to me. "Don't be embarrassed, sweetheart. Shalom! You understand 'shalom'?"

"Oh yes," I said. "Of course."

"See? Hear that?" Goldie gave me a small shove towards him and he caught me at the elbows.

"Sounds like normal English to me," he said. He squeezed me reassuringly. "You relax, sweetheart, you hear? I say welcome. Welcome to our happy home. Peace. Shalom. I'll see you later."

» «

From about this point, the panic that had visited me in the car and again in the front hall moved in to stay. It allowed me to talk, smile, unpack, but all the while my head churned with plans for escape. I lay awake at night turning them over and over, inside out.

After a few days of this, when letters began to arrive from home, the panic took the form of homesickness, that crippling legacy of familiar sounds and smells and tastes now out of reach. Everything I saw or heard or didn't hear triggered a wild upsurge of nausea and tearfulness. I watched "Tarzan" on the television. I buried myself in *National Geographics* with sections on Africa full of lions I'd never seen and alien tribes. It didn't matter. I courted familiarity even in the unfamiliar.

I ate almost nothing. The homesickness had filled up my stomach and I was never hungry. I picked and pushed the pieces around the plate, steeling myself against the family's perplexed whispering and Sam's persistent comments.

"Look sweetheart," he coaxed. "We could use a few more like you in the clinic, but for the meantime, do Goldie a favor, take a few bites of chicken, hey? Some kasha, no? Well," he'd say at last, with a shrug of ethnic resignation, "I guess she just don't like our food."

Marsha stared at the watery ground beef and cabbage on my plate. "What do you eat in Africa?" she asked. "Baboons?"

» «

Goldie seemed sure that things would cheer me up. So we went to the family's wholesale houses, where they bought me a fake fur coat and hat, dresses and skirts, bermuda shorts, costume jewelry. I saw myself transformed in wild reds and aquamarines, with sparkles in my hair and a fixed smile on my lips.

"You're one of us," Goldie assured me. "Why shouldn't I do for you what I would do for my own daughter?"

Her benevolence delighted her. She decided now that I needed the time of my life. "We gonna keep that smile on her face," she said to Sam and Marsha.

So off we went to Coney Island, to their beach cabana, to "Stop the World, I Want to Get Off." Marsha and I drove in Sam's new T-Bird to meet her friends at pizza parlors and soda fountains and the local bowling alley three nights a week. At eighteen I felt agèd with these fresh, smooth-skinned, straight-toothed American high school students. My own world of nightclubs and cha-cha-cha and Latin sophistication had left me without the ingenuousness to enjoy folk singing and boys my own age. I longed for someone to talk to. Someone who would understand my predicament. And other things too. How ugly everything was to me. The house. The clothes. The voices. The squat, bare bowling alley with its echoing din of loudspeakers and bells.

The longer I stayed, the dimmer became my dreams of escape. Everyone except me assumed that I was there for a year. I tried often to hint at the possibility of leaving, but no one seemed to notice. I knew that if I confessed my misery to AFS they would set about finding me another family. The thought of another family silenced me. It was I who was the misfit, not the Grossmans. And who could tell where they would move me to? Wyoming? Arkansas? Places I couldn't even pronounce.

I wrote my parents of a mild case of homesickness. They phoned immediately. My father repeated his old boarding school tales of homesickness and cold showers. He cautioned me to stick it out, grin and bear it, pull up my socks, play the game. My mother told me how proud they were of me, how everyone was proud, this one and that one. Mention of this one and that one brought tears to my eyes. I could hardly speak for the weight of the year ahead of me. The bargain I'd struck. Fifty-two weeks. Three hundred and sixty-five days as the guest of strangers.

» «

Two weeks before school was to begin Sam brought the suitcases down from the attic. Neither Goldie nor Marsha would tell me what they were for. But Goldie announced that we were off to the wholesale houses again. For evening wear this time, she said. Something *really* dressy. I was mystified. My own evening clothes had hung untouched for months. Apart from the bowling alley and a few hospital bazaars there was no night life at all in Far Rockaway.

At dinner that night Sam rapped on the table for our attention. He cleared his throat. Goldie and Marsha winked at each other.

"Here you are," he said, "from a foreign land, and yet no stranger, our daughter for this year."

"*Tell* her, Dad!"

"Grossingers," Goldie whispered.

"Excuse me?"

"*Grossingers!*" she shouted. "Never heard of Grossingers? The Catskills! *Boy* have *you* got a treat coming!"

"What about the *food*, Ma! Tell her about the *food!*"

"The food, the food!" sang Goldie.

"And the *pools!* Indoor and outdoor! The *clothes!*"

» «

The following Friday morning Goldie took Marsha and me to the beauty salon. We emerged teased, sprayed and stiff and drove off to the Catskills like paper roses in a pot. Sam was ecstatic.

"My three beauties!" he chortled. "Boy oh boy! We're going to have to tie 'em down!" And to me he added, "For you, darling, I'm wishing only the best! A nice American boy to keep you here with us! Nice *Jewish* boy, lots of dough. Can you imagine *that?*" He slapped Goldie's thigh. "A wedding! The whole family flying here from Africa!"

"Hey, hey Sam! She's gotta meet him first! There's a big demand you know." Goldie eyed me analytically. "How do we know she's gonna like one of our boys?" she asked.

» «

At Grossingers, before dinner on that first night, we gathered in a large hall with the other guests to view and be viewed. Marsha wore an aquamarine sequined evening gown held up by shoestring straps and a padded bra. She had matched her eyeshadow exactly to the color of the fabric and wore long false eyelashes which kept unsticking at the edges. "Oh shoot!" she hissed and darted off to the Ladies' Room.

I stood about, excruciated in my new gold lamé, with shoes and a tiara to match. Goldie, behind us, prodded us forward with words of encouragement. "He *cute!* . . . *He's darling!* she would say of some smooth-looking character in a dark suit and loafers. And the boy in question would turn in profile, this way, that way, to show the cut of his cloth.

But Marsha and I were ignored. Goldie coached us too closely. The other mothers hung back, seemed to have a more remote code of communication with their children, and never shepherded more than one of a sex at one time.

Ignominiously we shuffled into the dining room and were seated at a large table with several others.

"See what I told you?" Goldie whispered. "Ever seen such clothes in your *life*?"

She was right. Chunks of gold and precious stones circled fingers and arms and necks, hung from ears like ripe fruit. Hair, dyed and teased, stood out in horns and wings. Silver and gold fabrics glittered in the light of the chandeliers. There were furs everywhere. Beaded bags. Jeweled spectacles. No one stared at me in my lamé and tiara. No one giggled as I did. I felt absurd. I blushed. I wanted to turn and run.

Sam broke off a piece of halah and then scooted the plate over to me. "Take, take!" he said, spraying crumbs all over his neighbor. "Eat! Eat!"

"Sam!" Goldie whispered urgently. "First we have to be welcomed! And they haven't said the *blessings*!"

But Sam ignored her and addressed the table at large. "This lovely little lady is visiting us all the way from *Africa*!"

People turned to look. Some smiled in disbelief. Even the supercilious young waiter next to our table stared down at me.

"She's our daughter for the year," he went on. "A nice Jewish girl, can you believe? Here darling—." He held up a an empty wine glass. "This is to a sweet year. May all your troubles be little ones!"

The crowd at the table murmured and smirked. But before they could ask me questions a loudspeaker crackled on. A voice welcomed us on behalf of the family Grossinger to this their happy home. We were to eat and enjoy, it said. To partake with them of the Sabbath meal. And we should be honored to have in our midst a cantor famous

the world over. He had come there to bless the Sabbath wine and to
sing at services. Welcome. Peace. Shabbat shalom.

"*Now* you'll see what food is!" Goldie whispered. "Just take a look
at the menu!"

The people around me were already ordering two and three dishes
at a time. They laughed at the sight of the waiters staggering in under
heavy trays. And when the platters and bowls and chafing dishes
descended all around us, they ate without even a smile of embarrass-
ment. They complimented each other on the spans of side dishes.
Leaned over with forks poised to taste. Nodded and rolled their eyes in
approval. And then, when the last dessert dish had been removed,
they wiped their mouths extravagantly and trooped off to the hotel's
synagogue to hear the famous cantor.

An organ played softly as we walked in. No one talked. At eight
o'clock exactly the rabbi and the cantor, like two plump brides in
white satin robes, walked down the aisle and climbed to the podium in front.

I listened carefully to the cantor's singing for hints and snatches of
familiar tunes. But the organ played and a choir sang and the melodies
themselves sounded more like my old Anglican school hymns than the
meandering Eastern prayers I knew from shul at home. There was
none of the chaos of our own services — women waving and talking in
the balconies, men swaying and chanting and beating their breasts
below. This service was orderly. It didn't seem Jewish at all.

The rabbi stood up. He clasped the podium and raised his eyes
above our heads. Addressing God in English, he begged for wisdom
and gave elaborate praise. The congregation raised their books and
begged and praised in turn. He spoke of Jews the world over. They
gave thanks for the land of Israel. He spoke of suffering. They catalog-
ued their blessings. The whole service began to sound like a literate
version of one of Sam's dinnertime homilies.

Marsha nudged me. "Why aren't you reading?" she whispered.
"It's disrespectful!"

» «

"Shabbat shalom, sweetheart!" Sam shouted as we turned to leave. He kissed me on the lips. He kissed Goldie and Marsha on the lips, too. He threw an arm around my waist and another around Marsha's. "Wasn't that just *beautiful*, girls?" he asked.

"Beautiful! Beautiful!" Goldie chanted.

And then suddenly my head cleared. Just like that. Standing their amongst these strangers, these alien Jews, with Sam's wet kiss still on my lips, I knew what I had to do. The cantor's voice and the rabbi's words that had filled them with such comfortable reverence for their Jewishness, the strange sounds of the organ, the chorus of voices, had worked a miracle for me. I saw that hints would not do. Nothing but the truth would do. I would simply have to sacrifice my parents' pride in me and their standing with this one and that one. I would confess the whole of my misery. I would beg them to let me come home.

Early the next morning I wrote the letter. I spared them nothing, not even Sam's patients or Goldie's period pains. I ran out to the mailbox and thrust the envelope down its throat as far as it would go. Then I skipped out in the crisp morning air. I stood at a distance and looked at the hotel. Saw for the first time how beautiful it was. A real building made of stone, open on all sides, with paths and trees around it. And the air smelled of lawn clippings and freshly turned soil. The sky was blue and clear. Trees grew all over the hills. For the first time since leaving home I felt back on earth. I was even hungry.

» «

Back in Far Rockaway my secret became heavier as the week progressed. It burdened my dreams so that I awoke with a fright. I didn't hear what people said to me. The family teased me about being in love. Who was it, they wanted to know? One of the boys from Grossingers?

By Friday afternoon I had almost grown used to the wait. When I returned from the library I found Goldie sitting in the kitchen, mute. I noticed that she had missed her appointment at the beauty salon. Her hair stuck in strands to her face as if she had a fever. The polish on her nails was chipped and dull.

"Are you all right, Goldie?" I asked.

"Am I all right?" she asked, addressing the air above my head.

It had happened. I could barely breathe.

Goldie shook her head from side to side and then slowly and apparently painfully pushed herself up, wiped her hands on her apron. With her head held high she began to leave the room. "Wait here, if you please," she said. "I'm going to get my husband who has patients, emergencies, but never mind that. He asked that I should call him when you came home."

I sat there, mute in my turn, my heart clattering so loudly against my ribs and in my throat that it drowned out all the thoughts and phrases I had prepared for the occasion.

Goldie and Sam appeared together at the kitchen door. They stood still and looked at me in silence, like some latterday American Jewish Gothic. They moved slowly to the table to sit. Goldie opened her mouth to speak but Sam laid a hand over hers.

"It has come to our notice," he said at last, "that you wish to leave this home and move out."

Goldie shook her head sadly. I opened my mouth to speak but Sam held up his hand and closed his eyes.

"Today I receive a call from an important person — a Mr. Bolito. Bolati. Who knows? The head of FAS."

"AFS," I corrected.

"Yes, thank you for that. Well, this Belliti says to me that you are unsuitable to our home. They made a mistake, he says, and now they will take you away. 'Mistake?' I says. 'What mistake? *You*, Mr. Beltini, *you* are the person making the mistake.'" He looked at Goldie and shook his head. "A nudnik from Yonkers, I sounded like. 'She's our baby, our girl,' I told him. Then he says to me" — Sam's grasp tightened on Goldie's hand — "he says, 'The girl is not happy. Unhappy,' he says. 'Miserable. She writes letters to her parents about it and they phone all the way from Africa.' They phone to ask *him* to help — not me, mind you, they don't phone me, a *medical doctor*. They phone *him*, Mr. Head Goy, Brentano, whatever. 'Well,' he said to me at last, 'if you must go, you must go. That's all. And tomorrow. Already. The sooner the better'—*his* words, not mine. Goldie here, I worry about her, for your information. Like a mother to you she's been. And our

Marsha, that wonderful child. Who knows? You've been more than a sister to that girl who has no other. Did you think of that when you wrote those letters? Huh?"

There were no words to deal with this. I shrugged slightly under their glare. "Marsha is very resilient," I muttered.

"What is this?" Sam asked Goldie. "Is this the girl we've loved as our own? Wished for only the best? Opened our heart?"

Goldie nodded. A few tears squeezed out and rolled unchecked down her cheek. Sam looked at me and then led my eye with his to the sight of Goldie's silent weeping. He watched me watching and then turned to leave. "It takes a heart of stone," he said.

The phone rang out. Sam answered it. He closed his eyes and held the receiver out to me. "Long distance," he said.

"Hello?"

"*Darling!* Is that *you?*" My mother's voice boomed through the muffled beeps and crackles.

"Yes."

"How are you, my darling? Are you all right? That's the *first* thing we want to know."

"Fine, fine." I stared at the telephone dial in a hopeless attempt to forget that Sam and Goldie were standing in the doorway listening.

"Darling! We received your letter today and we're *most* upset! We phoned Bolito *immediately* and told him to get you out of there *pronto!*"

"I know," I said.

"*What?*"

"I said I know!"

"Has he *fixed* things, darling? You mustn't stay in that *awful* place a minute longer than necessary! When will you leave?"

"Tomorrow."

"When? What?"

"TOMMORROW!"

"Chopsticks!" My father's voice, modulated for the distance and interference, rang much clearer. "You're a chump not to have told us all this before. Why did you wait so long?"

"I can't talk," I said.

Goldie sniffed loudly.

"We would have fixed things before, you know," he went on. "Capital chap, this Bolito. Sounds quite competent. What your mother and I *cannot* work out is why he put you there in the first place."

"You asked for me to be put in a Jewish home," I said. By now I was oblivous to the Grossmans.

"But dash it all, they can't *all* be like that over there," he said.

"Dad! Don't worry about me. I'm fine."

"*She's* fine!" Goldie said.

"We've fixed things with Bolito, darling," my mother shouted. "I'm *very* anxious for you not to do *anything* that you'll regret for the rest of your life."

My heart leapt. "What do you mean?"

"Bolito's arranged everything, darling. He asked us to leave it to him to explain."

"*What?*"

"Call us from New York," she said. "Reverse the charges."

Explain *what?*"

"Bye, darling!"

Click.

» «

They were already standing behind their chairs when I came into the dining room—Sam, the patriarch, with his women on either side of him. I stood in the doorway—turncoat, renegade, damnèd ingrate.

Sam grasped the back of his chair. "This is the Sabbath," he said. "A holy day for Jews all over this land and this earth of ours. Tonight we gather together to join in the Sabbath meal with one who will leave us soon, namely tomorrow, to go from us and our home. May peace be with her on her chosen path." He looked at me and then at Goldie and Marsha. "None of us, God forbid, should blame her. She is young. She has a life. We hope that one day she will think of us and this home she had, and she will not be miserable. We wish her shalom." With that he blessed the wine and we sat down.

"Beautiful! Beautiful, Sam!" Goldie said. "I wish we had the tape recorder."

"Who can think of tape recorders at a time like this?" asked Sam, slowly tucking his napkin into his collar. He said the blessing over the bread.

We ate our soup in silence. And then the chicken. Every now and then Sam would lean over, lay a hand on Goldie's arm, and pat her reassuringly. Marsha, whenever she could catch my eye, narrowed her own in accusation.

But I was concentrating entirely on making myself as still and silent as possible. I took great care with my knife and fork lest some unexpected clatter draw more attention in my direction. I wanted nothing to point up further the extent of my ingratitude. So engrossed was I in this game of self-control that we seemed to arrive at dessert with relative speed. After dinner I rose and asked to be excused.

"Why ask?" said Sam. "You're free to come and go."

"I'm very sorry," I said. "Thank you. Thank you for everything."

The fact that I was not weeping, however, did not escape Goldie's attention. She signed and wiped her hand across her eyes. Sam patted her hand and then looked up at me.

"Sleep well on your last night in this home," he said.

» «

Early the next day Sam hauled my luggage into the Cadillac. Ethel watched in her bathrobe and curlers from an upstairs window. She banged on the window and waved. Children on the street stood back as we pulled away from the house. Goldie drove in silence, her lips pursed into an expression of hurt dignity. But Marsha chatted loudly all the way in. She laughed gaily, threw her hands in the air, as if we were driving to a celebration.

When we arrived outside the AFS building Goldie walked stiffly around to the trunk and held it open for me while I unloaded the luggage onto the sidewalk. Marsha watched me from the car. "Five weeks !" she said. "Can you believe it's been five weeks?"

Goldie slammed the trunk shut. "We wish you luck," she said, "Sam and Marsha and me. Shalom to you and yours."

Then she climbed in and they sped off down 43rd Street and out of sight.

» «

A door opened and the AFS receptionist called me in. "Go straight upstairs to Mr. Bolito's office," she said. "Leave your bags here. Your new family is waiting."

"New family?"

"They've been waiting half an hour. Up you go."

I took the elevator to the second floor and stepped into Mr. Bolito's office.

"So this is the young lady we've heard so much about!" said a ruddy-faced man of about fifty in a Brooks Brothers suit and brown penny loafers. "I'm Greg Lawson, your new dad. And this is Mrs. Lawson — Nan. And here," he said, gesturing to a girl of about my age, "is Dede."

Dede bounced up and kissed me coyly on the cheek. "This is *sooo* neat!" she said. "We've been waiting *sooo* long for a foreign student! And now it's like a fairytale come true." She flashed a smile at Mr. Bolito.

Mr. Bolito eased himself out of his chair and came up to put his arm around me. "And you'll find Darien very different from Far Rockaway."

Everyone laughed.

"Where's Darien?" I asked.

"Connecticut," he said. "You're a very lucky girl you know."

"Yes," I said, observing with by now familiar alarm the pink bow in Mrs. Lawson's hair, her baby print peter pan blouse and coordinated wraparound skirt.

"Well, come Precious, let's go," she said in a high, girlish voice. "If we're lucky we'll still make the brunch at the club. Oh!" She held one perfectly manicured but unpolished hand to her mouth. "I *almost* forgot! Are there any foods you don't eat, Precious? I mean are you — what do they call it now?" she asked, turning to the others.

" 'Kosher,' I think," said Mr. Lawson.

"Yes, *kosher*! You know —," she giggled, "— we always thought we'd get a Scandinavian or a German, being such fanatics for the slopes. But we're *dee-lighted* to have *you!*" She slipped an arm through mine. "It's *fascinating* to think of all the different customs and food habits the world over, isn't it? It's just that, being that we're Episcopalian and all, we eat *everything*, you know!" She giggled again and patted one buttock. "No good for the derrière, you know?" She squeezed my arm. "So we were just wondering, Precious, whether you would be — what was that word again?"

"Kosher."

"Yes, kosher."

"I'm not kosher." Suddenly I felt nauseous.

"Well, I'm *starved*. Let's go!" said Dede. She led the procession out to the street where Greg Lawson loaded my luggage into the Mercedes, and we all climbed in, waved to Mr. Bolito, and cruised down 43rd Street.

SHARON NIEDERMAN

A GIFT FOR LANGUAGES

1.

Dr. de la Torre loved her work. Hazy mornings, strolling from her brown shingle cottage on Hilegas to her office on campus, she immersed herself in scents of eucalyptus and good coffee, the Mediterranean softness of the air, and the sense of engaged, passionate life being lived on the streets of Berkeley. Unlike so many others who had come of age in the 1960's, she didn't feel she had to prove her right to exist by trying to fix the world. She knew she deserved everything she had.

She hadn't always been Dr. Rosalind de la Torre. Born Rosalie Zelnick, she'd kept her ex-husband's name. His Buenos Aires family had called her Rosalinda; she had shortened it to Rosalind.

This morning she took more than her usual care dressing. She knew she'd be on display at the Comparative Literature Department meeting this afternoon when she gave her evaluation of the new curriculum proposals. Brainy women had a special obligation to look particularly chic and sexy, she believed, and she prided herself on never looking like a teacher or a librarian. Rosalind favored pure, intense colors — clear red, royal blue, black — in interesting textures and styles that looked trendy, and at the same time as though they would always be fashionable. She cultivated her appearance of elegant, expensive simplicity as carefully as she cultivated her taste in films, food and music.

From her well-organized closet she chose a fuchsia sweater dress with a hemline well above her knees, patterned black stockings and little Italian boots. She'd purchased her underwear in Paris. The outfit would catch her colleagues slightly off guard, giving her the bit of extra space she needed to evaluate her interactions and stay ahead. Being the youngest in the department to hold her position — assistant professor at thirty-two — she constantly faced the judgments of people who wanted to stop her before she got started. There was definitely an art to being just provocative enough. Always a good student, she'd mastered this art as thoroughly as any of her languages.

Rosalind loved the peace she found in the early morning. As she moved about her house, she again admired each lovingly selected object and furnishing. She dearly wanted her home to be a reflection of her unique and excellent taste. Although she knew good things, money wasn't the real factor here. Even before she'd earned a decent living, she'd bought things she loved. Really special things weren't easy to find, and she'd learned to regret missed opportunities. Her house was eclectic, comfortable, and, she thought, quite perfect. Brass arc lamps coexisted harmoniously with leather chairs, a burgundy cut-velvet sofa, muted old carpets, oak tables, lacquer chests and stained-glass windows. Cream-colored walls provided a warm background for her art and photographs.

She still reveled in having an entire place just to herself. With a fireplace. After all those years of sharing a bedroom with Grandma in that claustrophobic Bronx apartment, she still hungered for privacy. Back then, Grandma got the bed; she slept on a cot. She was never alone. At night, Grandma snored terribly and woke Rosie to help her to the bathroom. When Grandma bathed, Rosie helped her out of the tub and dried the enormous wrinkled brown body. So many tasks, repeated over and over, but they never seemed to help. Grandma was just sick, and she never got any better. "How are you today?" Rosie would ask when she gave Grandma her medicine in the morning. "What's the good of complaining?" was the answer each day. With her parents working all day in their dry-cleaning store, Rosie always worried something terrible might happen to Grandma. Then again, she half hoped something might. She didn't know which was worse — the smells or the superstitions.

Over and over, Grandma told her the stories that made up her life, half in English, half in Yiddish. How she left her Polish village at fourteen and never saw her mother again. How she came to this country in steerage, sick for days. Lived on the lower East Side with her mean, grudging uncle and worked in the sweatshops, picking fuzz from bolts of cloth. Sundays weren't so bad. Then she and her girlfriends got all dolled up and strolled down Second Avenue or maybe went to Coney Island.

When she was sixteen, she met Grandpa, a second cousin, at a family wedding. "I waited four years for him," Grandma told her. "Then, the night before my wedding, his sister, your Tante Sophie, came to me and begged me not to marry him. 'He's no good,' she told me. 'He'll ruin your life. He runs around, can't save his money.' Was she right about the money! He never was an easy man to live with."

Rosie never knew how she came to understand Yiddish; she seemed just to know what the words meant. Later, German came easily to her in high school. Thank you, Grandma, she thought. Poor Grandma never learned to read, except for the racing forms. Just sat in front of the television until she died.

Meanwhile, her parents fought. About everything. "Your mother," yelled Rosie's father, "is driving me crazy. And in my own home yet!" But the apartment was cheaper than a nursing home.

Out of rebellion and hope, her parents had been leftists. All that remained of their youthful idealism was their disbelief in God. Their atheism tortured Grandma, who mouthed prayers morning, noon and night and invoked God continually. Oh God, help me. Oh God, save me. Oh God, you didn't hear that. Oh God oh God oh God. She lit her candles, Shabbes and Yahrtzeit, muttering her prayers alone.

Naturally, Rosie read a lot. Library books were free, and reading didn't bother anybody. Jane Austen, George Eliot, the Brontës, then Dostoevsky and Tolstoy. "Always got your nose in a book," was her father's customary greeting.

Well, she'd made it pay. A smart girl, hadn't they always said so? Her father saved his first kind words for when she won the Regents scholarship at sixteen. "Good girl, Rosie," he said, ruffling her hair. "We're real proud of you." He sounded like he meant it. Then he retreated behind his newspaper. Of course he was pleased. Now it wouldn't cost him a cent to educate her.

So she escaped to Buffalo. That was her biggest achievement. Bigger than the *cum laude* degree. Bigger than the graduate fellowship, and even bigger than the Fulbright. All she'd ever really wanted to do was to create a life different from theirs. And she'd certainly done that, she thought, looking around her domain with satisfaction. She owed them nothing. She'd done it all on her own.

When Joachim (who sat next to her in Seventeenth Century literature, smoked a pipe, and was definitely dark and handsome) asked her to marry him, she welcomed the change to get even further away. They sailed out of San Francisco for Argentina, and no one saw her off. His family doted on her, called her "La Flaca" (the thin one), waited four years for her to become pregnant. Her mother-in-law, Paolina, oversaw Rosalinda's housekeeping; exhibited her at countless family dinners, organized shopping expeditions with Joachim's sisters and summers at Mar del Plata. She had no life of her own. While Joachim worked in the family import-export business, she spent afternoons at the movies. In Buenos Aires, she learned that freedom and empty time were not the same thing at all. One afternoon, she saw *Hiroshima, Mon Amour,* and the intense longing and grief the movie aroused broke the daze of her boredom and isolation. She knew she had to leave. She returned to New York, taking one suitcase and her perfect Spanish.

Days, she typed at an office in the city; nights she slept at her parents' apartment, in her own bed. Her high school girlfriend, Terri, came in from Berkeley for a visit. Rosalind had to finish her degree. Why not California? She started packing the day her acceptance came in the mail. From the moment she arrived, Berkeley felt like home. Now it felt like her true love: the place she was faithful to, would cross oceans for, that always welcomed her, that she knew so well, that held pleasures and discoveries for her always.

2.

If he hadn't called her name in the café, Rosalind wouldn't have noticed Dr. Hoffmann. She stopped in for brioches to take to the office when she ran into him, sitting alone, wearing his émigré beret and reading his *New York Times.* His appearance chilled her. How small he looked, shrunken, like Picasso or Sartre when they were very old men;

his face so deeply lined, the flesh pulled tightly around the bones, revealing the very structure of his skull.

"Rosalind, my dear, how beautiful you're looking this morning," he said in his charming accent, smiling and taking her hand in both of his. She hadn't seen him all semester, though he'd never mention the lapse. He seemed so openly happy to see her, she blushed. Since his wife, Alicia, died the previous year, she'd drifted apart from her mentor. His neediness at this time made her uncomfortable. She told herself that trying to see him through this lonely period would only use her up.

But now, looking into his kind, intelligent face, she wondered how much of the need was his; how much hers. She hated seeing how badly he'd aged. He couldn't be near eighty yet, she thought. Ten years gone now since she'd first been his student — his prize — then his assistant, typing and editing his manuscripts on archetypes in world literature. Nothing in her life equaled the excitement she'd felt over her first conversations with the eminent Dr. Karel Hoffmann. He'd been the first to recognize her potential, not just to accept her but to believe in her ability to make a real contribution. She hadn't seriously thought of getting her Ph.D. until Dr. Hoffmann insisted she go on, and helped her find the fellowship.

He and Alicia had lost everyone when they fled Germany. Rosalind fit easily into the design of their family life, joining them for holiday dinners, helping them entertain, or just staying for supper to continue working with Dr. Hoffmann into the evening. In their refined world, filled with artifacts illuminated in niches like saints — pre-Columbian carved jade, an enameled Fabergé music box, a Japanese cherrywood bowl from the hands of a Living National Treasure — plus Bokhara carpets and the best wine and music (Alicia played Bach so beautifully on their Steinway), Rosalind became the person she'd always wanted to be. She felt she had entered the warmly lit home you spend your life walking past on the street, wishing you could go inside.

But she couldn't stop just now. She was in a hurry to meet Brian Miller, a student from European Classics, to discuss his term paper. Brian was very bright, in a class of not very exciting students, and, she had to admit, very attractive. Quickly, she made a plan to go to the opera with Dr. Hoffmann Sunday afternoon. They'd catch up then.

3.

Brian Miller, age twenty-two, senior in business administration from Crescent City, just below the Oregon border, waited for her — his six-foot frame leaning against her office door. Brian had sufficient irregularities about his looks to save him from anonymous, athletic wholesomeness. Rosalind noticed in particular the tiny gap between his two front teeth and the thick dark brows emphasizing the amused expression in his light-brown eyes. Outwardly ignoring the deliberate way he sized her up, she actually applauded this little show of audacity from one of his generation — this new breed with its intelligence neatly channeled into material striving, its grim predictability, and its lack of curiosity.

Rosalind, always in command in front of a class but not unfriendly, had often been party to confessions, both intended and oblique, during the intimacy of office hours. Precisely because of the respect her manner and scholarship inspired, this generation trusted her with its heartbreak and confusion. She, in turn, translated their appeals into practical suggestions for improvement. The exposure did not alter their mutual sense of propriety. On the fingers of one hand, she could name the students who had, in ten years, ever moved inside the circle of discrimination she inscribed around herself.

Now this Brian sat across from her, his arrogance intriguing as well as annoying. He sketched out his ideas for his term paper. She knew perfectly well he'd never have enrolled in the class were it not a requirement for graduation. He was the sort who only wanted to get through school so he could get out there and make as much money as he could the fastest way possible. When he finished speaking, he looked at her with a frankness that had nothing to do with library research, sending her a direct sexual charge. So much for the world of the intellect.

"What do you think of it?" he asked, showing his lopsided grin.

"I think you'll do very well," she replied, the air thick with double entendres.

"But don't you have any suggestions?" he wanted to know. He had to be aware of the game that had been set in motion. She wondered: How long had he intended to approach her? How much class time did he spend calculating the right approach? There was no law against imagination and no way to control your students' thoughts. Her behavior, however, was impeccable. She could afford to let this play out a bit. A little flirtation, like a little Belgian chocolate, could help get you through the semester.

"I can't think of anything to add to what you've put together," she said. "But if I do get any interesting ideas, I'll let you know." She gave him a smile he could interpret any way he chose and turned to her papers.

4.

When Dr. Hoffmann entered her silver Saab Sunday afternoon, Rosalind was struck by his frailty. His movements had become slower and more cautious than she remembered, as if his batteries were losing their charge, and she registered with dismay the grayish cast of his complexion. Rosalind rejected the flash of panic she felt and turned her thoughts to practical matters. Was he getting proper medical attention to get him through this period of rundown? Vitamin B shots could do wonders. Did he need a temporary housekeeper? Would he call her if she could help him find someone?

Of course she wanted to take care of him, comfort him — but how could she just drop everything? She was impossibly busy, as always. As they drove across the Bay Bridge in the misty sunlight, Rosalind chattered about her classes, plans for her publications and new books she'd discovered, avoiding the silence of unasked questions.

In the years they'd attended musical events together, the San Francisco Opera had always been their favorite setting. In its fin-de-siècle opulence, they returned together to the world gone by, which was no less vivid for their sharing it in imagination rather than memory.

When she took Dr. Hoffmann's arm and walked up these steps, life became for Rosalind perfectly civilized and elegant, as delicious as the exquisite Sacher torte one would savor with excellent company at the Café Voltaire.

But today, the professor tottered heavily at her side. Discreetly, she helped him up the steps. Inside the high-ceilinged lobby, he bought her a red rose, and tears burned her eyes as she pinned the flower to her black velvet jacket. She averted her head and started toward their seats.

This afternoon, the spectacle and finery of *Cosi fan tutte* failed to hold her attention. The image of Brian Miller returned as it had all week — lanky, relaxed, assured — just damn sexy. She could no longer meet his eyes in class. His eyes drank her in as she lectured, paced, and turned to write on the blackboard. His attention excited her and inspired her performance. No matter that her cleverness was mainly wasted on those dull undergraduates. She took pleasure in recalling how Brian lingered outside the door after class. She'd simply outwaited him until he finally sauntered off.

Of course, these little reveries were just whimsy. She could tune him out any time she chose. Pretty visions of Brian alternated with Rosalind's worries about Dr. Hoffmann, whose breathing beside her sounded irregular. She wondered if they ought to cancel their customary supper at Jack's and head straight back across the bay.

As she helped Dr. Hoffmann back to the car, he lost his balance, stumbled and took a bad fall. Seeing him crumpled on the sidewalk, Rosalind gathered all her resources and willed herself to remain calm. She focused on the task at hand. With effort, she raised him to his feet. He was shaken and badly bruised; clearly, their night on the town was impossible. Not wanting him to see her fright, she tried her best to keep up a soothing conversation on the way home. Undeniably, something was seriously wrong, and she drove like a demon. When she got him into his house and turned on the lights, he looked too sick to leave alone.

"Can I make you some soup?" she asked, as she looked for blankets to wrap him in and pillows to prop him up on the sofa.

"Fix yourself something, Rosalind," he said. "But don't let me keep you."

She brought out a tray with mugs of consommé and toast.

"Shall I call your doctor?" she asked.

"That won't be necessary."

"Really, Dr. Hoffmann, if you don't mind my saying . . . "

"Please don't concern yourself, my dear."

In the end she won, and it was a good thing she'd insisted. Dr. Duncan checked him into the hospital "for tests."

When Rosalind finally returned home from the Medical Center, it was after nine. Wound too tight to sleep or concentrate on work, she thought of a hot bath with soothing mineral salts, clouds of steam. Instead, without pausing to think, she went to the phone and dialed Brian's number.

"Hello?" he answered in his slow, level voice.

"Hello, Brian," she said, with a lilt he'd never heard in the classroom.

He took a beat. "Dr. de la Torre?" he asked.

She gave him a pretext that seemed reasonable for them both. "I was just going over your outline, and there are some parts I think we ought to discuss."

He understood her immediately, as she'd known he would. "Is this a convenient time for you?" he wanted to know.

"Tonight is fine," she said.

He was at her door in half an hour. She offered him a Courvoisier and poured one for herself. Within the hour, they were in bed together, no questions asked. She had chosen well. This boy knew a great deal; at moments, she swore he knew everything. A slow, accurate, and unself-conscious lover, his attention to her cost him no sacrifice. He left around two a.m., and she finally fell asleep, too exhausted to think. Except that in the few seconds before she dropped off, she again saw Dr. Hoffmann's face as he lay on the sidewalk.

5.

Barely present, Rosalind sat at Dr. Hoffmann's hospital bedside, wondering how soon she could respectably leave. Seeing him completely helpless, barely able to speak or move, tubes in his nose and arms attaching him to machines, she couldn't help thinking: Why not just have it over with? Although the stroke had left him paralyzed, she knew he still recognized her. She had loved this man as much as she'd ever loved anyone, but at this crucial time she just felt weary and numb. There was no fitting way to say goodbye. She refused to imagine the void his passing would leave in her life and in the world.

She gazed at the green treetops outside the window and thought of the afternoon ahead with Brian. Her body responded with an involuntary shock of pleasure. Brian's healthy, uncomplicated maleness short-circuited her analytic mind and lit up her sensations. With him, she didn't have to think. She only felt. While he was not what she'd term a grand passion, she had to admit he'd become her compulsion. She constantly craved the pleasure he willingly provided. Yet his offhandedness went counter to the urgency she felt with him.

She knew nothing more about him now than when they'd started last month. She couldn't help wondering: Did he have a girlfriend? A sweet bubblehead back home? Or a campus trust-funder from Ohio? In bed and out, she worked at trying to get him as obsessed with her as she was with him, but he behaved as casually as if she were just another experience of many. Still, she insisted to herself, Brian was "safe." Only a student, ten years younger, he was a prime example of a generation that replaced content with form. At least he was smart enough to behave. He arrived and left on time, and he always called when he said he would.

Rosalind had gone to his apartment only once. He lived in a way she'd left far behind and had no desire to revisit, with his cheap wall posters, empty refrigerator, ugly throws over uglier chairs, loud, unfamiliar rock music blaring through the walls, and, pervading all this, the smell of stale beer. By contrast, her own sandalwood-scented sheets, down pillows, and firm queen-sized mattress made their encounters—which began in the fading late-afternoon light and ended in darkness—far more pleasant and private.

Despite her nonstop desire for Brian, Rosalind refused to make the mistake of believing she was in love with him. Falling in love was the worst thing that could happen to a woman. Hadn't she seen this disaster repeated often enough? No matter how gifted or accomplished the woman — and Berkeley was full of brilliant, beautiful women — love provided a socially condoned route to self-destruction. Love automatically took precedence over work, money, reputation, ambition — the entire professional life that a woman had struggled so hard and honorably to create. Love succeeded where the world had failed to knock you out of the game. The fact of physical need couldn't be helped, but why pretty it up? Rosalind knew better than to believe love would improve her life.

Dr. Hoffmann seemed to be asleep. She bent and kissed his parchment forehead and left the room, each tap of her kidskin pumps reverberating along the corridor. Now she could go home and get ready for Brian.

6.

Rosalind didn't cry at Dr. Hoffmann's funeral or at his memorial service. She ached with her frozen grief. Nothing to be said, nothing to be done. She could only sit alone in a dark room. The image of Brian failed to magnetize her thoughts.

Finally the tears began. A relief. Then came panic so overwhelming and unexpected that she ran to the bathroom, vomiting. She locked the doors, unplugged the phone and sat on the floor, hugging her knees and swaying from side to side.

Wanting to scream, then hearing a broken howl unlike any sound she'd ever produced, she remembered the mourning rituals of her ancient European great-aunts. All her life, she'd tried to shut out their hysterical keening. Now she even smelled them: mothballs and Evening in Paris.

Rosalind knew what to do. She found candles and matches. She went to the closet, grabbed her I. Magnin black silk dress, made a half dozen gashes with her scissors and dressed herself in mourning. Then she took her beautiful pastel sheets, ripped them down the middle and covered every mirror in the house. *So the departing soul doesn't startle itself.*

Now she knew. She wasn't smarter or stronger or better. She had only reinterpreted her grandmother's immigrant endurance for her own purposes. She would rather die than be like her wheezing, kvetching grandmother. She would rather die *than be Jewish like her grandmother:* worn out, despised; prevented from freely choosing a life; resigned to feeding only on crumbs, crumbs that wouldn't be missed and devouring them quickly when no one was looking. Though Rosalind had fed on the finest delicacies, an abundance of delectable imports arrayed on white linen in a summer garden, still she hungered.

TILLIE OLSEN

DREAM-VISION

In the winter of 1955, in her last weeks of life, my mother — so much of whose waking life had been a nightmare, that common everyday nightmare of hardship, limitation, longing; of baffling struggle to raise six children in a world hostile to human unfolding — my mother, dying of cancer, had beautiful dream-visions — in color.

Already beyond calendar time, she could not have known that the last dream she had breath to tell came to her on Christmas Eve. Nor, conscious, would she have named it so. As a girl in long ago Czarist Russia, she had sternly broken with all observances of organized religion, associating it with pogroms and wars; "mind forg'd manacles"; a repressive state. We did not observe religious holidays in her house.

Perhaps, in her last consciousness, she *did* know that the year was drawing towards that solstice time of the shortest light, the longest dark, the cruelest cold, when — as she had explained to us as children — poorly sheltered ancient peoples in northern climes had summoned their resources to make out of song, light and food, expressions of human love — festivals of courage, hope, warmth, belief.

» «

It seemed to her that there was a knocking at her door. Even as she rose to open it, she guessed who would be there, for she heard the neighing of camels. (I did not say to her: "Ma, camels don't neigh.") Against the frosty lights of a far city she had never seen, "a city holy to three faiths," she said, the three wise men stood: magnificent in jewelled robes of crimson, of gold, of royal blue.

"Have you lost your way?" she asked, "Else, why do you come to me? I am not religious, I am not a believer."

"To talk with *you*, we came," the wise man whose skin was black and robe crimson assured her, "to talk of whys, of wisdom."

"Come in then, come in and be warm—and welcome. I have starved all my life for such talk."

But as they began to talk, she saw that they were not men, but women;

That they were not dressed in jewelled robes, but in the coarse everyday shifts and shawls of the old country women of her childhood, their feet wrapped round and round with rags for lack of boots; snow now sifting into the room;

That their speech was not highflown, but homilies; their bodies not lordly in bearing, magnificent, but stunted, misshapen—used all their lives as beasts of burden are used;

That the camels were not camels, but farm beasts, such as were kept in the house all winter, their white cow breaths steaming into the cold.

And now it was many women, a babble.

One old woman, seamed and bent, began to sing. Swaying, the others joined her, their faces and voices transfiguring as they sang; my mother, through cracked lips, singing too—a lullaby.

For in the shining cloud of their breaths, a baby lay, breathing the universal sounds every human baby makes, sounds out of which are made all the separate languages of the world.

» «

Singing, one by one the women cradled and sheltered the baby.

"The joy, the reason to believe," my mother said, "the hope for the world, the baby, holy with possibility, that is all of us at birth." And she began to cry, out of the dream and its telling now.

"Still I feel the baby in my arms, the human baby," crying now so I could scarcely make out the words, "the human baby before we are misshapen; crucified into a sex, a color, a walk of life, a nationality . . . and the world yet warrings and winter."

» «

I had seen my mother but three times in my adult life, separated as we were by the continent between, by lack of means, by jobs I had to keep and by the needs of my four children. She could scarcely write English—her only education in this country a few months of night school. When at last I flew to her, it was in the last days she had language at all. Too late to talk with her of what was in our hearts; or of harms and crucifying and strengths as she had known and experienced them; or of whys and knowledge, of wisdom. She died a few weeks later.

She, who had no worldly goods to leave, yet left to me an inexhaustible legacy. Inherent in it, this heritage of summoning resources to make out of song, food and warmth, expressions of human love — courage, hope, resistance, belief; this vision of universality, before the lessenings, harms, divisions of the world are visited upon it.

She sheltered and carried that belief, that wisdom — as she sheltered and carried us, and others — throughout a lifetime lived in a world whose season was, as yet it is, a time of winter.

NIKKI STILLER

A STATE OF EMERGENCY

> "Many times man lives and dies
> Between his two eternities,
> That of race and that of soul."
> W.B. Yeats

Anything can upset my mother, from a hangnail to a toothache. Particularly *my* hangnail or toothache. I don't understand how a woman who survived the McCarthy Period, the Russian Revolution, and my own adolescence can tremble at the sight of a cockroach or be rattled by a trip on the crosstown bus. Perhaps the kind of character shaped by waiting in a cellar for the latest pogrom to pass enables you to deal with catastrophes but makes waiting for a cab a melodrama. I don't know. I do know that my mother has involuntarily transmitted her fear of subways, swimming, impure drinking water, and catching the common cold to me.

Only twice since my father died have I witnessed her primal drives wake up and make demands. Once, a deep-fried sea bass in a Hunanese restaurant stirred something that forty years of self-denial had not quite smothered. And once, in Paris when we were on our way to Israel, she sent me all over the Left Bank in search of *jus de prunes*. The French must have other ways of dealing with constipation. It seems we came to an agreement long ago: she suffers for me, I live out her fantasies. She suffers when I stay home on New Year's Eve.

There was a time when our world extended beyond my future. My mother had been political; she had marched on picket lines; fed organizers; led meetings. She had kept the books of her cell in the CP as well as those of Charlie Mykonos and Jimmy the Greek, and had gotten both herself and my father into trouble. For almost a decade she pretended she was flighty and could not remember a single name when the FBI came around to chat. At the end, she and my father, native born but nervous, were worn out from the threats of deportation. When Adlai Stevenson lost for the second time, they stopped voting. Then the family dissolved before our eyes: Uncle Yuri married a southern belle, we moved to New York, and my grandmother died. When my father's fifth business collapsed, taking him with it, my mother became a kind of recluse: either she was to be found at the office or in bed with a headache. What sustained her was her belief that I would grow up into a professor. Our Jewishness sustained her very little; it consisted of feeling sorry for ourselves on holidays.

Our decision to resettle in Israel could not therefore be construed as the inevitable outcome of a committed Zionism. It was more like a desperate attempt to save whatever was left of our lives, or perhaps to change them completely. If our apartment in New York was dark, the one we would find in Tel Aviv would be light. If our wages barely covered necessities and we spent far more than was necessary on luxuries, in Israel we would live simply, on rye bread and fermented milk if need be. If we barely recognized our neighbors here, there we would be one big happy family. Didn't they say *Kol Yisrael haverim?* A young Parisian customs officer, checking our passports and observing that we held no return tickets, beamed, *"Ah, c'est beau! Une maman et sa fille se ménagent en Israel! Mazal tov!"* Not even the surly El Al stewards or the dinginess of Lod Airport could disabuse us of the notion that this place and our fate were special.

On my first trip to Israel the year before, I was overwhelmed: by the crumbling stucco facades, the flies on the felafel, the sharp-tongued matrons with plastic net shopping bags who eyed me suspiciously as they gave directions. I located a post office, phoned my mother in New York, and shrieked, "What am I doing here? Why didn't I go to Switzerland?" Then I realized how expensive and futile this was. But seeing Israel for the first time, my mother was charmed. She fell in love, for example, with the Jewish policemen in their lemon- and orange-sherbet-colored uniforms. Not even the flying Saharan cockroach in our bedroom—which I had to kill with a chair—fazed her. She became, to our neighbors, the blonde Anglo-Saxon: blonde from a bottle, Anglo-Saxon because she spoke English. "You see," she exulted, "you live long enough, anything can happen."

The Middle Eastern air, so deceptively soft, does one of two things:

it either bombards your stomach with exotic bacteria or it robs you of your critical acumen. To my mother it did both. On her only trip to Jerusalem, she became violently ill from eating St. Peter's fish. After that the holy city always called to mind a bellyache. But the thought of Tel Aviv's prostitutes seemed to testify to Israel's normalcy. Once in a café by the sea which the ladies of the evening frequented, my mother could not get over the beauty and proud bearing of the girls. After a while, it occured to me that there was something odd about the strength of their backs, the curvature of their jaws. When a diminutive creature, plump as a pullet, reported to the pimp, I saw the difference. "Ma," I said, "these beautiful women aren't women at all." My mother, who had been a virgin until she was in her thirties, merely chuckled, "Well, well, Jewish transvestites, what do you know about that?"

Such an infatuation could not last. One day my mother commented to Gveret Resnikoff downstairs that it was raining hard. "So?" said the old lady, "in New York it's snowing," and she walked away in a huff. "How do you like that," my mother sniffed. "Can't even open your mouth around here." Then the local grocer dropped a piece of cheese on the floor, dusted it off, and wrapped it up for her to take home. The girls in the bank were seen foraging for carbon paper in the wastebasket. Finally, having bought a chicken at the rotisserie, she found that both its wings were missing. She went back to demand an explanation. "I was hungry," shrugged the matron in charge, "so I ate them."

Annoyances multiplied. Aspirin was costly; the toilet paper had no traction. The electric heater had to be dragged from room to room over the lizard-cold tiles. The ways of Israeli business frustrated my mother, too. A day after arrival, letter in hand, she reported for work only to discover the company had fired the man who promised her the job. A second try took her to an office where the manager seemed surprised that an American should be looking for a position at all. Her third correspondant suggested that, like his grandmother, she should be taking the sun and minding children. Murray Rogoloff, the Immigrant's Friend who sold *toasterim* and *blenderim* to newcomers, urged her to work for him. But the former F/C through the general ledger of

Morgenthau Shoes tired quickly of explaining to Russians that they needed money in their bank accounts before they could pay by check. Finally, she was hired by an elderly importer of English books who looked like Rumpelstilskin. She detested her function, that of spy, in the workroom above the fish market where a dozen people shivered around a single gas heater and spun Mar Karensky's figures into gold.

Each of these stints lasted about a week. Since she started to have dizzy spells — perhaps it was the African sun? — I began going with her to interviews. At Ha-Aretz, Ltd., an international investment firm, a stunning redhead ushered us into the carpeted suite of Mar Shimon Bart, Vice President. Mar Bart offered us a drink — aquavit? scotch? — from his liquor cabinet, and discussed the state of the economy with my mother, and the state of Israeli higher education with me. It was difficult to contradict him, but he seemed to be enjoying himself. He cancelled an appointment with his wife in order to take us to his favorite Bulgarian restaurant, where the proprietor was as obsequious as the eggplant was oily. Bart's limousine took us home. He called frequently for the next week or so, inviting me to the theater or to his club in Herzliya. I declined these invitations; the job disappeared. When my mother complained about this to the American philanthropist who underwrote Ha-Aretz, Ltd., she received a letter from Mar Bart's attorneys, a hundred strong on the letterhead. Mar Bart was an outstanding citizen, a pillar of Israeli society, they asserted; in accusing him of moral turpitude, my mother had cast aspersions on the state itself. Unless she apologized to their client personally, the letter stated, they would sue.

But the final blow to my mother's pioneering spirit was of a different kind. Taking a skirt to the local seamstress, she found the shop closed and a sign in the window. She could not read it. My mother had not even wept when she became a widow. Now she cried all the time. Her father had arrived in America with as little knowledge of English as she had of Hebrew. "I'm not going to die of a stroke like my father," she repeated. She cashed the Social Security check she had been keeping in reserve and packed her possessions. ("You, an American, have only one coat?" asked Gveret Resnikoff in disbelief.) Convinced she had left me in a nation of lechers, my mother returned to the lukewarm bosom of her family.

Her letters urged me to follow. It was not long before she acquired a job, leased an apartment, and stocked two closets to the top with boxes of Kleenex and rolls of Soft-Weave. She loved her wall-to-wall carpeting and gloried in her control over the thermostat. Writing to me, she kept dropping heavy hints about the buying power of dollars and about the marriages of various acquaintances. She knew that I taught in a second university to pay the rent, that the libraries held few books in my field, Renaissance Linguistics, and that my boyfriend's mother grumbled about my lack of a dowry. Didn't I want to come home?

The promise of a lifetime's supply of typewriter paper would not have made me admit it, but I was of two minds in this matter. On the one hand, I enjoyed a newfound companionship: people dropped by the apartment daily; in fact, if I wanted to be alone, I had to pretend I was making love. I could walk home after a concert unaccompanied; I could assert my right to a seat in the bus without wondering if my competitor would pull a knife. My analyst treated me at half price. I liked the open doors of the terraces, the dry heat, the nine months of perpetual sunlight. Yet, while I wasn't overtly nostalgic, I thought about food a lot: rare roast beef, hamburgers with ketchup, sweet gherkins, twenty-eight flavors of ice cream, blueberry muffins, lobster and shrimp. How often, I asked myself, had I in fact eaten lobster when it was available? Once a month? Once a year? But reason did not help.

Other things drove me wild: taxes were always changing, making our paychecks fluctuate; the card catalog was in Hebrew and gave me headaches. I got annoyed with people who did not know automatically that West Hartford is a suburb. All of us, *Anglo-Saxonim,* would bitch about getting up in the morning and having to examine that patient, the state, always on the critical list, with its fluttering cabinet and its soaring inflation. Instead of saying "How are you?" to each other, we asked "How's the lira doing?" Intellectual discussion, of verbal clusters in Dante or the great vowel shift, was shattered by a plane cracking the sound barrier. You couldn't help it. Sure, you could go right on talking without its making the slightest bit of difference to the fellows above, but you just couldn't concentrate in the same old way.

There were days when one moment I was fine and the next moment felt that I had been dropped on an alien planet. I would waken to the sound of carpets being beaten on the neighboring terraces. Traveling by bus to friends in Ashdod, I would suddenly become aware of the other passengers munching sunflower seeds and spitting their shells on the floor. And the holidays! Sukkot, Shavuot, Tisha B'Av, Simhat Torah—on all of them I asked myself: What am I doing here?

Yom Kippur was the worst. I had spent the New Year itself with a family who filled my spiritual emptiness with pancakes; who thought the Diaspora would be ended through the sheer force of their hospitality. But it is kind of hard to invite people to a fast. As evening fell, men and women drifted toward the synagogue like so many shtetl ghosts. I became bitter. Here I was in a modern state, in the latter half of the twentieth century, and I had to put up with this medieval nonsense. *I would not fast.* I saw myself catching a flight back to the States, marrying a Gentile, joining the DAR. I realized I had never felt less Jewish. I found myself alone.

The day itself was much longer than I had anticipated. The bread was stale. I ran out of butter. Somewhere in the early afternoon, my clock stopped. When the sky seemed to darken, I turned on the radio to find out if Reshet Aleph had resumed broadcasting. They were playing Beethoven's Fifth, that anthem of collective transcendence. How odd, I thought, on the Day of Atonement.

Feeling light-headed—I had eaten only a dry bagel and an egg—I wanted to get something to eat on the way to my friend Nili's, where I was due after sundown. The streetlights were not on; I wondered whether Yom Kippur was over. A few cafes on Dizengoff were serving and the usual macho types—shirts open to the navel—were stationed at tables outside. I noticed that they weren't eating; even their coffees were untouched. Their *transistorim* were attached to their ears. One of these men turned around to stare at me and made a remark. It was not the usual comment. "*Selichah?*" I said. "Excuse me?" His companion repeated it: "We're fighting for you, *gvirti.*" I looked over my shoulder. I thought he must be addressing someone else.

Only when I reached Nili's, where her mother was reenacting the siege of Moscow, did I begin to realize what was happening. "What are you doing out in the street?" cried Gveret Markovitz, wringing her hands and clutching at her dressing gown. "You have to prepare! Veh iz mir! Again! Veh! Veh!"

"Oh, Maman," yawned Nili, a French teacher, "It really won't last all that long you know." Gveret Markovitz began drawing up a shopping list for me: sugar, flour, candles. Nili drew her wrapper closer about herself—they had just gotten up from an afternoon nap, I guess—and curled on the sofa. "Can you imagine," she said almost dreamily, "there's a war on again."

I could not imagine, but I left soon, as directed, carrying the tins of sardines and packets of cream cheese Nili's mother had pressed on me. The city was very quiet. I was the sole passenger on the bus, but the driver only nodded to me and did not speak. At home, I hung a blanket, gaily striped like my bedspread, over my window; the room took on an oriental quality, like a tent in the desert. I wondered how much was known abroad, how my mother was taking this. The radio reported hundreds of casualties, and I wondered how bad the fighting really was. I felt vaguely guilty, but argued against myself: had I brought this trouble upon her as usual? From inside a tent it is very difficult to tell anything.

The next morning a group of girls just under army age came up to me on the street. "Are you an American?" they asked. I said I was. "What do you think of us now?" they beamed. "Don't we conduct ourselves well in a state of emergency?" In the following weeks, it seemed true. Not that the lines were any more orderly in the post office, not that Gveret Kresky did not think she had a right to go ahead of Mar Joseph. But people made gallant gestures on behalf of the war effort. One of my superiors, who had barely deigned to acknowledge me, called to see if I needed several liters of milk. I don't drink milk. Friends and relatives of soldiers bombarded them with sweets; the radio begged them not to send custards and whipped-cream cakes through the mails. The elderly were given seats on the bus.

We moved from one radio broadcast to the next. Some of us, to our surprise, were actually mobilized. Mark, stoop-shouldered and mild, as unlikely an army candidate as you could find, was posted to the Gaza Strip; Jerry, a Victorian scholar, stood guard on the Golan

Heights. He would tell us about his basic training later. When he asked his sergeant why he could not pull the pin on his grenade, the sergeant informed him that he would first have to take the grenade out of its box. We were not sure if this was a joke or not.

Nili cut bandages in a hospital. I took care of a drafted colleague's pregnant wife. We got together at each other's houses at night, those curious nights when teams of older men came around to check on blackout observance, waving their flashlights and making so much noise you would think they were going to be heard in Cairo. Ordinary things, like a woman hanging out her laundry in the moonlight, were awe inspiring. Sometimes the opposite was true of special measures. During an air-raid warning in the middle of the night, I wrapped my trembling limbs in a blanket as instructed, took up my candles, and went to the shelter. I stood outside while the Sobols, an aged couple who owned the house, bickered about who had the key to the basement and why the one in hand did not fit. Fortunately, the all clear sounded.

I did not hear from my mother for several days. Just at the point when I was beginning to feel neglected, the call came. For once we had a clear connection: "I'm at Uncle Saul's," she said, in a calmer voice than usual. "They're giving me a hard time. They say the embassy is evacuating Americans."

"So?" I said, "Nu?"

"Do you want to leave, too?"

I remember I stood near the open terrace doors, the blackout blanket framing the view. A group of children — school was back in session — passed, chattering. They wore diminutive *sandalim* and carried satchels. I was amazed as always that they had already mastered Hebrew. From the garden next door came the smell of guavas, the national perfume I normally detested. I envisioned embassy types, blond and ruddy, departing by ship; and the narrow strip on the map where, if you twist your head to one side, you can read what country it is. This was the first time I had entertained the possibility of leaving.

"No, I don't think so."

"They've been nagging me to ask you," said the new person, "but I understand how you feel."

"You understand?"

"Of course."

"You *hated* living here."

My mother sighed. "What has that got to do with it?" She asked me if I needed anything; I told her the mails were full of cream cakes as it was. "Three minutes are up," the operator intervened. "Paula—" said my mother, "there's one more thing. I'm proud of you." The operator interrupted again and we said good-night.

My mother's calls were few, though I half expected them with each counterattack. When I did hear from her, she did not ask me if I was taking my Vitamin C or if I would find the funds for research. She spoke in a voice I identified—dare I say it?—as that of a goy, someone connected with harvests and crop failures and floods. I do not know if she took extra Valium or whether, between juggling figures at Mrs. Becker's Dress Emporium and worrying about my broken engagements, she had also heard Beethoven's Fifth. Though I was not on the border and thus in no immediate danger, I began to understand how the mothers of sons who die in wars do not follow them to their graves and how the wives of heroes remarry.

A week or so after the cease-fire, the telephone rang with peculiar insistence one Saturday night.

"Who could that be at this hour?" asked the new boyfriend. I could have told him.

"You're home!" exclaimed my mother.

"Of course I'm home. Where would I be, picking strawberries? It's two in the morning."

"You weren't hurt?"

"Hurt? How?"

"On Dizengoff, in the movie"—terrorists had bombed a cinema that day—"I know how you love movies."

"Ma, I'm all right, I swear."

"You're sure?" I told her I was very sure.

"All right," she conceded, "I was worried." I knew then that the crisis had passed. Shortly afterwards I began to dream again of Howard Johnson's mocha chip ice cream, central heating, and a library with a good Renaissance collection.

FAYE MOSKOWITZ

A LEAK IN THE HEART

Spring comes softly to Michigan; winter is more outspoken. The wind grows quiet and sun cuts through gray snow to warm the earth below. Overnight a few tender snowdrops appear in dark, wet patches where the snow has melted. The wet places grow; ice chunks relax and fall apart. One day the pavements are dry and little girls in sweaters come out to chalk hopscotch squares on the sidewalks.

 A leak in the heart, the doctors called it. Shifra, her own heart throbbing like a thumb caught in a door, carried the baby Chaya home and propped her in a high chair. Day after day she stuffed her with graham crackers swimming in milk, or pablum or pieces of zwieback sprinkled with sugar and softened in boiling water. Perched on a stool in front of the baby, Shifra tasted each spoonful and blew on it to make certain it was not too hot. She opened her mouth wide in empathy every time the baby swallowed but the food brimmed up, welled over and seeped out of the corners of Chaya's mouth. The food leaked out faster than Shifra could spoon it in and one afternoon, just before the Sabbath, the baby died.

An old woman Shifra had never seen before washed the baby and bound her jaws with a bit of flannel. After a while, the director of the burial society carried the bundle away. Shifra's mother came and brothers and sisters with their wives and husbands and they hid the baby clothes and took down the crib and put away the high chair, but in the kitchen Shifra found a small bowl with a flake of dried cereal stuck to its side and she said, "David, I can't look at this place. Get me out. I'll never come back here again."

There was a way for a woman in her situation to behave; Shifra conducted herself properly, she thought. She merely did what she had seen other women before her do. On Sunday she fainted repeatedly in the airless chapel, and twice at the graveside a brother had to restrain her from throwing herself into the raw, red-clay slit. Back at her mother's house, she observed the Seven Days sitting on a low mourner's bench staring at her stockinged feet, her young face yellowed with grief like old ironstone.

Shifra and David exchanged few words during the mourning period. When she thought to look at him, his eyes were as shrouded as the mirrors of the house, everywhere draped with sheets. Even at night the two were not together. She shared a room with her mother and sister to make space for other relatives in the crowded flat while he slept on a cot in the living room. One morning, finding her dressing alone, he curled his fingers around her hair, still in a thick braid for the night, and this time she averted *her* eyes, blushing to think she and David had ever been close enough to do the things necessary to make a baby. She could swear he had that look of wanting about him then . . . there in that house of mourning. It seemed to her she must be perfectly still, her arms stiffly at her sides, touching nothing, feeling nothing, loving nothing. In December, not long after the official mourning days were over, she convinced David to take her away from Detroit to a small town she had heard of, some sixty miles from their family and friends.

Shifra spent most of that winter inside the house. Early each morning, David left for the junk yard where he had found work with a Jewish proprieter who did not force him to work on the Sabbath. She cleaned house endlessly, polishing floors that already glistened and washing clothes that were scarcely soiled. The bungalow was small, and sometimes she woke up with little to do. Then she paced herself carefully using an intricate system of tasks and rewards she had invented for herself: wash this wall and you may sit down for a glass of tea; iron this shirt and you may look out at the snow. Cleaning was good; she was certain of that. She was not certain of much else. If only she could remember what it was she had done to offend God so, perhaps she could make some sense out of what He had done to her.

Endless inner conversations bespattered her mind; the thoughts at times so intense they squeezed out her mouth in spite of herself in short, humming groans: "Memory keeps things alive but I know David is letting go of Chaya . . . animals are like that . . . existing as if there is no past. Everything is present for them . . . no memory except for where the food is and the warmth . . . forgetting their young as soon as they are taken from them. He used to call her his diamond, the star in his crown . . . oh, how I polished her, my sweetness. She shone as though she had been dipped in pure fresh oil . . . now she is in the dirt . . . everything is dirty. When I was carrying her, David told me, showed me things I could do for him . . . when we couldn't be man and wife. He said it was allowed. He said, I am only human, after all. I have my needs. I asked him then, what kind of women do those things? He said, Shifrele, I beg you, and I did what he asked. Was that the sin? God, help me find the dirty spot and I will bleach it and wash it until everything smells sweet and clean again. . . ."

One night toward the end of winter, Shifra and David lay under their feather bed talking for a few moments before going to sleep. As she had done for months now, Shifra pillowed her head in the crook of one elbow and held on to the side of the bed with her other hand so she would not sink into the mattress' sag and touch David's body with her own. Slowly the coal fire in the basement burned itself out and the timbers of the little house creaked and expanded with the increasing cold. Out of habit, the two still spoke in whispers as if to avoid waking a sleeping child.

David told her of the salesman who came to the shop and sold Mr. Arnhoff a set of books containing all the knowledge in the world. He described the gold-stamped red bindings that looked exactly like leather and the hundreds of colored illustrations. Longingly he spoke of the shiny metal globe to be delivered when the final payment was made. Shifra wished she had a letter from home, or anything, to share with him. Her mother wrote Yiddish very well. Sometimes Shifra would receive a letter from her, the characters crowded onto the page with a blunt nib, the vowels liberally peppered underneath each word. She always saved the letters until after supper so she would have a contribution when David told his stories. Otherwise she had little to say to him. Nothing ever really happened to her anymore.

Today, of course, there had been the visit in the afternoon but she was too ashamed to tell him about it. A young neighbor, carrying a plate of cookies, had called on her but when she answered the door, all her English had drained out as though her brain were a colander. She had stood at the door, earlobes burning, babbling, "The same to you, the same to you."

Finally she had taken the plate and almost closed the door in the woman's face. A hundred times later that day, she imagined another scene in which she and the pretty blonde neighbor drank tea from china cups with their little fingers delicately crooked. They spoke of many things and her English was perfect. Instead, she had stood for half an hour behind the door, heart pounding, balancing the plate. Later she dumped the cakes in the garbage and gingerly washed the dish in the basement tubs. Goyim cooked everything with lard. God alone knew how she would get the plate back or for that matter, whether she was to return it at all. Who could understand the customs here?

David's voice droned on. She tried to follow his words but he confused her with the names of strangers and she resented the excitement that seemed to creep more and more frequently into his stories. Secretly she mocked his clumsy English. "I'm free, white, and twenty-one," he kept telling her. What did that mean? Soon he would be speaking nothing but English and she would be more alone than ever. She only pretended to listen for she did not really want to hear about his life outside. The child had been like a strap that held them close. Now, unbuckled, they had to struggle to keep together.

Shifra counted the faded roses blooming along the walls, their bisected petals and leaves lovingly rejected by some unknown paperhanger. Through the open door into the bathroom, she could see the long pull-chain to an overhead light floating back and forth in the warm blast of the floor register.

» «

Chaya had favored a certain toy, tiny wooden chickens attached to a platform with a red ball hanging down. Shifra dreams now about that toy. She is a gaudy yellow chicken. Someone pulls the string. Up and down goes her head, pecking, picking at painted bits of corn. But her mouth is painted and she cannot open it and the corn is painted and she cannot eat it. Another jerk of the string; her painted beak goes up and down, up and down.

Now her eyelids are pulled down as though lead weights are attached to each lash. Moist, drowsy, floating she imagines she feels the child, an infant again, nuzzling at her breast. Far down inside, her womb contracts and easily she unfolds, muscle by muscle, like a cat.

"Oh, that's good," she murmurs. "So good."

Suddenly she wrenched herself awake and whispered hoarsely, "Devil, let me be!"

She pulled the sleeves of her night dress back up over her shoulders and turned to glare at her husband. "What are you doing to me? Are you crazy?"

"Shifrele," he said. "You are *making* me crazy."

"What if I get pregnant again? What if this child is sick, too?"

"Don't worry. I promise you I'll be careful. I'll stop in time. Everything will be all right."

"All right! That's what you always say. That's what you said before, remember? So tell me then; what else do I need now? I'm listening to you. Go ahead. Tell me that I need another baby for the evil eye to fall on."

"Ah, you don't know what you are saying."

"No, *chacham,* only you know what you are saying." She sat up. "It's too soon; I'm the stupid one but I know it's not right."

Another time, David might have tried to stop her. This time he did not move as she crawled out of the warm bed and struggled into a faded chenille robe. He did not call her back as she felt her way down the cracked rubber treads to the front room.

Shifra fumbled for the switch, and the plaster clipper ship on the mantel glowed in a sickly artificial sunset. A red bulb, shining from between the sails, turned the green frieze sofa a mud-brown. Even the white doilies, stiffened in sugar and pinned to the chair arms, looked tired and dirty in the cruel light. Cheeks burning, warmed by her anger, Shifra fell asleep, sitting straight up in a slippery leather chair. Outside it was too cold to snow but on the windows near her, the frost crocheted a delicate pattern of lace.

» «

In Shifra's dream the pretty blonde neighbor woman wears an orange dress and carries an infant whose heavy head bobbles against her breast. The baby has red cheeks and round blue eyes that seem pasted on to its face. On one side of the infant's neck is a grotesque swelling like a misplaced goiter. A string of mismatched yellow seed pearls winds around its neck, almost hidden in some places by flaps of flesh. Shifra can see something below its belly that resembles the neck and spout of a watering can but she is not sure what it is.

The blonde woman asks Shifra anxiously, "Do you think there is anything the matter with my little girl's hands?" The baby's fingers are as long as its arms and are webbed in between. Shifra flounders for words. She feels almost guilty because her own child is perfect. She forces herself to touch the sick baby: "I'm sure your mama and papa have had you to a doctor." The father (who is somehow David), answers cheerfully, "Don't worry. Everything will be all right. I'm a doctor. I've checked the baby and its little bowels are perfectly clean."

Shifra has a vision of that strange baby hanging upside down on a hook like a naked chicken in a butcher shop.

A heavy icicle cracks loose from the eaves and shatters into brittle shards on the frozen ground. Shifra pulls the robe more tightly around her and dreams it is Succoth, the Feast of Booths, and she is a child at home in the shtetl Horodok. Her father enters the house carrying a small wooden box. "Shifrele," he says. "Come, see what is here."

She watches as he reverently pries open the top of the box.

"Tochterle, this has traveled all the way across the seas from the Holy Land." He lifts the lid and tenderly pulls away the grayish cotton wool that surrounds the fragrant yellow citron. Shifra can hardly breathe. The citron is perfect, without a blemish.

"Papa, I would like to be shut up in such a box, wrapped in cotton wool. Then I could stay the same forever."

Her father frowns. "What you are saying is a sin. You don't know what you are saying."

"Have I made a sin? Papa, why have you stopped smiling at me?"

Shifra's body was heavy when she awoke. Her veins felt as though they were filled with sand instead of blood. Like someone getting out of bed after a long illness, she was not sure she remembered how to walk. Raising the window shade, she could see an icicle drip-drop steadily into an ever enlarging circle in the snow.

» «

Upstairs the featherbed was thrown back and the sheets were cold to her touch. David was gone. Downstairs, in the drafty kitchen, heavy graniteware utensils sat neatly on the wooden shelves she had covered with oilcloth to hide the chipping enamel underneath. She unlocked the back door and snatched in two bottles of milk, their paper caps perched crazily on stalks of ice. He must have left even before the milkman came. God knows where he went. With a sharp knife, she sliced off the frozen cream at the neck of each bottle and dropped it into a pitcher. David always took cream in his coffee.

Two chairs, lined up as if with a ruler, were tucked under the porcelain-topped table. David was gone. The coffee pot was still in the cupboard. He didn't have anything to drink before he left. Who did she have but herself to thank for this. She had pushed him too far. He was a man, after all. Where would he go on a shabbos? He never worked on Saturday before. Arnhoff let the goyim run the shop on Saturdays. Outside was cold and alien; inside everything was familiar and in its place but David was gone and things were not in order. She put the cream away and noticed that cold water plicked slowly from a block of ice into the drip pan under the ice-box. Everything melts but me, she thought.

Gradually, thin, gray morning light had surrounded the house. Her throat felt weedy, like an old downspout grown over with ivy. "Let him hang himself," she said, clearing her throat. The sun could not penetrate the thick shades shrouding the spotless windows. Shivering, Shifra crept down into the dark cellar and threw a mouthful of coal to the furnace that ate and ate and was never sated. "There," she said, grunting with the weight of the shovel, "you and all my other enemies: choke on it!"

A fat black spider, underbelly marked with white spots like a domino, slowly lowered itself down a filmy thread in front of her face. She swung the heavy coal shovel, catching the thread on her arm. "Mama, help me," she screamed, running up the stairs, tripping on the robe, brushing her arms again and again against her sides. "Get off, get off!" Feeling the furry legs in her ears, down her back and crawling up to catch in the hair between her thighs.

Finally she stopped screaming and instead, a thin high-pitched wail trickled like blood out her nostrils and through her clenched teeth. She went in the front room and forced herself to sit down on the sofa, and then she flicked on the radio, silent during the long weeks of mourning. A sweet tenor voice rattled the cone. "Did you ever see a dream walking? Well, I did." She thought of the strange, sick baby. "Did you ever see a dream talking? Well, I did. . . . "

"Who are you talking to? Gottenyu, what is going on here? This house is bewitched! When is that bastard coming back?"

The radio blared on but Shifra could no longer understand the English. Her teeth chattered with cold, even as a perverse wave of perspiration drove sweat down the sides of her body and the cleavage between her breasts. She rocked back and forth on the sofa, unaware that she moved her body to the brassy rhythm of some far-away dance band.

"Ten o'clock. Bulova watch time." Early yet. In Detroit, the women would still be sitting in the balcony of the shul, whispering, ignoring the shammas as he banged his fist on the lectern and shouted for order. Why think of that now? She didn't want to be with those women who, for envy of her grief, would tear her apart like a herring. She didn't want to be sitting there with them, catching the drip from her nose with a sodden handkerchief bound round her wrist, her prayer book forever blistered by tears.

She had always hated the stench of the place, the stuffy women's section smelling of fish and garlic that wouldn't wash off the fingers and of the naphthalene that seemed to be part of the very texture of the greasy black dresses the wives all wore. She wouldn't stay there and become like them, waiting for the pores of her face to open through the years and fill with tiny carpet tacks of dirt. Away from their example, perhaps her own skin would stay milk-white instead of gradually darkening, looking as if in perpetual shadow.

Ah, but what difference did her youth make? Long ago, the soft, sweet brown rot set in and one day she would push her fingers through her own flesh to touch cold bone beneath. Shifra, her mother had said, look at your baby one last time, and when they lifted the lid, the stink of rotting flesh so astonished her, she slammed the top down on her mother's fingers.

Shifra rocked and rocked on the davenport, her arms crisscrossed on her belly. She felt a warm wet smear between her legs. My God! This, too. Bessie's Flora became a woman when she was only nine years old. The American teacher brought her home and told Bessie, I felt sorry for the kid. She didn't know what was going on. She just raised her hand in class and said, Miss Chase, I have red paint all over my chair.

It still happened to her mother. Disgusting. She *joked* about it. Called the rags "schlamazel's kerchiefs"; told her daughters, the holidays are early this month. Well, there it was; life was nothing but blood and stink, then dried-up breasts dropping to wrinkled bellies and fingers reeking of rancid fish. My mother knows, she thought; she laughs about it so she won't cry. My sister knows. Even Bessie's Flora knows, poor baby, but she doesn't know everything in store for her. . . .

Like the binding of a well-thumbed book, her mind cracked open to a particular scene: Mama? Here it comes again! Where is the doctor? You *said* he was coming. When is he coming, Mama? But I *am* trying. I'm trying to lie down. See, Mama, I'm trying to lie down. Yes, I know David is here but I don't want him to see me like this. Get him out of here! I don't like the way he looks at me. Devil! You said it would be all right. Take my hand, Mama. Help me; here it comes. Oh, God in heaven, Mama, LOOK WHAT I'VE DONE TO THE BED! Is that what it's like? But it's so ugly . . . so ugly . . . so dirty. I don't want it. Here it comes and I don't want it . . . .

Shifra didn't know how long she sat there on the sofa trying to wipe the scene out of her head but at last she thought, I will have to do something about this. In the bathroom which she had bleached and scoured ivory-white, she began to clean herself. Knocking over a stack of snowy towels in the linen closet, she pulled out some small squares of bird's-eye cotton. Each month, after her period, she soaked and washed the old diapers but still faint rusty spots remained. She leaned on the wash basin, the room whirling.

Overnight, the hard water from the tap had dripped a filthy orange stain into the white bowl. There was no end to the dirt. She cleaned and cleaned and it was still dirty. With trembling fingers, she shook gritty powder into the basin. On the soft-yellow cleanser box, a downy chick stepped out of an egg shell.

Heart fluttering like a bird in her breast, she saw the sliver of steel, David's razor hanging from a nail; she remembered the Shabbos goy coming toward her carrying the writhing chicken by her spindly yellow legs, the earth frozen to steel squeaking under his heavy boots, coming toward her, telling her through the yellow tobacco-stained hair around his small mouth, this is what we do to little birds who try to run away; throwing the hen on the ground in front of her, lifting her wing, spreading it, a pulsing feathered fan, the knife glittering, catching the sun, slitting the tendon. All the while, the chicken screaming, rasping rhythmic screams as she, Shifra, had screamed then, as she had screamed when the baby tore itself out of her body, as she had screamed one other time, as she screamed now, imagining the cold steel slicing through bushy hair and biting into the vulnerable flesh under her armpits. *This* is what we do to little birds. . . .

She ran in short, tight circles around and around the tiny room until, exhausted, she dropped to the floor and placed her cheek against the cool porcelain of the footed tub. She lay there for many minutes, her mind white and empty. Then she said out loud, almost laughing, "Run away? Where can I run? To where the black pepper grows?"

Shifra stood up stiffly and washed her hands, twirling the oval bar of Sweetheart around in her hands. She dressed and went down stairs. He would be good and hungry by now, probably cold, too. Was it his fault? Who could change the world? She shrugged into a heavy coat, tied a babushka around her hair and pulled open the front door. The sun, mirrored in countless melting surfaces, blinded her for a moment. When she could see again, she turned towards the heart of the town and set off to look for David.

BETTE HOWLAND

THE LIFE YOU GAVE ME

So my father is going to be all right.

That's what my mother said as soon as we met at the airport. That's what the doctor said when he came out of surgery. That's what my father said himself, just before he went in, making it snappy over long-distance: "This is costing you money."

That's what I thought all along.

He's always been all right before.

» «

Before. That would be ten years by now.

The voice over the telephone sounded encouraging.

"Mrs. Horner? Sally Horner?"

Uh-huh, he's selling something, was my first thought. What'll it be? Magazine subscriptions? Rug shampooing? I can never make up my mind what to do about telephone solicitors. Is it better to say no thanks and hang up on the spot, so they don't waste any breath? Or to stand there, frowning, with the phone to your ear, and let them finish?

I stood there.

"This is Reverend Nightswan? Chaplain at Covenant Community Hospital?"

Still inquiring.

Didn't I tell you? Collecting for charity. But what's he calling me for? What does he want from me? How did he ever get hold of my name?

"I'm calling about your father? He had an accident?"

"How?"

Owww.

A grappling hook got tangled in seaweed.

"Now take it easy now. Don't go getting all excited. There's nothing to upset yourself about. He fell? Off a ladder? Fixing the roof on the house? It looks like he maybe cracked a couple of ribs. He broke his nose. Things like that. We should know pretty soon. They're still checking him over."

Oh, yes. Wasn't that just like him? Easy to picture my father up on a ladder. Haven't I seen him dozens of times? The wide back and heavy shoulders. The polar bear neck. The legs powerful, foreshortened, condensed by their own strength and weight. That's nothing new.

But wait a minute. What's going on here? I don't get it. My parents don't have a house anymore. What roof? What house? What business does the old man have — climbing ladders?

Reverend Nightswan spoke.

"We thought you might want to come down?"

"Now?"

I was still frowning. My father does that. Talks into the telephone as if he's getting a bad connection or bad news. His thick forehead bunched; the phone squeezed to his raspy cheek; raising his voice to make himself heard in the next room — the next world. He says he can't help it, he's used to working in the plant, shouting over machines. I believe him. I got sent every now and then to pick up his paycheck. Through all the open transom windows the noise made a tunnel: clubbing, bludgeoning, plundering air.

He doesn't know his own strength, says my mother.

We have the same vertical groove over one eyebrow; more than a frown — almost a scar.

"You mean right now?"

"Well, yes. Now. Now would be good. Now, that is, if it's all right with you."

"Yeah, sure," I said. "Okay. Now."

»«

It was a warm bright day. Earlier a pair of window washers had been at work, ropes and planks butting the cemented slabs of the building. I heard voices, looked out, down they came. Thick boots, army pants, cigarettes in curly beards. The sponges slopped and slurred. Water blurted. It ran on the glass as over stones glazed in a stream.

The sky looked like that. Transparent. Luminous.

Out of the clear blue sky it came to me: What if my father was dead?

That must be it. That was what they had called me for. That was what it was all about. The chaplain. No wonder. You know yourself how they are; they never tell you the truth. They don't like to break the news over the phone.

I pictured a form under a white sheet; my father laid out like a large piece of furniture. The hulk of the chest, the humps and ridges of the toes, the sloping head, the bump of the nose.

Didn't that guy just say, though, that my father's nose was broken? He wouldn't say that, would he, if my father was dead? No, no one would say a thing like that. Not a broken nose.

He must be all right, then.

He was going to be all right.

I felt grateful to this Reverend Nightswan, whoever he was. My first guess had come pretty close. A limited-one-time-only offer. Can't last. Take it or leave it.

Now or never.

» «

There was something I wanted to say to my father. I knew what it was, what it had to be. Everyone knows that. Only I wasn't sure how to say it. But I always knew the time would come. Sooner or later. The stage would be set; the scene would be played; all of a sudden it would be easy.

All of a sudden I would mean it.

Still, I dreaded seeing him like this. My father's size and strength were more than physical. Mental, temperamental. Character traits. Mind Over Matter was his motto. Whenever anyone else got sick, he would tiptoe about the house, trying to speak softly — lowering his loud voice to sandpaper whispers — pulling down window shades, fetching glasses of water. He looked apologetic, respectful, almost — if such a word could be applied to him — scared; as if he had filled the glass too full and thought it might spill. He gave advice, pep talks, about keeping your head warm and your feet cool. And he meant it. Did he have a Hot Head? Cold Feet? But it was no good. What was the use? Others weren't made of such stern stuff; didn't his constitution (or, as he called it, his System) or his conscience; his maxims or morals. To see him brought down, laid low, damaged, hurting, like any other injured creature — was to see him disgraced.

All of which is not to say that my father was ever a simple man. Only that he didn't know his own strength.

But I did.

» «

The Emergency Room was busy. The benches facing front, lined up like church pews; peaked caps moving up and down — nurses scribbling away behind a high counter. I spotted my mother standing and talking to a doctor, a large dark man in a Hawaiian sports shirt and tinted glasses; but I could tell he was a doctor from the beeper in his pocket and all the ballpoint pens clipped to it. My mother's head came just about up to this row of pens on his chest; thrust at him — close — as if she wanted to take a bite out of him.

It surprises me how short my mother really is.

"He'll be all right, won't he?" she was saying. The doctor folded his arms, braced in steely watchband.

She turned on me.

"Well he's gone and done it now. Now he's really gone and done it. He fixed himself up but good this time," she said. "And I told him too. I told him no more ladders. He's not the man he was, you know. I begged him. Please. Don't go climbing any ladders."

"That's what I don't understand. I can't figure it out. What in the world was he doing up on a roof?"

"What was he doing? What do you think he was doing?"

She skimped up the arcs of two picked plucked little eyebrows — the only items little in that proud front, her face. Hair white; features dark; lipstick intense, vivid as a caste mark.

"Do you have to ask? Don't you know your father by now? A favor, that's what. For the neighbors, that's who. You don't suppose he'd be fixing anything for me? Not him. Not if the ceiling was falling on our heads. He's *retired*. I can't get him to look up from the newspaper. I have to plead with him till I'm blue in the face. But the neighbors are never afraid to ask. All they have to do is knock on the door. — It'll only take you a minute. It's nothing for you. — Oh no. Nothing. Some nothing. Go. Go take a look at him. Go see what's nothing. I just hope he learned his lesson. Maybe next time he'll listen to me for a change. That man. Talking to him is like talking to a wall."

I followed the doctor down the corridor.

We were at basement level; painted pipes in the ceiling, loud bare floors. His back was humped and husky in his flowery shirt, his arm swinging and flashing its watchband. I tried to picture a hospital room, a row of white beds, and in one of them my father. Looking out from a visor of bandages, a splinted nose.

My father spent his working years in a factory; he was a junk collector, a handyman — fixing and forcing. It wasn't as if he didn't get "banged up," "busted," and "clipped"; chunks taken out of himself on things jagged or rusty; his hairy-backed hands daubed Technicolor from stinging stains and dyes. Orange Mercurochrome, purple permanganate, smelly yellow-brown iodine. His nails were bruised and black as clamshells — more decoration.

His eye would squint, his lip grip. Pain, effort, concentration: all one to him.

But then, remembering his audience — my sister and/or me — and strictly for our benefit, he would give his thick curly head a shake — a shaggy shudder — a wet dog wagging; and pantomime a howl. A yowl. His mouth with its lead-weighted molars opening wide, wrapping all around the sound:

Yow-wooch!

Only nothing came out.

"Sunnuvugun," he'd say. "That was a beaut."

But where were we going? Why was it taking so long? Frosted-glass doors, elevator doors, sliding doors. Doors with portholed windows. The doctor's arm kept swinging. Our heels clicked. Everyone knows the sound of heels clicking in hospital corridors. Everyone knows the tread of the heart.

"In there."

He pushed a door. A long sheeted table stood wheeled under a lamp. The purplish light sputtered. A nurse had been giving the patient a shot, and as she stepped aside, still fussing with the sheets, I caught a glimpse — just a glimpse — of something dark. Black as fur. A forbidden sight: the naked hairy loins of my father.

She tossed some bloody cotton in a bucket.

He had not been cleaned up, prettied up, bound up, and bandaged. His nose was swollen and clotting; his cheeks too — puffed up, punchy — like a boxer's. His whole face was bigger than usual, a damp glistening gray, the color of steamed meat. And the sheets weren't tidy either. They wrinkled and twisted.

I must have come closer. He opened his eyes.

"Oh, Sal."

He looked surprised. Most of the time my father looks surprised; it's because his eyes are so blue. They stand out above the rough cheeks. They startle you too.

Say, what're eyes like you doing in a face like this?

"'Lo, Sal."

At the last minute, feeling that the ladder was slipping and giving way beneath him, he had had the presence of mind, the force, to hurl himself forward. So he had landed, not on the concrete, on the back of his head (and from the height of three stories, I guess that would have been that) — but on the soft earth, on his face.

He had been wearing his new glasses; so new, no one had had a chance to get used to them yet. The wire rims. The eyes expanded, blinking. They were safety glass and didn't smash, but the impact left their impression on his face — an exact copy.

There they were: two circles in his cheeks, a deep dent over the bridge of his nose.

The eyes opened; they shut.

The eyes opened; they shut.

He seemed to be staring at me through a pair of specs.

He looked very large, he looked formidable; winding sheets, swollen face, broken chest. It was moving, but not up and down.

Higher.

Then higher.

And a little higher.

A boulder being pushed uphill.

He seemed to be concentrating on the effort.

His lids were violet, an odd cosmetic effect. His lip gripped—stiffened—things better left unsaid.

This wasn't what I was expecting. Not what I feared, but not what I hoped. Clearly, this was more than a case of a couple of cracked ribs and a broken nose. This wasn't going to be so easy. No one was going to get off that lightly. The sheets were wrapped and wrung about him. They clung to him. They were the pain.

He nodded, eyes shut, chin to his chest.

"'S all right, Sal."

What did he mean, it's all right?

That he was going to be all right?

That things were all right between us? (Just like that?)

Or only that it was all right, I had done my duty, shown my face; now I could go?

One thing for sure, I was dismissed. This wasn't the time, and there was nothing to say. It was an old story. I had come to ask, to seek, to plead—and not to give.

I backed out, shut the door.

"Gone . . . done it . . . ," I heard him mutter.

The doctor was passing; I caught up with him.

"He'll be all right, won't he?"

He folded his arms. It was hard to hold his eyes, in the tinted glasses.

"We have to wait and see."

"But he'll be all right? He's going to be all right?"

He didn't seem to know what I was asking.

» «

Well? What are we waiting for?

We know what's coming, don't we? We know what direction it's coming from? Is it a secret? A rumor? We know what has to happen sometime. Why keep putting it off?

Now? You mean right now?

The woman sitting next to me on the plane was on her way to see her folks in Florida too.

"I'm dreading this," she told me.

Her parents were in their eighties, had been living in Florida the past ten or a dozen years. Up to a few months ago their health had been holding up pretty well; then both had broken down at once. Between them they had just about everything wrong: cancer, heart, kidneys, cataracts, diabetes. "You name it." There was no hope, of course; no question of recovery. The only question was *how long*. She hadn't made up her mind, didn't know what to do; didn't know what she would find when we finally got on the ground. She wasn't sorry the plane had been delayed.

"Though I guess I have to face it sometime."

There had been a freak spring storm, clear across the country — taking more or less the route we were covering now — dumping ice and sleet, cracking trees, downing power lines. The world was a snow swamp; the Everglades turned white. Knee-deep drifts, rafting logs, broken branches; limbs bent low under loads of snow like lush tropical vegetation. Everything bowed down in silence.

Now we were flying over yet another snowy landscape; three-dimensional cutout clouds. The plane was packed; stewardesses in ascots and aprons pushing carts, passing out drinks, paper napkins, sliding stacked snack trays over our seats. Their faces leaned and smiled, sunny with makeup. Ice cubes faintly tinkled in plastic glasses. Smokers in the rear section had lighted up, cigarette fumes seeping through the compartment; stale traces, a bluish tinge, leaking like the trail of a dye marker.

The aisle was lit with wintry brightness.

"It's awfully bad luck," she said. "It's really a very bad break."

Somehow she had been expecting to deal with these matters one at a time.

She was in her fifties (I'd say); round face, pouchy chin, small neat-tipped mobile nose. Bifocals. Frizzy gray hairs straggling from a smooth dark bun. (By no means as much tinsel as I have; premature gray runs in my mother's family. We like to call it premature.)

She picked up her sandwich in plump ringed fingers and eyed it suspiciously. "Wonder what's in this? Ugh. Don't you hate airplane food?"

She put it back on her plate and began to dissect it with her fork.

I told her that my parents had only recently moved to Florida, after talking about it for years.

"Mine were that way too," she said. "Kept putting it off."

Now they loved it; they were only sorry they hadn't made the move much sooner.

"Just like mine," she said. "Same with mine. Don't I know."

Luckily they were barely seventy; still in good health; still plenty able to enjoy themselves.

"Oh, mine were too," she said. "Mine were too."

She was glancing at the window, not really looking out, the light settled — a kind of sediment — in the thick bottoms of her lenses. She didn't need to look; she knew the terrain. She had been here before, she had covered this ground. She was drawing me a map.

Each time she spoke, she nodded and swallowed — as if given permission — and poked at her lips with the paper napkin.

"Mine too. Mine too."

I didn't say that my father had undergone surgery that morning.

It was an emergency. A couple of nights before, he had started to hemorrhage. He was in bed; he got up and put his pants on and drove himself and my mother to the hospital. She drives now; but not with him in the car. By the time they got there, some twenty minutes later, the pants, the front seat, and the assortment of rags he keeps in the car for old times' sake (there's not much place for his junk in their new apartment, their new lives) were soaked through; sticky-bright; red with burst blood. He had almost no pulse. He had been on intravenous feedings and transfusions. The doctors were expecting to remove a section of the colon: they were pretty sure it would be malignant. But if all went well and there were no complications, they were pretty sure he would be cured completely.

Who knows why they kept putting it off?

My father had been retired for years, had elected to take an early retirement, first chance he got. It was something new. Now there are bonuses; then there were penalties. It meant a considerable sacrifice of pensions and benefits. But he didn't want to be one of those, as he put it — as he was bound to — Living on Borrowed Time.

Besides, he had always hated his job. Not that he said so. Not that he had to.

I used to wake to the trudge of a shovel: my father scraping the coal pile, getting the fire going in the furnace, in the basement. Hollow pipes carried it all through the house. The hoarse flinty rumbling had something of the ring and register — the grumbling resonance — of his voice, and I would think of him as down there talking to himself. *Down in the dumps.*

That was not just a figure of speech with my father.

Outside it would still be dark. The snow on roofs, gutters, fences, clotheslines, nothing but gloom. The air was black-and-blue with cold.

That was when we lived on the West Side of Chicago, a neighborhood of two-story houses, mostly frame. In winter the sidewalks were blasted black from the dust of coal delivery trucks, clinkers and ashes sprinkled on snow and ice; in summer, from the squashed juices of the mulberry trees. Our windows faced west, smeared with angry red sunsets. I remember the day we moved in. I mean the day my father moved us in; hauling it all down three flights from our old flat, tying it on top of his car, hauling it back up the skinny front steps, the porch on stilts. Everybody else watched, neighbors old and new. Taking his burdens to himself — seized, crushed in his hairy arms — with his crouching legs and grim gripping face, he might have been in a wrestling match. A contest of wills.

Now please. Don't get me wrong. My father was never a show-off, a muscle-bound type, like these body builders and pumpers of iron in the slick magazines; arms and chests molded in epoxy. You didn't notice his muscles. Width. Heft. Pelted neck. Hairy withers. Ruddy flesh, almost raw. — Smell of head sweat. (It was running from the roots of his curly hair in shining creeks.) And always, always that impression he gave, and still gives, of being laden with strength. Loaded down with it.

When everything was piled up in what was going to be our new front room — all our misplaced, mismated store; boxes, bedsprings, bureau drawers, chairs upside down on the table; all looking pretty dismal and discouraging, dashed with light from bare dirty windows

— my father took my sister on one knee and me on the other. He made a speech:

From Now On. Got to Get Organized. Turn Over a New Leaf. All Pitch In. Do Our Part. Listen to Your Mother. Treat Each Other Right. Make a Fresh Start.

The dresser with the tilted mirror found its way upstairs to the bedroom; the wooden ice chest wound up in the kitchen; everything else stayed where it was. If not those selfsame boxes and drawers, headless lamps, black-bagged vacuum cleaners (why *three* Hoover uprights and no rugs? not that any of them worked) — then others. There was always more where that came from. Still, my mother talked about "redoing" — as if anything had ever been done. That was what everybody else said, and she wanted to be like everybody else. From my friends' houses I knew the sort of thing she had in mind. Carpets you couldn't walk on, sofas you couldn't sit on, drapes you couldn't open (the sun might fade the carpets and upholstery). Something too good for us to use. When she got her carpets, she said, "the Traffic" would take their shoes off at the door. When she got her towels, "the Traffic" would dry their hands on paper. When she got her bed-spreads, "the Traffic" would hang up their clothes.

"The Traffic": that was us.

She was giving aid and comfort to the enemy.

We must have lived in that house a dozen years (which surprises me; I thought it was a hundred), and all that time it looked as if we had just moved — or were just about to. How could she ever "have any-thing"?

After they sold the house and my father retired, they moved a lot; Lock, Stock & Barrel, which was about all they had to their name. They were like fugitives keeping a jump ahead of the law. So when they decided, after years of this, to move to Florida, everyone pooh-poohed:

A Retirement Village? Now I've heard everything. Are they out of their minds? All those *old people*? Phooey. And what will they do with themselves? Sit around and play cards? And the houses — all alike. You can't tell them apart. (A good thing they don't drink; they'd never find their way home.) Living in a fishbowl. No privacy. Everybody knowing everybody's business. Don't worry. They'll get tired of it. They'll be back. Just like all the other times.

When it comes to decisions, my parents like to change their minds a few times; otherwise they don't feel right about it, same way a dog likes to turn around and around before it lies down. But they put a couple of boxes in somebody's basement, and a couple more in somebody's attic, and piled the pots and pans and the portable TV into the back of the car and drove down. To Live Happily Ever After. From Now On.

» «

All at once the clouds ended. Came skidding to a halt at an edge of blue sky, as banks of snow and ice stop at the blue edge of the sea. I saw a curved shore, a stiff-frozen surf. I knew it was an illusion, but the illusion was complete. The plane was moving through light as a boat through water. The air was vibrating with clarity and brightness; the nose cones of the jets were tingling with it — ringing out — as if they had been struck with tuning forks.

The engines roar.

The light is loud and clear.

"Bad luck," she kept saying. "A very bad break."

Sometimes I wonder what we look like, to stewardesses. Passengers, strapped into our seats, our trays down in front of us. Infants in high chairs, maybe? Clamoring to be fed? Here we were, side by side, the two dutiful daughters — she with her prompt obedient manners, close-mouthed possessive nibbles that made me think of a squirrel in the grass; me with my napkin tucked under my chin (where it belongs).

So here I am at last. This is it; this is what it's like; I finally made it. Not just what I expected, though. Hard to say just what that was. Maybe I thought the scenery would be better. Panoramic. Valleys, vistas, mountain peaks. Pearly clouds, purple distances. The sun sending down planks of light. Yes. That's right. A *view*. This is pretty flat, you know. — Will I be her in ten years' time? Then what? What when I am in her shoes? She doesn't know what to do because she doesn't want to do it. Easy for me to say. But what will I do?

"I know it sounds awful," she said. "It's a terrible thing to say. And yet. Right now. If one of them, at least. Isn't it crazy? You always think it's the worst thing that can happen. And then all of a sudden it seems like the best thing."

Maybe it's just the only thing.

"But my parents are very happy," I said.

She nodded and swallowed and patted her lips: "Give them ten years."

» «

And now for the hard part. My father and I were not on the best of terms, not on the worst. No finalities, no formal estrangements. Words had been spoken — plenty of words; but not the most bitter. Not the Last Word. Nothing that couldn't be taken back.

We hadn't shot all the arrows in our quivers.

In his heart of hearts (I truly believe) my father held this against himself. Does a man have to live in this way? Should a man put up with such things? Disappointment, disaffection, disobedience? Unnaturalness between parents and children? Strictly observant Orthodox Jews have ways of dealing with offenders; settling matters for once and for all. They know how to cut their losses. An offspring who has transgressed, sinned against the tribe and tradition, can be read off — cast out — given up for dead.

The Prayers are recited; the Period of Mourning is observed; the Tears are shed.

Goodbye and good riddance.

My father admired these methods, and had long been threatening to use them. He had been threatening as long as I could remember. How Sharper Than a Serpent's Tooth It Is to Have a Thankless Child. That was one of his favorite sayings. (I could tell from his lofty look he wasn't making it up.) If I heard it once, I heard it a thousand times, and never without a thrill — a shiver — of guilt and shame: a sense of my destiny. This was prophecy!

Wasn't it his right? Wasn't it his duty? Give him one good reason why he shouldn't.

Was he a Jew for nothing?

There was only one hitch. My father is not a strictly observant Orthodox Jew. He does as others do. Sometimes he Observes. Sometimes he Looks the Other Way.

He observes — when he observes — in the Orthodox manner. He walks to the synagogue in skullcap and prayer shawl and stands up and prays with the book in his hands. The smooth circle on his head, the sprinkled drops of his Brilliantine, make him look stiff and anointed. His hoarse gristly throat locked in necktie and collar, his eyes blue and blinking above grouty cheeks. The room sways; fringes quiver; my father's rough raspy voice gets rougher and louder. When he turns the page, or loses his place, it drops to a mutter; his chin drops to his chest.

His lip is full, solemn — exposed.

Even these days, down in Florida, he insists on walking to the synagogue: two or three miles of heat, open highway, diesel trucks, potholes, exploding rubber; mag-wheeled pickups sporting the spokes of the Confederate flag on their bumpers, and horns that hoot 'n' toot and whistle "Dixie." He persists: There is no Orthodox synagogue to walk to. And my mother comes stumbling after, in billowy skirts and high heels, scared to death he will get knocked down and run over if she's not there to keep an eye on him. — What a target. His broad, brunt-bearing shoulders draped in stripes, silk and fringes; his curly hair whitened, thickened; the glasses pressing his cheeks. Every few minutes she stops to lean on him for support, to rattle the stones out of her shoes, to ask an old question:

Why can't he take the car and drive?

Why can't he be like everybody else?

But this went on only a few days out of the year: on Rosh Hashanah, Yom Kippur, and those occasions (ever increasing) when my father recited prayers for the dead. Of other holidays, my sister and I scarcely heard the names. We fasted on Yom Kippur, kept Passover faithfully, didn't mix meat and milk at the table or eat of "any abominable thing." But we didn't keep kosher. No separate sets of dishes, no meat ritually slaughtered, no chickens hanging by their feet — in dishonor — in the kosher butcher's window with twisted necks and pincered wings. My parents lighted candles in memory of the dead;

pink-labelled glasses filled with a white wax that sizzled. Afterwards we used them for drinking glasses; they matched and made a set. (Just about the only thing that ever did.) But in our house prayers and blessings were not said. I never saw my mother light candles on Friday night. Her own mother did. The old lady would mutter the prayer hastily to herself, under her breath, holding both hands up to her face: as if, I thought, the flames might be too bright for her. They never seemed that bright to me. Still I saw their reflection — refraction — in her eyes.

Once, on a trip, we visited the family of my uncle's bride; Pennsylvania Dutch Quakers living in the Lebanon Valley. They were plain, but not like the Amish farmers we had seen along the way, with their clip-clopping horses and dipping buggy whips. Mr. K. wore buttons on his pants, drove a car, used farm machinery. He was a tall wide old man and his hair had the solid whiteness of a salt lick. And his wife, for all her starched cap and apron, did not look as reticent as the Amish wives — sheltered under their bonnets and wagon canopies, the horses waiting, horse-patient, with black flies on their eyelids and black blinders. Her cheeks were broad and bright as crockery. (They really did remind me of all those cups and bowls, glazed and blazoned with slogans, selling at every roadside stand. "Too Soon Old and Too Late Smart." "The Butter Is All.")

It was August, and it was hot. The cows were mud puddles under the trees. The grass was so blurred with heat it didn't look cool; gassy, rather, effervescent; something like the green lights burping up the sides of jukeboxes, or a sweet soda pop, in vogue at the time, called *Green River*.

The house seemed lighter inside than out. Crisscrossed windows, white cloth, china cabinets gleaming with cut glass, silver, pewter, that had been in the family two hundred years. Platters heaped with fresh tomatoes, fresh peaches — sliced, juicy, running with their own ripeness — and dark sizzling meat.

We sat down to eat.

The meat had a strange flavor I had not tasted before. As soon as I bit in, I knew something was wrong. I stopped and looked up, mouth full, head over my plate. I wasn't the only one; my mother and my little sister were looking up too. We glanced at each other and we glanced at my father. He wasn't looking at anyone. His fork was lifted and his eyes were lowered. He seemed to crouch over the table, his head so low between his big shoulders I could see the back of his neck — which was as wide as a brick; and his ears — which were as red.

Curtains fidgeted at the windows. An electric fan blew on us as on hot soup. Our host and hostess were fanning us too, flapping at our faces with fly swatters, dish towels, anything that came to hand. Their glasses beamed — almost urgently solicitous. Beads of sweat prospered on their brows.

Through the screen I could see fields wavering vaguely in the heat, and the raised hackles of the hills.

My father laid down his fork and raised up his eyes.

"Very good," he said, reaching for the water glass.

He nodded. He gulped.

"Very good."

His jaws moved on their haunches; his molars collided. At once, as at a signal, we all began to chew. Life was going to continue.

Naturally, we knew better than to bring up this subject when we got back to the car. (Just as we knew not to talk when my father was shifting gears; there was something wrong with the clutch.) And what was there to say? That he had eaten ham — pig — for that is what it was; had permitted his wife and daughters to eat — rather than to give offense? No, there was more to it. For himself, he would not have been so touchy. What he couldn't bring himself to do was to let on — let these good kind people know that they were the ones who had given offense.

God knows, they never intended. Their daughter had up and married a Jew; she had gone off to live in the big city; of that much they were aware, but they had a pretty hazy notion of what it might mean. They were different too. The world was divided into town folk and country folk, and those who were plain and those who were not; and they had trouble enough keeping track of what set them apart from everybody else — without worrying about every little quibbling distinction, what the fuss was about, amongst all the rest.

So far so good. That much a Jew could understand. But there was

something else. I felt it then, and I can try to say it now. The china
cabinets, the crisscrossed windows; the white farmhouses, bricked
chimneys; the fenced fields; the animals harbored under the trees.
(Through the screen there was the stillness of a canvas someone had
painted on in numbers.) They had all this to uphold them in their
ways, sustain them in their differences. Our connection seemed more
puzzling. We had nothing but this: the grip of our rituals.

Sometimes it's hard to know the right thing to do.

I'm sure my father held this against himself as well. And yet he had
no use for Conservative, much less Reform; practices which would at
least have let him off the hook. He was always a man to take his own
measure; but what good are rules, if you make them up as you go along?

And still, you see what comes of it, living with compromise. (As if it
is his fault that there are things we have to live with — and things we
have to live without.) Let that be a lesson. If only he had been religious
enough — righteous enough — man enough — mad enough. But who
was he to perform such sonorous rites over me? Chanting Prayers for
the Dead? Weeping and rocking and tearing his beard?

How would it look?

What would he tear?

He doesn't even have a beard.

» «

So my father remains at a loss to express his dissatisfaction. He tries:
When he wrote his will, he cut me out. (I know; he showed me; he
couldn't wait.) Not What a Daughter Should Be, read the clause, in a
style I think I recognize by now. That was when at long last it dawned.
Dummy! I am, and always have been, just the sort of daughter he
wanted. What with one thing and another, all things considered — the
times we live in, the Spirit of the Age — I am What a Daughter Should
Be. Just What a Daughter Should Be. Just that and no more.

It's nothing to brag about.

» «

It was raining a little, a fresh-scented drizzle; it might have been salt
spray blowing from the ocean. The breeze felt soft as a scarf. I saw it

drifting around my mother as she stood in front of the spotlighted palms; floating through the folds of her skirt, the white filaments of her hair. Trees leaned, turned inside out like beach umbrellas. People were rushing to make their planes, lugging armloads of grapefruit. Grapefruit, grapefruit everywhere. In string bags, in plastic, packed in crates on crinkly green cellophane. Bald, thick-skinned grapefruit; yellow, uniform; perfect spheres. That was how to tell who was coming from who was going. The ones trying to take home replicas of the sun.

»«

My mother looks like someone in disguise.

She is stained teak color from the Florida sun, so tan her lipstick seems to be glowing in the dark. (Purple-pink; bougainvillea.) Her hair is cut short, shingled, clinging to her cheeks — her face enclosed in white petals — like the fancy rubber bathing caps ladies wear down here. Her shoulders stoop. (Since when?) Her elbows stick out. (How long has this been going on?) Her legs, big knee-knobs, are two thick black bones.

I recognized her anyhow. I always have, so far.

It was late — too late to go to the hospital tonight — the air so thick, spongy, saturated, I felt I could stop right then and there and peel it off me in layers, same as the northern sweaters I was wearing. But my mother was heading for the car, in a hurry, her high heels striking the sidewalk. She walks fast — especially now; luggage or no luggage, it would be hard to keep up with her. And she wears steel taps on her heels; it emphasizes her pace. Each step rings out — announcing her. That's her signal; you hear her coming. It's a practical matter, though; it saves shoe leather. All foresight, that's my mother. Alas, no hindsight.

She stopped. "I don't want you to say anything about that."

"About what?" I said.

"About that. You know what. What you just said. I don't want you saying anything about it to him."

The biopsy report wasn't back yet.

"But what do you mean? Is there something wrong? Something else? There's nothing to hide?"

"Never mind. I just don't want him worrying, that's all. He doesn't need to know anything about it."

"But, Mother," I said.

"No buts about it. You heard me. You're not to say anything, and that's that. That's all there is to it."

My mother may be short; but she has the manner, the bearing, the imperious white head and noble features (Roman coin? Indian-head nickel?) of a woman who is used to getting what she wants. Having her own way. And she has the reputation, besides: "Won't take no for an answer." And yet — as far as I know — and except in the most trivial circumstances — she never gets what she wants; she never has her own way (whatever that is). No one ever "listens" to her.

She doesn't let that stop her. No harm in trying. And maybe, if she can just keep it up long enough. . . . In the meantime, it's true; she doesn't take no for an answer. She doesn't take answers.

She went tap-tapping on, elbows sharp and crooked and ready at her sides; head thrust forward — sleuthlike, I thought — its whiteness all but phosphorescent under the eerie purple of the arc lamps. In the spotlights, palms dipped their green pennants. Her heels clipped the cement. Her pleated skirt whipped where her hips used to be. The drummer no one is marching to.

She glanced at me over the hill of her back:

"You'll do as I say," she told me.

» «

Once, when my sister and I came downstairs to go to school, our father was still sitting at the table, dragging the spoon through his coffee cup; one arm white with bandages, in a sling. He had cut his wrist on the power saw; the blood came up in black bullets, splattered the ceiling; he knew he had hit an artery.

He tied the arm in a tourniquet — tightened it in his teeth — and drove to the Emergency Room.

"That was a close call," he said. "Thought I was a goner."

(He did not smoke or drink or use what he called "phraseology."

"There'll be no phraseology in this house!" But he had plenty of phrases of his own. Customers, Characters, Fakers, Jokers, Schemers, Dreamers, Screwballs, Bellyachers, Stinkers, Sleepers, So-and-Sos, and Yo-Yos. Just to give a hint; a partial listing. But the greatest of these was Goner.

Goner! Goner! The very word was like a bell.)

And he shook his head and whistled appreciatively and went on stirring.

Later my mother took me aside.

"Daddy was very hurt," she said. "You didn't even say you're sorry. What's the matter with you? Haven't you got a mouth on you? Are you afraid to talk? *I'm sorry you hurt yourself, Daddy.* Is that too much to say?"

My mother, of course, was the family interpreter. She translated — explained — excused us to each other. That was her job, and she had her work cut out for her; but I used to think she made most of it up:

He doesn't mean it.

This hurts him more than it hurts you.

You know he really loves you.

He's *still* your father!

You see what I mean. Who'd fall for that? As if she expected us to swallow such stuff. — And just because she said a thing was so didn't mean it was so. Maybe my father had said something, and maybe he hadn't. Maybe she *thought* he was hurt. Maybe — and this most likely — she thought he *ought* to be hurt. Because it wasn't only that she put words in our mouths; she was trying to "redo" us.

She's so sensitive.

That was her excuse for me. That was how she sought to put an end to their endless quarrels; on and on, like the freight cars bickering in the switchyard: "Can't you see she's sensitive?" I happened to know I wasn't sensitive; unless it meant throwing up. I didn't even want their quarrels to end! Not in that way. I wanted an end that would be an end; something dramatic — if need be, drastic. I didn't care what or how.

"Don't provoke him." That was another one. Wishful thinking. I guess she liked to think that he could be provoked because that implied an opposite. But my sister and I knew better; our father's wrath was made of sterner stuff. We had simply got in the way of it; we were too small for it; it preceded us. Not that that didn't make us feel smaller.

"You're asking for it. You've got one coming. You're going to get a going-over."

Leaning on his elbows over the newspaper, not bothering to lift his eyes from the page. We could see blue roving from the bottom of one column to the top of the next. When he wasn't shouting at the top of his voice, stretching his throat and straining his vocal cords, his tone was something more felt than heard. Cadenced blows. The freight trains shuddering through the night; the grunts coming up from the basement.

Sure, don't provoke him. Go tell the trees not to provoke the wind. All that quaking makes it nervous.

These scenes are lapped by lurid flames of memory.

I seem to recall them taking place down in the basement, next to the coal pile. Spiders spilling down walls, pipes furred with dust, the dangling light bulb swaying violently on its wire. (His head was always bumping into it.) The furnace swelling and glowing with cast-iron heat; orange as the fire within. And so forth. But I know that can't be. It all took place in the kitchen, only the kitchen; the smell of wiped oilcloth, still wet; dishes slanting in the drainboard; the pink-labelled glasses rinsed and turned down. The light as dull as waxed linoleum.

I was the older one, so I went first. My little sister would cling to my mother's legs, hiding her face in my mother's apron and pleading:

Don't hit her! Don't hit her!

She kept peeping out to look and hiding her face again.

But oh, how it sparkled. What earnestness. What passion. What big beautiful tears slipped and slid down her big beautiful cheeks. I was impressed. She was weeping zircons.

Meanwhile, my father would be counting the strokes of the strap with words; lip gripping, eye squinting, forehead bunched in a frown. A man taking aim, taking measure, playing a hunch:

Let . . . That . . . Be . . . Lesson . . . Next Time . . . Know Better. . . .

At least I hoped he was counting.

The strap snapped against the leg of the table, the chair. That scared me: I could hear how hard he was hitting. Which just went to show how hard he was *restraining* himself. It was understood he was forever *restraining* himself, his a power that must be held in check:

This hurts him more than it hurts you.

He was a man who didn't know his own strength.

Came time to change places. Now it was my little sister's turn to bend over; mine to cling to my mother's legs and plead.

Don't hit her. Don't hit her.

How halfhearted it sounded, even to my ears. I never put up the defense for her that she put up for me. The most I could manage was a few snotty sniffles and a couple of sticky hiccupy secondhand tears.

Sensitive.

Why do I keep saying *little?* My sister was younger, yes; and she must have been little when she was born; but all I know is, when I had the mumps, my parents thought I was her — because my face got so fat — and switched us in our cribs. She was bigger and stronger and more precocious. Not only, at five or six, did she paint her nails magenta — fingers and toes (my mother hoped it would keep her from biting them — both — which it didn't) — she shaved her legs. That was her own idea; by that time we shared a bed, and the stubble on her knees scratched me to pieces. She was a great climber of fences and swinger from trees — strangers had been known to pick her up and spank her because she scared the wits out of them with her exploits — and, as the tomboy, our father's favorite. He had been disappointed when his firstborn did not turn out to be a boy. That was an open secret. On the other hand, I had a secret of my own. I knew I had spared him a much greater disappointment. Such a boy as I would have been.

Toward books my father's attitude was lofty, as of something he had sworn off, a reformed zealot. He had read a book or two himself, *Oliver Twist* and *The Merchant of Venice* — high school requirements — and he had a theory about the great and famous writers. Therefore, whenever he spotted me, sitting over the hot-air register (the warmest place in the house; the grill left red welts on my legs, checks and boxes just like the ones we used to draw for the game of X-and-O, and I figured people could play on them for the rest of my life) —whenever he spotted me, yet another pile of pages open in my lap—he would hitch up a mighty eyebrow and thicken his forehead:

"Now what? Not another anti-Semite?"

And yet he liked to quote poetry: Shakespeare, Longfellow, John Greenleaf Whittier, and James Whitcomb Riley; slogans, famous last words, scraps of wisdom from reliable sources—George Washington, Teddy Roosevelt, Ben Franklin's *Almanack*. We liked especially one lively version. You know how it goes:

> For want of a nail the shoe was lost.
> For want of a shoe the horse was lost.
> For want of a horse the rider was lost.

But he never stopped there. He went on. And on. A roaring voice, a rousing rhythm, his brows rollicking, carousing, his eyes razzle-dazzle, as when he teased us:

> The battle was lost.
> The war was lost.
> The country was lost.
> The cause was lost.

My sister and I listened with thralled faces. (One of the reasons we were so crazy about him—naturally, we were crazy about him—one of the reasons, strange to say, was that he was no disciplinarian. He gave us our lickings once a week, almost without fail; but he would never have thought to tell us to wash or eat or go to bed.) After all the hoarseness, the shouting, the excitement of battle, his voice would drop to a rumble—all the way to the basement. It came up through the floor, the soles of your feet:

The cause! The cause!

(We had no idea what a *cause* was.)

And all . . .

> *For want . . .*

> > *Of a nail.*

It would be nice to be able to report that my mother's accusations were unfair; that I had been struck dumb from depth of emotion, sympathy for my father, fear for his injuries. The fact is, it had never even crossed my mind that my father could hurt himself. Let alone that anyone else could. Let alone that I could. It never even crossed my mind that he could ask—want—need my sympathy.

"You go to your father," my mother said. "Right now. Right this minute. You march in there and you tell him. Say you're sorry you didn't say you're sorry."

There was a diagonal wriggling thing on the inside of his forearm —a fat shiny pink scar-worm—from his wrist halfway to his elbow, for years and years. For all I know it's there still.

» «

All night it rained.

A newsreel rain; so I saw it in my sleep. Rain slashing through the dark, slanting against the windows, lashing the glass like shackled leaves of the palm trees. Rain hosing down red tile and pink stucco and wrought-iron balconies; capsizing boats; swatting shutters; sousing trailer camps and truck farms and ten thousand lonely gas pumps. The palms and palmettos were kneeling in rain. Everything turned inside out, even the waves.

The morning was dark; the sky low and gray, the streets sleek and streaked with light. It took me a minute or two to realize they were flooded, the parked cars covered to hubcaps and bumpers. The neighbors were standing out on porches and stairs, squinting at the sky— helicopters flying low, props beating. The air was thick with sound. They were boats out fishing.

On the first floor all was activity; dragging out soggy swollen carpets, putting out chairs to dry. A car was coming through, slowly nudging sluggish water. Everyone clapped. It got slower and slower and chugged to a stop in the middle of the street. The driver got out, holding his jacket up over his head—pants rolled to his knees, legs eddies of hair—and ran off, plinking and plunking and hiding himself, like a mobster or convicted public official ducking the cameras.

The palm trees swayed, waving sliced streamers, tattered banners. Each and every leaf—notch—blade—was dripping light-sap, tipped with pods of light.

There was some discussion of the relative advantages of first floors and second floors.

On the first floor you get more dampness, more bugs, more noise, and — as you see — you can expect now and then a little excitement. On the second floor, you can't use the screen porch as an outside entrance, and it might be a little hotter; it is believed that the Builders skimped on the roofing insulation. (It is believed that Builders skimp where they can, wherever you can't see, wherever they think they can get away with it. That is the nature of Builders. Especially in South Florida.)

In spite of that, it is clear that the second floor would have the advantage over the first, but for one thing. It's the second floor. You have to walk up. That's fine for now. But for *how long?*

Builders in South Florida are like God in the universe. Their handiwork is everywhere, but they are nowhere to be seen. They move on, leaving Gardens of Eden all over the place, and nothing quite finished.

It was hard to tell if it was still raining or not; the smooth water stirring, ever so slightly, as if something might be blowing on it — a breath peck-pecking. The sun had disappeared; favors withdrawn. The helicopters kept passing through misty swamp. They had discovered another leak in the roof, another defect in the Plans.

» «

This development is now five years old; the ones who have been here that long are old-timers. It started out as a row of single-story, white-stuccoed duplexes. They were prefabs, and must have seemed pretty bare to begin with. I wouldn't be surprised if — in spite of wear and tear, water stains, dry rot, mildew — they look better now. Because now they are drenched in green; bunches and clusters of thick subtropical vegetation; names like sea grape, cocoplum, gumbo-limbo, nicker bean. (I've been reading the botanical labels on the nature trails again. Strange bedfellows.)

And there is plenty of space. They are on the canals, which are everywhere in South Florida; from muddy ditches, humble fishing holes — hardly enough for an alligator to wallow in, if that's what alligators do — to the Intracoastals, wide enough for drawbridges and

seagoing vessels. People drive their golf balls into them and sometimes their cars.

But that was before the Boom. The new developers (the first had
gone broke and everyone seems to think it serves them right) put up
two-story structures; now there were four to each unit. And they built
them closer. Pretty soon they weren't prefabs anymore; but they kept
getting closer. They didn't face canals, either; they faced each other;
over archways, walkways, stairways; and there was less and less space
in between for anything green. Crimson hibiscus; spiky Spanish bayo-
net; the feathery shafts of the coconut palm.

Now you pay extra for a view: the golf course, with its mounds and
flags and thistled grass; or the distant stands of gray-green scrub oak
and pine. The scrawny scruffy forest primeval of Florida. They look as
if they might have been trees once; but they all drowned and died, and
these are their ghosts.

Still, the crows seem to think they are trees.

Someone will buy them and chop them down too.

» «

The sections have names like Seville, Tuscany, Isle of Capri. Each
condo has a letter; each apartment a number. So small wonder, what
with fourteen thousand people living here, if visitors have a hard time
finding their way. Everyone has stories of would-be guests who drive
through the gates, past the guards in their kiosks, into the midst of all
the look-alike buildings, parked cars, gridded streets, white lines,
yellow stanchions; shiny brown Dempster Dumpsters on each and
every corner. And pretty soon they get lost; they give up; they go
home. Maybe they call the next day to apologize.

Everybody laughs at such tales. They know what it looks like: like
every other development. Construction is everywhere, spreading
westward, from the ocean, from the Intracoastals, from the Interstate;
the setting sun winks and shimmers in the empty eyeholes of new
buildings. — White. That is the color of Florida. In spite of the blue of
ocean and sky and the living green of practically everything else. The
white of limestone and fossilized seashell; that's what the whole state
is made of, and that's what it's built of. Dug up; crushed for lime and

cement; for roads and bridges and sparkling white high-rises. Also the color of clouds and golf balls and concave sails and gulls' gliding wings; of pretty white yachts leaving pretty white wakes. And Florida is so flat; it seems intentional. God must have meant it for condominiums. All those raw roofs rising instead of spooky trees; almost, like them, a mirage — the white dust scarcely settled. And all those billboards, promising that The Best Is Yet to Be.

And so? So what! This is Florida.

What could be easier than to heal this landscape; repair the breach, the damage and disruption, cranes, bulldozers, quick construction, transplanted populations. The flora down here is nothing like what you know up North — shy crocuses, shrinking violets, all those tendrils so bashfully wrapped up in themselves, peeping from leaves. These are tropical plants; they know how to compete. They shriek green; they screech it. You can see they belong to a more primitive age — when reptiles flew; pterodactyl plants, ridged and spiny, still can't make up their minds whether to wear feathers or fins. And none of your pale bulbs, either, that never see the light of day, and roots reaching deeply, secretively underground. In Florida, plants carry their roots with them; whole forests crawling on their bellies, recumbent trunks with roots that noose and lasso. They have claws, tusks, fangs, beaks. They can take anchor anywhere — the shallowest places; an inch or two of soil; on water; on other plants; on nothing at all — on air. The Spanish moss that beards the scenery — all those hanks of gray hair hanging like scalps from arthritic trees — that's an air plant. And so is that thing that might be the greasy-green cluster on top of a pineapple; it favors and festoons the gawky cypress. And what about the mangrove? Its roots grow up, not down; creep, crawl, grope, feel, latching on to whatever happens to come along — treasure troves of drift and debris. What the strangler fig does you might guess. And the banyan — the beautiful beautiful banyan (said to be the tree under which the Buddha found enlightenment, and why not?) — the banyan, with its tiers of leaves, puts down roots like trunks: porticoes: a veranda-tree, spreading green dominions. Looped, coiled, draped and doubled in roots — rope-roots — enough to hang itself, or to let down a ladder from heaven.

But the palm, the palm is the original prefab plant. Height means nothing; even the roots of the royal palm are a handful, a bunch — as if you had yanked up some grass by the scruff of the neck. All you have to do is dig a hole or stick it in a pot, and aim a colored spotlight on it.

» «

It's not true, what people say, about the toilets and the telephones. You can hear the phones ringing, sure, if the windows are open; and if the speaker happens to be a woman — the gravelly abrasive mannish voice some women get as they grow older (sea gulls on Social Security?) — yeah; you can hear that too. But you don't hear the plumbing. Absolutely not. That's a lie.

I'll tell you what you do hear. You hear everyone getting up in the middle of the night. Everyone has to, at least once.

Maybe you hear creaking: footsteps. A thud: the seat going up. Silence. Then you wait. A drip . . . a drop . . . an experimental dribble. More silence. Hey, you! You up there! What happened? What are you waiting for? Did you fall back asleep? Do you have to, or don't you? Are you going to do something and get it over with, or are you just going to stand there and think about it? Ah. That's right. That's better. That's more like it. Did you get out of bed for nothing?

What's public about that? What could be more private? People minding their own business? We have heard the chimes at midnight.

» «

The guards in the kiosks with their caps and their badges, waving you on with their clipboards, are a necessity, yes. People here are from the urban North; lower-middle, middle-middle-class Jews, Italians, Poles, other so-called ethnics — and they know all about it. That's the way we live now. In the older retirement areas, down in Miami, built before the days of guards and gates, the residents are sitting ducks. They may as well be on a Game Preserve. They are attacked — as the old are everywhere — with a ferocity that suggests other intentions; a kind of desecration; a destruction of our symbols (no matter how decrepit).

Nowhere are there more old people than in South Florida. And nowhere is the contrast greater, between youth and age. It's instructive to watch the aged, sitting on benches at the beach, watching the youth go by. They come down for spring vacation with surfboards under their arms — chained, fettered to them. So tall, so tan, so firm of flesh, so sound of limb, so white and solid of tooth and bone. Their sun-bleached, moon-blanched, wheaty-blond hair; their eyes as blue as their cut-off jeans. Meanwhile, here sit all the old ladies with freckled arms and wattled elbows and lavender hair that looks, I swear, as if they get it done in funeral parlors. And all the old gents lined up, with their hooked backs, their shoulders squatting at their ears. All the plastic teeth, the pink rinds for gums, the glasses so thick they give a vindictive sparkle. Pelicans perched on the shore — scythey necks sunk into their feathers, beaks buried in their breasts.

The waves roll in the generations, heaping up entangled sea life. Oozy weeds, unmolded jellyfish, driftwood and pickle jars toothed with barnacles, the deflated balloons — blue bubbles on strings — of the man-of-war. Also: Styrofoam buoys, hairy coconut noggins, Frisbees, light bulbs, bottles, gym shoes. Bottles I can understand (how come no notes in them?), and maybe gym shoes; but light bulbs? Why light bulbs?

The air is bright, particulate; the glint and grit of white sand. The gulls flap up, spilling wings — scraps of light — glittering currents. The sky scatters blessings.

You have to understand. It's not just that the climate is nice, the weather sunny and warm — blue-skied, cloud-scudded. It's the air: it floats. One sniff and you're grateful. It smells of orange groves and salt water and, best of all, earth; pungent and potent as under the glass roofs of greenhouses. It's not just balmy; it is balm. Healing. A restorative. Heart's ease. Help for pain.

Who can blame them? Who would want to leave this? We get it all wrong. Beauty is here to stay. Beauty doesn't vanish. We do.

» «

The guards at this development tend to be older than the residents. That is a fact. My father gave a lift to one who — taking off his cap and

rubbing the nap of his thick white hair first this way and then that—
owned up to eighty-six. He said he was getting "sick and tired of
retirement." Since then my father has been considering: What to do in
case of emergency? What if violence should threaten? What if there
should be an attack? How will he, my father, protect these poor old
souls—the guards—and come to their rescue?

The guards in the kiosks are a necessity, maybe; but first and
foremost, they are symbolic. Everybody knows it. The residents
themselves call all this "the Reservation." This is the line of demarca-
tion, the border.

"How long are you here for?" "What's the weather doing back
there?" That's what they all want to know. Because it's nothing down
here; that's not what they're keeping out. It's what's back there; what
they have left behind them.

More than dirt, crime, crowding, corruption; more than hard
winters, blithering snows, icy streets; cars that won't start, sidewalks
that need shoveling. It's a notion of life. Something they want to
forget. Something bleak and somber they have traded in for things
undreamt of in their philosophy.

It's the Future.

All their lives they believed in the Future; they struggled and slaved
and sacrificed for the Future. Not that they had much choice; it was
understood they had been born too soon. Things were going to get
better. In the Future. The everlasting Future. And now all of a sudden
they see the truth. The Future? What Future? What's everybody talking about? Is there even going to be such a thing? For the first time in
their lives—for this once and once only—it's an advantage to have
been born too soon. They won't have to stick around for the Future.
They leave it to us. See how we like it. Right here, right now, right
inside these gates—this thin line of trees—they have just as much of
the Future as they want. They have caught up at last with American
life, and they are going no farther.

The Future stops here.

Enough is enough.

» «

My mother was on the telephone saying something about a flood. In her shortie nightgown, shoulders lifted, shrugging — the better to keep the thin straps up — her back a pair of brown water wings. Petals of white hair were clipped to her cheeks. She put her hand in front of her mouth when she saw me coming. A reflex, an instinct; she can't help it; she hides her mouth when her teeth are out.

It makes her look timid, flinching; someone stifling a scream, warding off a blow.

"It's true. I mean it. It's not just here. It's not just us. It's everyone. Everywhere. No one can get anywhere today. I don't think he believes me," she said to me, talking behind her hand. "Right away he blames me. He thinks there's something the matter with the car."

This is something new, so I guess the teeth must be too. A complete upper plate? When did this happen? Her lip is pinched, puckered; she is trying to hold a bunch of pins in her mouth.

That's the way she talks; lips mincing, afraid to move; afraid she'll lose all her pins.

"What? The doctor was there? Well, good for him — Can I help it if the doctor was there? Maybe there's no flood where he is. Maybe he came in a boat. He can afford it, I'm sure. He said what? Back already? So soon? Oh, it was? Oh, it was. Oh. It was."

She held out the phone, her hand to her mouth, pumping up her little scarified eyebrows, biting down on her pins. Her hand is large and bumpy. She wears knuckles; other women wear rings.

"'S all right. 'S all right."

A deep basement grunt. The old repercussions.

Don't keep saying it's all right. It's not all right. We want to be with you.

"Take your time," he told me.

» «

My mother hides her mouth; I don't know where she hides her teeth. Haven't seen anything pink and white blooming in water glasses. Maybe she keeps them under her pillow? She hides her mouth even when she sleeps. On her back, the covers pulled to her nose, her hands — pawlike — gripping the sheets. I don't call this vanity. It's not the ugliness of old age she wants to keep to herself, it's the affliction. There is such a thing as self-defense.

I didn't mean to pry, but I saw. I saw, anyway. I looked in while she was sleeping. The covers had slipped down, her mouth had slipped open; sagged to one side—ajar—the way it does when she sleeps. Someone had let the air out of her. It's funny, you don't realize how much of a face is mouth: the armature, the support. It was the rest of her face that had collapsed; almost her whole face was mouth—the dreadful minced lips. It looked big, bigger than ever.

It looked like an exit.

"I *told* you not to say anything," she said to me. "I *told* you not to. Who asked you to?"

Her eyes are light brown, a yellowish tinge. Now that her skin is so tan, they are the same color as her face. The part—behind her hand —that is illuminated, moving.

»«

I get a funny feeling in my parents' new home. Everything is new. Carpets, drapes, lamps; sofas with arms for cozying up to, cushions to get chummy with. A glass-topped coffee table with edges green as ice. There is even a china cabinet, shelves for displaying knickknacks (what folks down here call "momentos"). But where did it all come from? That is the question. Your guess is as good as mine.

People "redo" when they move to Florida; that's part of the ritual. I thought at first there were no cemeteries in the state; there are, you don't see them. They look like the farm fields they were just the other day; still standing, right next to them, surrounding them, without fences, the crops planted in parallel rows. (The cemetery gates, with their "Green"-this and "Garden"-that, pass easily for the promise of new developments.) Instead, you see warehouses; blocks of them, windowless white boxes. Some people bring all their worldly possessions—according to my mother—all that "dark ugly old furniture," all their "dark heavy winter clothes," And then: "Who needs it?" They put it all in these warehouses, and store it—as she says— "forever."

So I feel the way I might if I didn't know the people who live here.

Not sure where to sit, what to touch. I walk around seeking what is familiar to me. The pots and pans, heavy hammered aluminum (they never looked new, so they don't look old); the portable TV (a suitable "momento," it does nothing but snow). Pictures of weddings and graduations. The decanter has a gold star pattern; it must be from Israel, where my sister lives now. (She'll be back; she moves around as much as I do.) Maybe those demitasse cups were housewarming gifts, like — I'm sure — the two bottles of Sabra they put out when company comes, and put back when company leaves.

I keep looking at the china cabinet. Candlesticks, candy dishes, figurines; things that rattle and chink and catch the light. I look so much, I make them nervous. Shelves tremble, glass shivers; ceramic eyes *shine:*

"Psst. Watch out. Knock it off. Here she comes again."

"What? Her? Oh no, not again. What's she up to, anyhow?"

"She wants to see if we're *worth* anything, dope."

"Well I like that! Of all the nerve."

So that's the way it is? That's a fine how-do-you-do. My parents are getting on in years, they're living in a Retirement Village. My father is lying right this moment in a hospital bed — they just took out half his gut; my mother is napping on the couch, hands nailed together atop her breast, a mouth like a punctured tire. The Last Act. And I'm inspecting their possessions? Looking it all over, to see how I like it?

So that's the kind of person I am.

That's nice to know.

All of a sudden, it came to me: My parents have never had *things* before.

Not like other people have; not like everybody else; possessions, acquisitions, matters of taste — choice — pleasure — pride. Considerations of a sort which rarely entered our lives. No wonder all this is new to me; no wonder it's such a strange sensation. I'm not used to looking upon their belongings as anything of value, sentimental or otherwise. But especially sentimental. The luster of associations, of memories. As anything to be kept; worth keeping; to be passed on; potentially mine.

Keepsakes.

Someday, in the ordinary course of events, it will fall to my lot to get rid of all this. And what am I supposed to do with it then? Will someone please tell me? Where can I put it? How can I keep it? I have no place of my own. I've been storing belongings in this one's basement, that one's attic, for years. And I don't want to get rid of it; separate it; any of it. I want it all just as it is, every last bit. Intact.

This is the scene of their happiness.

Maybe I can rent a warehouse?

» «

What funny people. My parents. Still don't understand my sister and me. How come we live the way we do. Why we don't "have anything"; never seem to settle down. (Why can't we be like other people's children, acquiring things, habits for a lifetime?) The same way they can't understand why and how come we never learned to speak Yiddish.

Our grandparents spoke a crude and broken English, and we thought that other language they spoke — harsh, guttural to us — was crude and broken too. Our parents spoke Yiddish for privacy's sake. How else could they conduct this grim business of their grownup lives? They talked *about* us in Yiddish, all the time; but never *to* us. Sitting at the table in morning darkness, my father dragging, dragging the spoon in his coffee. (He was awfully fond of sugar; kept heaping it in until there was nothing left in his cup but silt — sludge — glittering sand.) Oh, we knew what they were saying all right. Someone had got sick, or died. Someone had lost money, or a job. Someone had done something wrong — though she didn't know what; and was going to get a licking — though she wouldn't know why.

Like oars thick in weeds, the sound of their voices slapped in our ears, got tangled in sleep.

They had learned Yiddish at home; their first language, the primary language, the expression of feeling and family life. For them it meant a separation between that life and the rest. (What they called "this cockeyed world.") But for us it meant a division within the family itself; barriers between parents and children; bitterness fated; something banished and denied.

And yet I knew all along that Yiddish was the primary language, an original tongue. All other speech would never be more than a polite translation. This was the Source. Things were named by their rightful names, names that could hurt; given their true weight and force. Nothing could be taken back. It was all Last Words.

» «

My mother, for all she looks like a stabbing victim, keeled over on the couch, is making purring noises, humming to herself, her motor left running. She does that now, both sleeping and waking. If this is old age, she sounds contented with it. And I forgot to say: we took off our shoes when we came in the door.

That's family for you. Right back where I started.

There is nothing here I would ever choose — and nothing I can ever part with.

» «

So. Here we go again. The distant, the steadfast, the enduring. My father's stern and rockbound features. Elevated. Snoring. His head is huge — precipitous. Steep banked brow. Broken nose. Quarried cheeks. The skin not so much pocked and pitted as granular, eroded; the mica flash of whiskers beneath.

A pile of sandstone on a high white pillow.

His lips are smooth in his rough face.

» «

My father's snoring is an old scenario. Action-packed adventure. Good guys vs. bad guys. Hair-raising rescues and narrow escapes. Storms at sea; sword duels; catapults and cannon. All this and more, courtesy of *Liberty Comics* — *Wonder Woman, Batman & Robin,* and *The League of Justice;* James Fenimore Cooper and Victor Hugo in *Classic Comics* editions; fairy tales dramatized over Saturday-morning radio to sound effects that whistled and swooned; and mealy-papered, close-printed library books that began with dashes — and took my breath away: "One day in the year 177 –, in the village of M — "

My father was David *and* Goliath; Samson *and* the Philistines; Jack *and* the Giant. Daniel and the whole damn den.

And to think he had been such a puny kid.

At the time of his Bar Mitzvah, almost fourteen, he was still the shortest one in his class. He posed for his photo in cap, knickers, prayer shawl, some tome open on the lectern table beside him; and you can see how he has to hoist his elbow and hitch it up in order to lean against the table. The face is already his face; a mug, a muzzle, a kisser. It's as if he had stuck his head through a hole in a cardboard poster, like those trick shots you take at carnivals and amusement parks.

He sprouted, in the proverbial manner, overnight. It took the rest of him a while to catch up. At the time of his marriage, ten years later, he weighed one hundred eighty-five pounds and looked gaunt. Starved. The heavy-boned, hollowed cheeks, the lumpy throat and cliffy brow of the young Abe Lincoln. There are props in this one too; his white bow tie, the white carnation in his buttonhole, the stiff paper cone of his bride's bouquet and the swirling train of her veil (a curtain someone swiped off a window) — all belong to the studio. Like the backdrop they are standing in front of; a waterfall, a stream, frothy bushes, frills of trees. After this is over, after the click, after he yanks his head out of the box, the photographer is going to take it all back, put it away.

It was the stock story, told in all those comic books. *Superman, Captain Marvel* (there was a Marvel family, and I'm not sure but what there may have been a Marvel dog), and all the rest, had ordinary everyday identities; but when they tore off their shirts, or their specs, or shouted out the magic word *(Shazam!),* they became their true selves — hero selves — and invincible. A story retold in the smudgy back pages as well. Those ads featuring the famous "97 lb. weakling," in his roomy bathing shorts, with legs like white worms, and two little — oh pitifully little! — dots on his chest. On the beach he is mocked by bullies; they laugh at him and kick sand in his face and on his blanket. He sends for the *Charles Atlas Course;* and the next time those wise guys show up, are they in for a surprise. A real shocker.

There would be a photo (actual) of Charles Atlas himself; legs solid in skimpy trunks, chest massy, head bowed; looking unmistakably like my father—something grim-lipped, stoical in this self-made strength. What had worked for him could work for you.

Mind Over Matter.

There was a moral to these stories. Is there anyone in the world who doesn't know it by heart? All those pip-squeaking, four-eyed, timorous alter egos; all those heroes who could fly through the air and laugh at bullets. Escape! Escape from this weak and helpless condition of childhood! Growing up was growing invulnerable. That's what we thought.

My father used to emerge from these struggles victorious. Now it seems from the rattles and sighs and phlegm catching in his throat, from those two noisy excavations, his nostrils, that he might be getting the worst of it; taking his lumps. I hear blows.

» «

The room overlooked the entrance to the hospital—three or four stories high, pink stucco sticking up for miles around. The usual landscaping outside the glass doors: grass laid down in patches— squares—rough green toupees; spindly, scantily clad palms bending and bowing in colored spotlights. These were buttressed with poles as thin as they were. And the usual digging: a new wing being added, the parking lot expanded, mounds and pits all over the place. Today the holes were water and clay. The roads were still slimy with mud, the grass and fields blubbering with it. Everywhere, stranded tractors, bulldozers, trailers, and the rusty beat-up pickup trucks of migrant workers.

The green peppers stood row on row, polished to ripeness. But the bosses weren't taking any chances on sending their equipment out into all that muck; they were afraid of ruining their machinery. They walked up and down in squelching boots, talking here and there to angry pickers. Most of the pickers weren't talking to anybody; not even to each other. They sprawled on the trucks. Some of them seemed to be wet—soaked to the skin—as if they had spent the night out in the rain. It was their stocking hats and processed hair, stuck to their heads like large wet leaves.

All along the roads lay frayed flattened shoelaces that turned out to be dead snakes. Hundreds of dead snakes, and pale pink blood-prints.

» «

My father quarrelled with his mother. Never mind the whole story — because what's the whole story? — but anyone would have said he was in the right. For all the good. And shouldn't he — of all people — have known better? Who was it who was forever telling me? Might Made Right. Two Wrongs Didn't. Sleeping Dogs Lied.

He had been the dutiful son; he had *shown respect*. (One of the truly mystical phrases of my childhood. I couldn't figure out what it meant. I had never *seen* any *respect*.) It was the first and only time he ever stood up to her. How was he supposed to know she would make so much of it? Backs turned, doors slammed, telephones banged down, letters sent back in shreds. How was he to know she would die suddenly, one foot on the floor, trying to get out of bed?

The phone call. The rush to the house. The trucks standing outside. A long red fire truck, a hook-and-ladder, motor running — shuddering — pumping noise by the gallon. The street seemed flooded and dammed.

It was a stone-faced two-flat with a brief front lawn, and all the doors and windows were open. My father ran up the steps. A fireman in shovel helmet and hip boots was coming out backwards, an ax at his belt, carrying one end of something. Black rubber or oilcloth, same as his slicker. Two men were holding up the other end and shouting directions at him:

Keep Going Watch Out Easy Does It Keep Going

He glanced over his shoulder, bumping down the stairs.

His boots sank in soft mud and sprinkled grass seed.

The next morning I heard my father getting up. He always rose mute, with a mouthful of phlegm, and headed straight for the bathroom — holding up his pants, holding out his lip — looking neither left nor right until he'd had a chance to spit. I heard the floors resounding under his heavy bare feet, then the hoarse rash noise. First thing he always did.

That had been the hardest blow of his life. He told me so himself. (Sometimes he forgets when he's talking to me and when he's not, and who wouldn't get confused, after all these years?) Why he would want to pass on such pain; why he should be so bound and determined to inflict this bitterness, I can't say. But we have to pass on something, don't we? Otherwise, what's the good? What are children for?

» «

A plastic bag, hooked to a plastic tube, was slowly slowly seeping light-sap, one clear liquid bead leaked at a time. Another, larger bag, clipped to the side of the bed, was sudsing and slushing. The arms over the covers hairy and sunburnt; a circle of sunburnt skin round the neck. A sprinkle of grizzled hairs — singed, frizzed — they'd crumble if you touched them. The width, the depth of the chest — the coarse sheet-blanket stretched across it — seems pretty much what it has always been; the forearms still viny with tendon and vein. But the upper arms and shoulders don't bear the load they used to, don't pull their own weight. They seem to slope and slump from the humped muscles of the neck.

The hair is cocoon white, and of that texture. It looks frivolous above porous yellow earthworks.

An eyebrow tugs.

A lid lifts.

I see blue.

"Oh, Sal. Well well well. Look who's here. 'Lo, Sal." An iron door scraping on its hinges. "So you made it, I see? So you got here all right? Everything all right, then?"

"Fine fine. How about you?"

"This? This is nothing. A Rough Customer, that's all."

"Which do you mean? It or you?"

"Oh-oh. My daughter's here. She's ribbing me. She's giving me the business."

Still looking at me out of one eye. Still whispering — lip stiff, as if he has to spit.

"And your mother? Where's she at?"

"She's coming. Don't worry." A little trouble with the car. I'm not supposed to mention, among other things, cars and floods.

There is a deep deep dent over the bridge of his nose, right between the eyes. From the accident, still? Or is this from his glasses? We're used to them by now; so used to them, we forget. We think it's the lenses that make his eyes so blue — blinking — on the brink. The truth of the matter is, the new nose is an improvement over the old one; not so roughhewn. High-crested, flattened at the tip. Abrupt. Abutting. If you'll pardon the expression, a real butte.

I put my hand on the middle of his forehead. The middle of his forehead is the size of my hand; a saddle, a slope. The heavy ridge over each brow smoothed as with the stroke of a thumb.

I see what it is. I see what it is. With my mother age is a disguise; she puts it on with a wink. (Some wink.) But with my father it is another matter altogether. Age is revealing him; the essential in him; completing the job. It scares me. Hacked, chipped, chiselled, gouged. The mark of the craftsman's hand, the craftsman's tools.

In his mortared face the niche of blue eye is like a glimpse of the sky in whiskered stone walls; monuments or ruins.

He doesn't mean it.

This hurts him more than it hurts you.

You know he really loves you.

He's *still* your father!

Who would have thought? That all those things my mother says would turn out to be true?

This is the way my father shows his love.

What's more. What's more. This is the way he feels it.

» «

I saw her coming, in flats and slacks, arms swinging at her sides, white head moving briskly along with the rhythm. Florida white. White as gulls' wings. Turning out her feet smartly, the way she does; such conviction in her step I could see the soles of shoes.

Whaddayaknow. Taps on her toes.

And she shall have music wherever she goes.

I opened the vent. "Here she comes now."

Very distinctly the taps could be heard, singing out on the sidewalk — announcing and identifying her. Arms, legs, shoulders, flat brown cheeks, Indian-head nickel nose — all of her seemed to be pointing one way, heading in the right direction.

My father must have heard the sound, familiar enough to him; and it must have brought to mind what I was seeing. And a whole lot more. Because he shut his eyes and laughed to himself, his chin and his voice in his chest, his thick forehead bunched in a frown — as if it hurt him some, all the same.

"'S her all right. Know her anywhere."

The glass doors glided open; she glided through.

Puddles were beginning to gleam in the parking lot. In the colored spotlights the palm trees bent their bundled sheaves. Over the chilled dried racketing of the air conditioner the night air was coming in; mammal warm. You could all but catch it and keep it.

I put out my hand. I shut my eyes too.

Yes. Please. Give them ten years.

E. M. BRONER

 THE DANCERS

She was a nanny goat, great udders hanging, whiskers on her chinny-chin-chin.

She went with Billy Goat Gruff until he was reinstitutionalized.

Her kids wandered out of the pen.

She knits for extra money besides her disability payments.

"This is a muff," she says.

It looks like a catcher's mitt.

"This is an animal pillow."

But which animal?

"This is a hat for you."

Not for me. For a small child.

"The hat is for winter warmth."

But it's not double thickness.

"I must occupy my time, you see. The days are unoccupied." She smiles as she says this. Her teeth need fixing. She holds her jaw in pain. But she will see no one in white, not the dentist, doctor, psychiatrist, pharmacist, barber, or florist.

Her hair is matted, uncombed.

She will see no one in suits, not professors or businessmen.

But she is comfortable with some uniforms: the guards at the art institute, policemen, waitresses.

II

Most of us don't have to see ourselves. She had to see the extension of leg at the barre. She had to see the bend at the waist. She had to carefully study the position of the pale, heart-shaped face, the flip of her dark hair in its ponytail.

Her mother held her waist and bent her. Her mother placed her arms in the correct position.

They move together, Shiva or a crab, two pale faces, luminous in the early morning light of the studio. Straight dark hair escapes from rubber bands and whips their faces.

The mother choreographs; the daughter performs.

When they exercise together, they time their movements to the beat of the goatskin drum. The drummer holds it between her legs and watches the pair. They are a double-shelled creature, long arms swimming, legs kicking across the ocean floor of the dance studio.

They are always partners, leaping across the room in a pair. They exercise on the floor, hands clutching one another, a rocking boat, a circumference of mother and daughter.

III

They picnic at the sea.

"I was born by the sea," writes Isadora Duncan, "and . . . all the great events of my life have taken place by the sea."

Duncan writes in *My Life* that dance comes from the rhythm of the waves.

Every May 27, the mother and daughter have gone to the seashore of their city or a summer resort. They have worn togas — the mother is a gifted seamster — and they walk into the water while the togas drop from their bodies.

The mother is full-bosomed. When the sheets unwind from her body, she emerges like a sea goddess.

"Isadora says the body is our greatest architecture," says the mother to the assembled photographers.

The daughter is more modest, and so is her body.

"She is my Isadorabelle," the mother tells the press about her daughter.

They plan to follow the map of Isadora's life, giving dance performances to pay their way. It's easy enough to start out in San Francisco, walking into the sea. They must then find the means to travel to London, to visit the British Museum and sketch the Greek vases, as Isadora did. They must continue on the pilgrimage, to Paris, there to visit the Rodin Museum and the Louvre. They will be the Victories of Samothrace, the bodies of Venus.

Mother and daughter hope to dance in Vienna and Berlin. They must make arrangements to meet the great artists of Europe, the German writers and actors, the Russian musicians and the dancers, as Isadora did.

When you speak with the mother and daughter, you will see that they are somewhat practical. They will not relive Isadora's South American tour, with the political disturbances now in that continent. On the other hand, now that democracy has returned to Greece, they must visit Athens and be photographed at the Parthenon.

They speak of traveling in the month of May, when Isadora was born and when she birthed her son.

But in May the daughter travels out of her head.

IV

"What are you doing?"

"Teaching dancing."

"Where?"

"On the sidewalk, crossing the street, in the court of the museum, in the university parking structure, at Melvin's Finer Delicatessen."

"Who are your students?"

"Passengers, drivers, pedestrians, streetwalkers, cops on corners, grocery-store owners, museum guards, movie ticket takers, parking attendants, waiters and countermen."

The mother is leaping across the room. Her long hair is chiaroscuro, changing from dark to white. The mother has her private key to the dance studio and rehearses before classes begin or after they end. There is no drum accompaniment. A vein throbs in the mother's forehead.

V

"How can we write the truth about ourselves?" asks Isadora. "Do we even know it?"

The mother knows her daughter is a gazelle, a frightened forest creature. Her daughter is a racehorse. The daughter is as stretched as a drum skin. Her daughter has a musical ear and can learn languages by speaking to a passerby, to a shopkeeper, a fruit-stand owner. The daughter's tongue is athletic. "Rs" trill, are swallowed, are rolled. The daughter's throat is a bird's—sounds vibrate deep within it; notes sing out.

The bird has flown into a high branch. Sunspots blind the mother's eyes when she looks upward for a sight of plumage among the foliage.

VI

"I have made up this song. Listen to it."
"I can't hear the words."
"They are made-up words."
"What are you carrying?"
"An instrument."
"But the strings are missing, and the sounding board is cracked."
"That's the way I like my music."

The daughter has a bag lady's body. Her breasts hang with memory of the sucking of a litter, never born or given away. Her stomach is a melon, pregnant or delivered. Her legs do not extend on the barre. The movement of her arms is posturing. Her eyes cannot spot. If she turns, she careens and crashes into the other dancers. She accompanies herself on what she thinks is the beat of a drum.

She is denied entrance into the dance studio.

VII

The daughter awakens at night and startles. Her bed is empty. Where did that other person go, and who was he? Where had she met him? Were they comrades at the mental institution, doing art therapy together? Was he the musician on the street corner when she danced and lifted her skirt high, saying, "Whoo! Whoo! What have we here?"

He came to find out what was there.

Was he the cop who gave her the ride when she was hitching?

There are too many mysteries to unravel.

But sleep is the biggest mystery of all.

It drives her out of bed. It is a stake in her forehead. It fits splinters under her fingernails.

Sometimes she tries to outwit sleep and dozes in the daytime. Something catches on her window and will not let go. It is a leaf, a praying mantis, a cricket, a leafy spirit that means to cover her with others of its tribe until she can never be found under the leaf mound.

There are scratchings everywhere. Someone had a duplicate key made to her door and stole her Bedouin drum. Someone came through the window and took her stringless instrument with its cracked sounding board.

Someone came in and made off with her knitted caps, animal sweater, and muff.

Someone came in and stole her thoughts.

It could have been her clever mother.

VIII

What has the mother tried?

Being dry-eyed or crying her eyes out.

She studies the stars and constellations.

She asks, "What happened to my beautiful child?"

Were the planets in retrograde? Were the gods angry?

These are the questions Isadora would have asked at the edge of the sea on that terrible day when her babies were drowned.

"Only twice comes that cry of the mother which one hears as without one's self—at birth and at death," wrote Isadora.

Isadora was thirty-five when she saw the coffins of her children with "the golden heads, the clinging, flower-like hands."

The mother is forty-five when she sees her daughter's arms flop, her bosom stretch pendulously, her feet swell, and gain sizes and widths. The mother sees her daughter's eyes vacate their original site.

IX

"Where are you?"
"Drowned."
"In the sea?"
"In my tears."
"In a lake?"
"In a teacup."
"Down a well?"
"In a bowl of consommé."

X

One day I said to my daughter:
Which twin has the Toni?
One day I said to my daughter:
Whose hands are the younger?
One day I said to my daughter:
Whose hair is natural and whose naturally tinted?
What did your daughter answer?
Her hair answered by becoming gray.
Her hands answered by becoming chapped and sore.
Her legs answered by losing their muscle tone.
Her head answered by going back ten years.
She has an old address in the old neighborhood. She has never
graduated from intermediate school. She giggles or cries or shrieks
with laughter. She asks passersby to help her. She asks taxicab drivers
to take her hundreds of miles. She asks college professors to hire her to
teach their classes. She asks publishers to publish her unwritten mem-
oirs. She asks strange men to father her children. She asks newborns to
fend for themselves.

XI

Recollection
Mother, what did you dream?

I dreamt that my daughter performed those dances that were beyond my powers.

Mother, what did you dream?

I dreamt of my daughter's face on a poster at Carnegie Hall.

Mother, what do you dream now?

I dream that my daughter is sane.

XII

Mother, what are your dreams for yourself?

I want to dance without a partner.

I want to eat at a table with a single plate.

I want to sleep with only one pillow dented in the double bed.

XIII

What happens when a thought is completed by another person? When a laugh is echoed by another's? When shadow and substance are one?

The mother flees. It doesn't matter where: the Connecticut College of Dance to learn new techniques; Martha Graham's Dance Studio in New York, Dance Therapy in Santa Cruz.

XIV

Good friends offer advice.

One knows a psychologist of behavioral modification in Denver, Colorado.

One knows a psychiatrist who does chemotherapy at a clinic in Ann Arbor.

One knows a psychosurgeon.

One knows an old friend, a social worker, who will talk to the daughter.

The daughter knits her ill-fitting hats, sweaters with uneven length sleeves, pillows of animal species not yet born.

Will you knit me a scarf? I'm cold.

She knits a scarf you can see through.

Will you knit me a hat for my head of thick curls?

She knits a cap that ties under the chin and fits a six-month-old.

Will you knit me gloves? My hands are freezing.

She knits a muff with large open spaces.

Will you make a sweater of soft blue?

The sweater is brown.

Will you make the hat to match?

The hat is blue.

Will you make the gloves a similar color?

Each finger of the gloves is a different color.

XV

The mother sends in her application to participate in the dance program. She drives her VW bug, loaded with leotards and tights. She takes her favorite herbal tea, her herbal shampoo and henna tint, her cracked-wheat cereal.

She expects at any minute, during the class hour, her daughter will enter and disturb the lesson.

She expects, at lunchtime, that her daughter will pour milk from the carton onto her tray.

She expects, at bedtime, that there will be a soft knock on the window. Her daughter will be perched on the ledge.

At the end of three weeks, she knows no one can interrupt the dance lesson. No one will enter the lunchroom uninvited. No one will scale the brick wall of her dormitory.

The mother drives home singing. The leotards are stiff with sweat. The tights have worn knees. She has a bruise on her toe. Her legs have muscle tone. Her breasts ride higher. She looks in the mirror and smiles at the driver.

As she approaches her city, the mother breathes shallowly. At the expressway near her exit, the mother pants.

Her front door is broken. Pictures of Isadora, Isadora's lover, Gordon Craig, and photos of Isadora's children have been yanked off their picture hooks. The mother walks on the shards of Isadora's life.

She calls the police. She takes out a warrant against the daughter. The daughter is charged with trespassing.

The daughter has walked on the mother's eyes until they swell with tears.

The daughter has walked on her mother's feet, scraping her instep.

The daughter has walked on the mother's heart, injuring the pumping action.

XVI

The daughter steals the mother's credit cards. She buys wonderful presents like cosmetics, wallets, handkerchiefs of Irish lace for the garage attendant, the professor whose class she asked to teach, the museum guard, the fruit-stand owner.

Saks Fifth Avenue bills the mother.

The daughter has taken the mother's favorite clothes and stuffed them down the clothes chute.

The daughter would place the mother in a house without Isadora's photos, in a house without dance costumes or formal dresses.

The daughter wants a house like an institution with bare walls and floors and assigned clothing.

XVII

The daughter no longer looks like the mother.

The mother stops looking for her daughter.

The daughter is not to be found in the usual places or the ordinary memories.

The daughter has said farewell to herself, and yet keeps breaking open her mother's front door.

The mother has several choices.

"How could I go on—after losing my children?" asked Isadora.

The mother can cut herself open with the can opener and spill out the beans. She can empty herself into the garbage disposal.

Or

The mother can become the daughter's twin. She can wiggle her fingers adieu to herself; she can let tickles of giggles escape her unsmiling mouth. She can drive her VW, with her practice clothes, to the local institution.

XVIII

The daughter does not give the mother time to make decisions.

The mother must appear before the credit department at Saks.

The mother must appear at her local police precinct.

The mother must speak to the college professor whose class is being disrupted.

To the museum guards whom the daughter distracts.

To the shopkeeper and fruit-stand owner where the daughter filches small items.

To the garage attendant whom she follows to all the levels of the parking structure.

XIX

It is May, years of May are passing.

The daughter is graying and her forehead is lined.

The mother's long hair hurts her head. She is always with migraine.

The mother goes camping. She spreads her tent by the sea, as Isadora did. The mother swims in the early morning. She begins to look at the children. She sees families at the seashore, little children with sturdy arms and legs. She dances with them by the water's edge.

When the air turns cool and the daylight is shorter, the mother unpegs her tent. She walks to the shore. In her hands are shears. She cuts off the heavy hair that binds her head and throws it into the sea, as had Isadora.

XX

The mother will train other Isadorabelles. The mother will look down rows of extended legs at the barre, at heads held high, at the tunics that give her children freedom of movement.

The mother knows that she will never bear her own again. It is unbearable.

As it was for her to see the daughter's babies taken away, one after the other. The daughter had forgotten about her milk-filled breasts. The daughter had forgotten the hospital formula. The daughter tries to feed her babies raisins.

"A raisin-bred baby," she laughs.

The mother can never raise another daughter.

In the city, the front door is fixed. Mail is waiting in the mailbox. Photos are pyramided on the wall. There is Isadora as a caryatid at the Acropolis. The mother has been a caryatid for too long.

Her short hair rests lightly, like moss, like a laurel crown on her head.

There is a soft rapping at the door. The mother hesitates. There is a gentle scratching at the window. The mother stands frozen. There is a calling from outdoors.

"Mother! Mother!"

The mother thinks it might be coming from the clothes chute or from a closet of clothes that had been ripped from their hangers and trampled upon.

But the mother's home is undisturbed.

The mother thinks she recognizes the voice. Someone once called her by that name.

She thinks of phoning the neighbors. She begins to phone the police.

The doorbell rings.

The mother has ordered nothing from the pizza parlor, and her news route has not started in the fall. No one should be ringing her bell.

The footsteps on the porch descend.

The mother sits up all night.

XXI

Near every city is a lake. The next morning the mother drives to water. She walks through the woods. The beach is difficult to find. The paths are not clearly marked.

The water is cold, and sand blows and stings her eyes.

Leaves drop and stick damply to stones.

The mother stands at the shore. She hears rustling in the trees. Autumn rain falls in large, wet drops and separates leaves from trees.

"Mother! Mother!"

Her daughter has traveled here. Has traveled back to her own mind. Her daughter's young body is hunting for itself. The daughter's face is not her mother's. It is both older and younger.

"I've come to say good-bye," says the daughter.

Their lips touch.

"Where are you going in the great world, O?"

"I'm going to London and Paris, to Athens and Moscow. I'm going to find the children who drowned."

"Will you return to me, O?"

"Not 'til our eyes are different colors, our laughs different melodies, and our maps have different continents."

"And after your eyes are their true color, and after your laugh is free, and after you've sailed the whole world over, will you return to me?"

"Only then, only then will I return to you."

They part at the sea.

LESLÉA NEWMAN

THE GIFT

To be born a Jew in the 20th century is to be offered a gift. . . .
Muriel Rukeyser

 Lilly is five years old. She is going out for a walk with her father. It is a windy day near the end of autumn, and Lilly is wearing her red wool coat with the real fur collar. Today is Sunday, and every Sunday Lilly's father takes her out on an adventure, so her mother can have a little peace and quiet. Sometimes they go to a diner for lunch, sometimes they go out for a little ice cream, and sometimes they just walk and walk through the streets of New York, with Lilly holding tightly to her father's hand.

Today they are walking through a part of Brooklyn that Lilly doesn't recognize. Her father stops to look at some books stacked high on a cart outside a bookshop. Lilly notices right away that these are grown-up books — not big and shiny like her picture books at home, but old and dusty. Her father picks one up to read and when he turns the page some of them crumble and bits of them fall into the street and mix with the dry brown leaves whirling around their shoes.

Lilly's father picks up another book, holds it up close to his nose, and begins to read. He reads and reads and reads. Lilly is getting bored. She starts hopping up and down, first on one foot and then on the other. She wants to keep walking maybe, or just go home.

All of a sudden, Lilly notices a man coming towards them. He is short, not tall like her father, and he is wearing all black — black shoes, black pants, black coat, funny black hat. And swaying back and forth in the middle of all this black, is the man's long white beard. Lilly gets more and more excited as the man draws near. She stops hopping up and down on her left foot and grabs her father's arm. "Daddy, Daddy," Lilly says, pulling at her father's sleeve with one hand and pointing with the other. "Is that Santa Claus? Why is he wearing those funny clothes?"

Lilly's father looks up from his book and sees the old Hasidic Jew coming towards them. He stares at the old man and the old man stares at him. The old man moves slowly and the face of Lilly's father does not move at all. Now Lilly is frightened. She watches the old man approach and it is as if her father is watching himself growing older in a mirror until he looks just like the old man, and it is as if the old man is watching himself growing younger in a mirror until he looks just like her father. Then the old man passes them and Lilly's father grows young again. He puts the book back on the cart, reaches down for Lilly's hand, and they start their long walk home without a word.

» «

Lilly is eight years old. She is standing in the kitchen with her back leaning against the counter, her arms folded across her chest and her lower lip sticking way out. Lilly's mother is making soup and Lilly is mad that her mother is paying more attention to the soup than to her.

"But why can't we have a Christmas tree?" Lilly asks again.

"Because Jews don't celebrate Christmas," her mother says, in a voice stretched so tight it sounds like it's going to break.

Lilly watches her mother's back and her pout turns into a scowl. That's no reason, she thinks, staring down at the blue linoleum floor. I hate you, Lilly mouths silently, as her eyes travel across the floor and stop at her mother's feet. Lilly is so mad right now that she hates everything about her mother — her scuffy white slippers, her baggy stockings, her flowered housedress, her yellow apron, the shmate on her head, even the knaydlach ball she is rolling between her two small hands.

Lilly tries once more. "How about a Chanukah bush then?"

"There's no such thing," her mother answers, turning around to face Lilly with the wooden spoon still in her hand. "Shush now, your father will be home soon. Do you want to pick out the candles?"

"No," Lilly says, and she stomps out of the kitchen to sit on the hallway steps. It is the seventh night of Chanukah and she has saved all the red candles — her favorite color — for tonight. But now she even hates them. Lilly doesn't want to light the menorah and recite the blessing. She wants to sing "We Wish You a Merry Christmas," and she wants a tree. A tree, Lilly thinks, with tinsel and little colored balls and strings of popcorn hanging on it, with lots of presents underneath it, and with pretty lights blinking on and off and a beautiful angel on top. Like they have everywhere, Lilly thinks, with her chin on her fist. Everywhere. At school, across the street at her best friend Kathy's house, even on TV. "Everywhere," Lilly whispers loudly so her mother will hear. "Everywhere but here."

» «

Lilly is ten years old. It is spring and Lilly knows better than to ask her mother if the Easter bunny is coming to visit their house. Jews don't celebrate Easter, Jews celebrate Passover, her mother has told her. Lilly doesn't like Passover very much. She doesn't get any presents, like at Chanukah, and she can't eat any of her favorite foods like tuna-fish sandwiches or vanilla ice cream cones with jimmies or Sara Lee chocolate frosted pound cake. Instead she has to carry peanut butter and jelly on matzo to school while all the other kids get to bring pretty blue and pink and lavender hard-boiled eggs in their lunch boxes. Lilly's matzo sandwiches make her thirsty and they're hard to eat. They get all crumbly and make a big mess on the table and all over Lilly's lap.

Lilly is smart though. She saves up all her milk money and by Friday she has fifteen cents — enough to buy a package of chocolate-chip cookies. She trades the cookies for half of Melanie Thompson's bologna and cheese sandwich. Right before she takes the first bite, Lilly looks around the lunchroom. She has a funny feeling in her stomach. What if God punishes her; or worse than that, what if her mother finds out? Lilly takes a bite, chews rapidly, and swallows. She looks around again. Everything seems normal. Billy McNamara is still shooting spitballs at Marlene DiBenedito, and Alice Johnson is still sitting all by herself, eating a banana with her nose in a book, pretending she doesn't care that nobody likes her. Lightning doesn't strike and Lilly's mother doesn't rush in hysterically to snatch the forbidden food out of her daughter's hand.

Lilly finishes the sandwich, feeling relieved and a little disappointed at the same time.

» «

Lilly is fourteen. She is getting taller. Her hips are getting wider. There is hair under her arms and between her legs and now she has to wear a bra. She hooks it around her waist, swivels it around so that the cups are in front, and pulls the straps up onto her arms. Lilly misses her soft cotton undershirts. She keeps them at the bottom of her underwear drawer.

Lilly is getting very pretty. Everyone says so; her mother, her father, her Aunt Esther, everyone except her grandmother. "Oy, such an ugly face you got. A face like a monkey," she says, pinching both Lilly's cheeks. "What are we gonna do with such an ugly monkey-face? Take her back to Macy's where we got her, that's what we're gonna do."

Lilly hates when her grandmother says that, though she likes to believe that she was adopted. She also hates it when anyone says she is pretty. I'm not pretty, Lilly thinks, staring at herself in the mirror. I'm too short and too fat, and my hair is too frizzy. Lilly wishes she was tall and thin, with hair the color of yellow crayons and eyes the color of the sky. She wants to look like the models in *Glamour* magazine. When she says she would like to be taller, her father offers to string her up on a rack. Very funny, she tells him. When she says she would like to be thinner, her mother tells her to go to Weight Watchers. Gross, Lilly says. But most of all, Lilly would like her hair to be straight.

Every other night Lilly washes her hair. First she shampoos it with Head & Shoulders and then she rinses it with Tame. She combs it out and before she even steps into her bathrobe, the ends are already beginning to frizz. Lilly scoops up a gob of Dippity-do and smooths it onto her hair. She divides her hair into eight sections and wraps each one around a pink roller, big enough to put her fist through. Then she ties a net around her head and sits under the hair dryer for forty minutes, until her hair is dry and her ears are bright red.

Now Lilly parts her hair in the middle and brushes it out, checking her reflection in the mirror for ridges or bumps from the bobby pins.

Before she goes to bed, she gathers all her hair up in a ponytail at the top of her head and wraps it around an empty orange juice can. Lilly sleeps on her stomach with her head hanging off the bed, before she falls asleep she makes a deal with God: I'll be good, she whispers into the darkness, if You promise that tomorrow You won't make it rain.

»«

Lilly is fifteen. She is going to the beach with her best friend Kathy. Kathy is tall, thin and blonde — everything Lilly would like to be. She even wears the perfect bathing suit: an itsy-bitsy pink bikini that Lilly would give her life to be able to fit into. Lilly wears a black one piece suit that she bought last week with her mother. Lilly hates going shopping with her mother. She always says things like, "I'm not buying you that — your whole tuchus is sticking out," or "Too bad, kid, you got those famous Goldstein hips." Try as she might, Lilly couldn't make her hips any smaller, no matter how little she ate or what diet she went on. She had to admit, though she hated to, that the Goldstein family had indeed left its mark.

I wish I looked like Kathy, Lilly thinks, as the sun warms her skin. She is lying on her back on a big blue beach towel, with her arms over her head so that her belly will look flatter. She squints into the sun and then looks behind her past her arms. There is a man lying a little ways away from them and he is wearing boxer trunks with nothing underneath. Lilly can see up his skinny hairy legs, to his thing, which rests inside his bathing suit against his left thigh. The man is sleeping, and his thing seems to be sleeping too. Lilly pokes Kathy on the shoulder.

"Look," she whispers, pointing with her eyes.

"Oh my God," Kathy whispers back, and they giggle and turn away and then look again.

When Lilly gets home from the beach her mother is on the phone. "She's fine," she says in a certain tone of voice that lets Lilly know her mother is talking about her. "She just got back from the beach and she's so dark, vey iss mir, she looks like a shvartze." Lilly doesn't know what a "shvartze" is, but from the way her mother says it, Lilly knows it is something Jewish and not very good to look like. Lilly runs upstairs to consult the mirror, but she doesn't look like anything much, except herself.

» «

Lilly is sixteen. She is sitting on the couch next to her father, looking at old photographs. The big album is spread across both their laps. Four black triangles, one in each corner, hold the pictures in place, though some pictures have gotten loose and stick together between the pages.

Lilly's father points to each snapshot and tells her who everyone is. "That's your Great Aunt Sarah," he says. "That's your Uncle Murray, that's your Grandpa Harry who died right before you were born."

"Who's this?" Lilly asks, staring at a photo of a young girl, about the same age that Lilly is now. She wears a white frilly dress and black shoes with thin ankle straps. Her father lifts the album up on his lap and bends down closer to the picture.

"Who is that?" he repeats softly to himself. "Oh for God's sake, that's your Aunt Esther with her old nose." Her father lowers the album and chuckles. "Look at that. God, that must be an old picture. Must be 1942, maybe '43." Now Lilly bends closer to see the picture. It doesn't look like Aunt Esther to her. The girl in the picture had her hands clasped tightly behind her back and she was wearing dark lipstick but she wasn't smiling.

"I didn't know Aunt Esther had a nose job," Lilly says to her father.

"Oh sure she did. Both my sisters had one — your Aunt Rachel and your cousin Robin too. Thank God you got your mother's nose. Look, there's you at the old house on Avenue J. Do you remember that house?" He lowers his own nose closer to get a better look at the page.

» «

Lilly is seventeen. She takes the train into the city with Kathy to visit the Museum of Modern Art. Lilly pretends to admire the paintings, though she really doesn't think they look all that different from the crayon drawings of her five-year-old cousin Nathan, which her Aunt Rachel has hanging on her refrigerator door with orange slice and banana peel magnets.

Lilly and Kathy go into the gift shop to buy some postcards, and then Kathy says she has to go to the bathroom. Lilly stands by herself, slowly turning the creaky postcard rack.

"Hey Chica, Hey Mama," a man's voice calls, and without turning around Lilly knows he is talking to her. She ignores him, just like her mother taught her, and stays right where she is, waiting for Kathy. The man comes right beside her and puts his hand on the postcard rack so it can't turn. He is wearing black pants and a brown corduroy coat, and he is short, about the same height as Lilly.

The man starts speaking to Lilly in Spanish and she shakes her head, holding up one hand. "Listen, I don't speak Spanish. I'm sorry," she says, and her voice is sorry too, as if she has done something wrong.

But the man doesn't believe her. "C'mon. No kidding me. You speak Spanish, yes?" He smiles and Lilly notices he has bright white teeth.

"No, you don't understand. I'm not Spanish. I'm Jewish," Lilly says, backing up a little.

Now the man's smile grows even bigger, as though Lilly has made a joke. "No," he says. "You are no Jewish. You are too pretty for Jewish. You speak Spanish, yes?" The man leans towards Lilly and now she feels afraid. She leaves the gift shop quickly and walks swiftly through the lobby towards the bathroom, where much to her relief she sees Kathy's face floating towards her above the crowd.

» «

Lilly is eighteen. It is Yom Kippur and today she does not go to school. She goes to services instead with her mother and father. Lilly puts on her new plaid skirt, her soft red sweater and a pretty gold bracelet. Then she laces up her red high-topped sneakers and goes downstairs where her parents are waiting for her.

Her mother looks her up and down and when her eyes reach Lilly's feet, she starts to scream. "What's that on your feet? Get upstairs and put on your good shoes."

"But Ma, you're not supposed to wear leather today. You're sup-posed to give thanks to the animals. Even the Rabbi goes in sneakers." Lilly stares at her mother in defiance.

"Since when is she so religious?" Lilly's mother asks the ceiling. The ceiling offers no reply and Lilly's mother turns back to her daughter. "I don't care if the Rabbi is going barefoot—you are not wearing those sneakers to shul. Now get upstairs and change your shoes. Do you hear me?"

Lilly hears her. She changes her shoes.

» «

Lilly is still eighteen. She is going away to college. She has survived high school, much to her great relief and astonishment. She is in the back seat of the car with her pillow, two blankets, a suitcase and a potted plant. The rest of her things are in the trunk and her parents are in the front seat. They talk and talk while Lilly pretends to be asleep. They talk about the pretty New England towns they are driving through; they talk about where they will stop for lunch and how hungry they are and what they will eat; and they talk about Lilly and how big she is, already going off to college.

They arrive at Lilly's college in the midafternoon. Lilly will be living in a suite with three other girls and she is glad none of them are there yet. Lilly doesn't want anyone to meet her parents. She is embarrassed by how loud they talk, and she is ashamed of her mother's shabby fake-leather coat.

Lilly's parents leave, and the three other girls arrive soon after dinner. Lilly sits on an overturned milk crate and watches them unpack. Their names are Debbie, Donna and Marie. None of them are from New York. None of them are anything like Lilly. Soon they all sit in the bare living room—two on the orange couch and two on the blue director chairs. They talk. Debbie says she grew up on a farm in Vermont, Donna comes from Illinois, and Marie is from Pennsylvania. Lilly tells them she is from New York—only the way she says it, it sounds more like New Yawk and the other girls laugh at how she talks. Lilly vows to practice her Rs, and she doesn't hear what Donna is saying.

"Are you Jewish?" Donna asks her again.

Lilly thinks for a minute. "No," she says slowly. "I used to be, but I'm not anymore." And suddenly Lilly is talking and laughing with her new friends and feeling free — free as a downy bird that has just pecked her way out of a baby-blue egg with a beak as sharp and pointed as her Aunt Esther's new nose.

» «

Lilly is nineteen and a half. She has a boyfriend named Eddie. Lilly and Eddie are in bed together. It is 11:30 in the morning and Eddie's roommate is at his biology class. After the class there is a lab, so he will be gone most of the day.

Eddie is smoking a cigarette. He leans back to grind the butt out in the ashtray on the floor. He has nothing on except a thin gold chain around his neck. Lilly is naked too.

Eddie lazily stretches his arms over his head and grins at Lilly. "I'm starving," he says to her, bringing one arm down to stroke her hair. "I wonder what delicious delicacies they're going to bestow upon us in the dining hall today?"

"Probably spam sandwiches and jello mold with floating fruit cocktail," Lilly answers, wrinkling up her nose.

"Hey, what's the difference between a Jewish American Princess and a bowl of jello?" Eddie asks. Lilly doesn't answer. "One moves when you eat it and the other doesn't," he says, diving under the blankets. Lilly opens her legs wide and hugs Eddie's head with her thighs. I'll show him a thing or two, Lilly thinks, as Eddie emerges from the blankets, pulling her close and sliding inside her. Lilly knows what is expected of her. She digs her nails into Eddie's back and moves for all she is worth.

» «

Lilly is twenty years old. Her dorm is having a Christmas party and this year she is Donna's secret Santa. She goes downtown to buy a little present to leave outside Donna's door. The trees that line Main Street are decorated with red and green lights that blink on and off, and the sidewalk is filled with people rushing about with packages of toys and wrapping paper grasped tightly in their hands.

Lilly turns down a side street where it is quieter and enters a store. The store is filled with Indian clothing made of 100% cotton, costume jewelry, cards, posters and knicknacks. An old man and an old woman sit behind the counter, eating. Lilly walks around touching a mauve skirt, inspecting a wooden elephant, picking up a pair of white cloth shoes. She walks over to the jewelry counter and looks at a row of silver earrings.

"For something special you're looking maybe?"

Lilly raises her head and looks at the old man who has spoken to her. He wears a yarmulka on his head, and the old woman next to him has a silver *chai* around her neck. They are sitting on little wooden stools with napkins on their laps, eating potato pancakes out of a plastic container between them. Lilly stares at the food.

"You want a latke maybe?" the woman asks, smiling at Lilly and holding out a pancake.

"No thanks," Lilly stammers, aware now that she has been staring. "I just came in for a tchotchke." The Yiddish word, coming from nowhere, flies out of Lilly's mouth.

"Tchotchkes she wants? Oy do we got tchotchkes," the man says, coming out from behind the counter. "Little animals we got, and wooden baskets, paper fans maybe you like?" He gives Lilly a guided tour of his shop and she picks out a hand-painted wooden giraffe.

Lilly pays the man and sees that now the old woman is eating some applesauce out of a jar with a plastic spoon. "Take, take a latke home, you'll have it for later," she says, handing Lilly a package wrapped in tinfoil. Lilly takes the latke and Donna's present and leaves the store.

When she gets back to the dorm, Lilly hides Donna's present under her bed and takes off her coat, hat and scarf. She takes the bundle of tinfoil into the bathroom and locks the door. The old woman has given Lilly not one but three potato pancakes. Lilly eats the latkes ravenously, then licks her fingers greedily, searching the tinfoil for any stray crumbs she may have left behind.

>> «

Lilly is twenty-one. This is her last year of college. She has learned a lot of things over the past three and a half years. She has learned about Art History and Abnormal Psychology and American Literature Since 1945. She has learned about drinking sombreros and Singapore slings, smoking pot and taking speed. But the most important thing she's learned is that she likes women better than she likes men.

Lilly has a girlfriend. Her name is Angie. They do everything together. They eat meals together in the big dining hall, they study together on the top floor of the library, and they sleep together in Angie's tiny single room.

One Saturday Lilly and Angie get dressed all in purple and walk downtown holding hands. It is Gay Pride Day and this is the first year there is going to be a parade in their town. They stand in a schoolyard with about three hundred people and there are balloons, dogs wearing bandanas around their necks and chasing Frisbees, even a marching band with a man and a woman baton twirler.

Now the march begins. Lilly and Angie get on line and start up the street. They feel very happy stepping to the beat of the drums. They walk up Main Street proudly, past all the little shops and restaurants they have gone into together many times before. People line the streets. Some raise their fists and cheer and others simply stand there staring.

At the top of Main Street the march takes a turn into a park. At one side of the park entrance stands a small group of people holding signs that say, "God made Adam and Eve, NOT Adam and Steve," and "Jesus loves the sinner but not the sin." On the other side of the park two girls are standing with a big sign made out of an old white sheet stretched between them. Their sign says, "NEVER AGAIN," and it is decorated with women's symbols, men's symbols and Jewish stars. Lilly looks at the sign and feels the tears welling up in her eyes and running down her cheeks. She turns her face away so Angie won't see, and wipes her eyes with the back of her sleeve.

» «

Lilly is twenty-two. She and Angie live in an apartment in town. Angie is in graduate school and Lilly is working in an office and daydreaming about becoming a famous movie star or winning the lottery and getting at least a million dollars.

Lilly is grouchy when she comes home. She doesn't like working in an office and she doesn't get to spend enough time with Angie, who is always at a meeting or studying at the library. Lilly eats dinner by herself, listening to the radio. The news is on. Otto Frank, Ann Frank's father has died today, in Switzerland, at the age of ninety-one. Lilly puts down her fork. *The Diary of Ann Frank* was one of her favorite books when she was a little girl. She walks over to the bookshelf to see if she still has it. She does. Lilly takes it down and begins to read. She gets so absorbed in the book that she crawls into bed at ten o'clock with all her clothes on, still reading. Angie comes in at eleven o'clock and finds Lilly asleep, with the book on the bed upside down beside her.

"Hi honey," Angie whispers, kissing Lilly awake. She slips into bed beside her and gathers her up in her arms. "I missed you all day," Angie says, kissing Lilly's warm cheek. "Hey, you still have all your clothes on. Let me undress you." Angie unbuttons Lilly's shirt and plants little kisses all across her chest. Soon her mouth finds Lilly's breast. Lilly cradles Angie's head in her arms and soon they are rocking each other gently and moaning together softly.

"You feel so good," Lilly murmurs as Angie unbuttons her pants and slides them down around Lilly's feet. Angie touches Lilly in the way Lilly likes best, and just as she starts to come, Lilly bursts into tears.

"What is it, baby? What is it?" Angie holds her as she sobs and sobs. "Never again," Lilly cries out, sniffling and gasping for air. "Never again," she repeats, crying uncontrollably now. Angie is puzzled, but she holds Lilly, stroking her hair and murmuring, "It's all right, Lilly. It's all right."

Suddenly Lilly is furious at Angie. "It's not all right," she says sharply, pulling herself away. "What if they came tomorrow? What if they're coming right now? Would you hide me? Would you?"

"Who, Lilly? Who's coming to get you?"

"The Nazis," Lilly says, a fresh batch of tears falling from her eyes.

"Oh Lilly, that's over. You're safe now. No one's coming to get you."

"What if they are? What if they're coming right now? Where would I go? Who would take care of me?"

"I would, honey. I would hide you. Of course I would. Lilly, I won't let anyone take you away from me. I'll hold onto you really tight, just like this." Lilly lets Angie encircle her in her warm arms, even though she doesn't believe her.

» «

Lilly is twenty-three. It is April and she has been invited to two feminist Seders. She stands in the kitchen looking at the Women For Peace calendar hanging on the wall. Angie is sitting at the table drinking lemon-grass tea.

"We can go to Amy's Seder Thursday night and Meryl's on Friday, okay?" Lilly asks.

Angie pours some honey into her tea. "Do we have to go to both?" she asks. "I'm getting a little Jewed out."

"What?" Lilly's body jerks itself forward. This is the woman who touches me in all my secret places, Lilly thinks. This is the woman I'm going to spend the rest of my life with. "What did you say?" Lilly asks, sitting down next to Angie at the table.

"Never mind," Angie says, letting out a deep sigh. "You have Seders for Passover, right, and the menorah is for Chanukah?"

"Right," Lilly says, leaning back in her chair. "And let's see. You have a tree for Christmas and a rabbit for Easter, and you put shmutz on your forehead for Ash Wednesday and you give up something for Lent on Good Friday, and . . ."

"Okay, okay, I was only trying. You don't have to get nasty," Angie says, staring out the window, the sky reflecting in her blue eyes.

"Sorry," Lilly mutters, but she doesn't really mean it. She's sorry Angie hurt her, and she's glad she hurt her back.

» «

Lilly is twenty-four. She and Angie aren't together anymore. It is December and Lilly is out doing errands. She goes to the post office and asks for five stamps. The clerk hands her a strip of stamps; three with pictures of Christmas trees and two with a child's drawing of Santa Claus.

"I don't want these," Lilly says, handing them back. The clerk gives her five stamps with American flags. Lilly isn't crazy about these either, but they'll have to do. She pays the postal clerk and waits for her change. The clerk hands her some coins and says, "Merry Christmas."

"I don't celebrate Christmas. I'm Jewish," Lilly says as she drops the money into her wallet.

"Oh, I'm sorry," the woman says, and Lilly can tell by her voice that she's not sorry for the mistake she's made, but rather for Lilly's misfortune. "Well, have a happy holiday then."

I'm not having a holiday, Lilly thinks as she shoves her wallet into her coat pocket. Chanukah was over five days ago. She leaves the post office wrapped in a cloud of angry silence.

» «

Lilly is twenty-five. She has a new girlfriend named Bernie. Bernie's real name is Bernice and she is Jewish. Lilly is going shopping for Bernie's Chanukah presents. She is going to get her eight presents — seven little ones and one big one.

Lilly walks around town and finds her way to the women's bookstore. There is a bulletin board with lots of buttons, and Lilly thinks maybe she can find something funny for Bernie. Her eyes search the little shiny circles until she finds something perfect: "This Butch Melts." Lilly reaches up to get the button and her eyes follow the motion of her hand, until they rest on another button: "I Survived a Jewish Mother."

Lilly looks away, then looks at the button again. "I Survived Kent State," she thinks. "I Survived Three Mile Island." But "I Survived a Jewish Mother?" Lilly takes the button down and brings it over to the cash register. The woman behind the counter looks up from the invoice she is checking.

"This button really offends me," Lilly says, with her heart pounding against her chest. The woman looks down at the button, then up at Lilly's face. "I'm Jewish too," the woman says. So, Lilly thinks. She says nothing. "Those buttons are made by a feminist company," the woman says, as if that explains everything. Lilly waits but the woman says nothing more. Lilly asks, "How many of them do you have?"

The woman opens a wooden drawer and fishes around among buttons, key chains and loose coins. She counts out eight buttons. "I'll take them all," Lilly says, handing the woman a ten-dollar bill. Her heart is still racing. Lilly puts her change in her wallet and her wallet into her shoulder bag. Then she reaches into her bag again, removes a felt-tipped pen and uncaps it. She scribbles on all the buttons and asks the woman behind the counter if she has a trash can.

"Get out of my store," the woman says. Lilly and her beating heart leave.

» «

Lilly is still twenty-five. She is going shopping for Chanukah candles. She gets in her car and drives to Waldbaum's. She asks the man in the courtesy booth where the Chanukah candles are. "Aisle six," he says. "International Foods."

Lilly is a little wary as she walks towards aisle six. That man is the same one who last spring told her that the matzo was in the frozen-food section. He had confused matzo with bagels.

Lilly turns down aisle six and her eyes scan the shelves until she comes to the Jewish food: borsht, applesauce, chicken soup in jars, potato-pancake mix, Shabbos candles, Yarzheit candles, but no Chanukah candles. Lilly walks up the aisle until she sees a man in a red smock pricing jars of picante sauce.

"Excuse me," Lilly says, "but I can't find the Chanukah candles." She walks back up the aisle with the man following behind her. The man looks up and down the shelves and points to the Shabbos candles. "There," he says.

"No, those are Shabbos candles. I want Chanukah candles."

The man studies the shelf and picks up a Yarzheit candle. "Is this what you want?"

"No. I'm looking for a box of forty-four candles, all different colors, little to fit into a menorah," Lilly says.

"A what?" The man puts the Yarzheit candle back and picks up a box of Shabbos candles. "Look these are very nice candles. Seventy-two in a box. Can't you make do?"

"Never mind," Lilly says and she leaves the store. How can Waldbaum's not have Chanukah candles, she wonders, as she backs out of her parking space and heads for another store. It is the same story at

Stop and Shop, Price Chopper, the Food Co-op and Store 24. By the time Lilly gets home, she is exhausted. She calls the synagogue, and a woman tells her she can buy candles at Goodman's Pharmacy on Grove Avenue. Lilly hangs up the phone and cries for an hour.

The next night is Chanukah. Bernie is coming over for dinner. Lilly comes home from work early to chop up apples for applesauce and grate potatoes for latkes. She is very happy, bustling about the kitchen and listening to *Fiddler on the Roof* on the stereo.

Bernie comes over at seven. She is tired; she has had a hard day at work; her head hurts. She asks Lilly to turn down the music. She tells Lilly she isn't very hungry. Lilly is disappointed. At least they light the candles together.

Bernie tells Lilly she can't stay very long. She's going to a Christmas party at Mary Ann's house.

"A Christmas party!" Lilly says in astonishment. "On the first night of Chanukah? I thought you'd want to spend the first night of Chanukah with me."

Bernie thrusts her hands into her pockets and shifts her weight. "Well, Mary Ann's having this big party and I told her I'd come. I didn't know the first night was such a big deal. Chanukah's eight nights—we can spend another night of it together."

"But this is the first night. Of course it's important." Lilly starts to whine. "And I made a whole dinner for you."

Bernie looks at the food on the stove. "Well, I don't like latkes so much anyway. They're too greasy," she says. "Look, why don't you come with me to Mary Ann's? I just have to stop at my house and get her present."

"You bought her a Christmas present?" Lilly is practically yelling now.

"Well, yeah." Bernie thrusts her hands deeper into her pockets and fingers her change.

"But Bernie, you're Jewish!"

"I know I'm Jewish."

"Then how can you buy someone a Christmas present?"

"Mary Ann's not someone. She's my best friend."

"So, did she buy you a Chanukah present?" Lilly asks, leaning back against the sink and folding her arms.

"No." Bernie stares down at Lilly's feet.

"Then why did you buy her a Christmas present? And why are you going off to celebrate her holiday with her, instead of staying here to celebrate our holiday with me?"

"What's wrong with doing something special for a friend that you love?" Now Bernie is yelling, too.

"Then why doesn't she do something special for you and buy you a present for Chanukah?"

"Because she's not Jewish."

"And you're not Catholic."

"Lilly." Bernie let out a deep sigh. "Christmas isn't a Catholic holiday anymore. It's a universal holiday."

"That's bullshit."

"Lilly," Bernie sighs again, "do you really think Mary Ann is celebrating the birth of Jesus Christ?"

"Yes."

"Well, she isn't." Bernie is pacing around the kitchen floor. She stops in front of Lilly. "She just likes having a tree and a party because Christmas was the best day of her lousy childhood every year and . . ."

"Well it was the worst day of mine," Lilly yells, flinging up her hands. "Go then. Have a great time. Kiss someone under the mistletoe for me."

"I will," Bernie yells into the night as she yanks open the door. Lilly closes it behind her and sits down to eat the latkes by herself, salty tears running down her cheeks.

» «

Lilly is twenty-six. She needs some new clothes. She goes downtown to a used clothing store called Clothes Encounters and begins to browse. Usually Lilly finds something she likes at Clothes Encounters, but not today. On her way out she stops at the fifty-cent bin to look at some scarves. She squats down and rummages around. Her eye falls on something white and shiny, trimmed with blue. It is a tallis. Lilly can't believe it. She rubs the shiny material against her face. How did it ever wind up here, she wonders. Lilly pays for the tallis and brings it home. She sits in her rocking chair, braiding the strands of the tallis together, just like she did when she was a little girl sitting next to her father in shul. Lilly is lonely. She and Bernie aren't girlfriends anymore. Lilly wants a new lover. Being a lesbian is lonely, Lilly thinks. Being a Jew is lonely. Being alive is lonely, she reminds herself. A tear slips down her cheek and Lilly wipes it with the corner of the tallis.

Lilly decides to call a friend but her line is busy. She calls someone else and gets an answering machine. Lilly takes a warm bath and drinks some chamomile tea. She sleeps with the tallis under her pillow, one hand stroking the shiny cloth the same way she would pet the shiny part of her baby blanket twenty-five years ago, to put herself to sleep.

» «

Lilly is twenty-eight. She has just moved in with her girlfriend Nina. Lilly loves Nina very much and Nina seems to love Lilly. Nina is not Jewish, but she knows some things about Judaism, like why the Jews were driven out of Egypt and who Miriam the Prophet was and how you're supposed to kiss the mezuzza when you go in and out the front door.

Nina tells Lilly that even though she can't be Jewish for her, she can be supportive. She says maybe she'll take a Hebrew class or a Jewish history class. Lilly doesn't like that idea. She doesn't want Nina to know more about being Jewish than she does. She tells Nina so, and Nina gives her a big hug. "It's okay, Lilly," she says. "I won't if you don't want me to. But it would be neat to know Hebrew so I could go to temple with you."

Lilly doesn't tell Nina she hasn't been to shul in ten years. Today they are going to an all-day Lesbian conference. There are lots of workshops and activities to choose from. Lilly decides to go to a writing workshop in the morning, and a cross-cultural relationship workshop with Nina in the afternoon.

Lilly enjoys the writing workshop. The workshop leader is very supportive and full of good ideas. The women write for half an hour and then go around the room sharing their work. Lilly is moved by the words that the other women read.

As they go around, a few women decide not to share their writing.

The leader says that's okay, there's no pressure. One woman apologizes. The workshop leader says, "It's really alright. Nobody's going to force you to do anything you don't want here. This isn't a Nazi concentration camp."

Lilly is stunned. She looks around at the faces of the women in the circle, all of them paying rapt attention to a woman in a green jumpsuit who is reading a poem about her grandmother. Lilly slowly scans the room. I am the only Jew here, she thinks, as the tears begin to rise.

After the workshop Lilly approaches the teacher. Her heart is beating in her throat. "What you said," she begins, faltering, looking down at her hands — this is a famous writer, Lilly reminds herself, but she continues — "What you said about this workshop not being like a concentration camp," she pauses again and then bursts out, "how can you compare not sharing your writing with being in a Nazi camp? Do you have any idea what went on there? This is nothing," Lilly says, gesturing with one hand at the room. "Nothing," she repeats.

The workshop leader is very sorry. She apologizes a hundred times. She supports Lilly. She says she's glad she brought it up. She tells Lilly that she is brave.

Lilly doesn't feel brave. She feels tired and a little apprehensive about the next workshop. She and Nina go to Room 307 and sit down. There are already about fifteen women there. The leader of the workshop smiles. She is a white woman.

"Welcome to this workshop on interracial relationships," she says. Lilly and Nina look at each other. "I thought it was cross-cultural relationships," Nina whispers. "It must have gotten changed," Lilly whispers back. "Should we stay?" Nina asks her. Lilly shrugs her shoulders. "I guess so," she says.

The workshop leader has the group break off into pairs and talk about the first time they met somebody from a different racial group and what that was like. Then they talk about an interracial relationship they are having right now and what they're learning from it. Then they talk about what barriers prevent them from having more interracial relationships.

After the third question, the women regroup in a circle for discussion. Lilly smiles at Nina when she comes back to sit next to her. They listen to the discussion. A white woman talks about how hard her parents make it when she brings her black lover home for a visit. Another white woman raises her hand. She tells the group that she is involved with a Jewish woman and that her lover's parents are Holocaust survivors.

"It's really hard to be around them," the woman says, "especially when they act in that stereotypically obnoxious Jewish way."

Lilly's body stiffens for the second time that day. She looks around this group of faces, asking herself again, am I the only Jew here? Doesn't anybody else have ears? Now everyone is listening to a black woman who is speaking. Lilly is afraid to look at Nina. She sits in silence, until the workshop is almost over. When there are only about five minutes left, she rises slowly and walks to the front of the room to stand next to the workshop leader. The woman turns. "Yes?" she asks, putting her hand on Lilly's shoulder, and Lilly bursts into tears.

» «

Lilly is twenty-nine. It is Rosh Hashanah. She stays home from work to go to shul. Nina offers to come with her, but Lilly says no, this is something she needs to do by herself. Nina says "gut yontif," the way Lilly has taught her and kisses her cheek. Lilly tells her later they will eat apples and honey together, so that the New Year will be sweet. Nina tells Lilly she has a little present for her. "Do you want it now or later?" she asks. "Later," Lilly says. "I don't want to be late for shul."

Nina leaves for work and Lilly gets dressed. She puts on black pants, a fuzzy white sweater and a pair of turquoise earrings. She laces up her red high-topped sneakers and wears a labyris and a Jewish star around her neck. She buttons her coat, thrusts her hands in her pockets and starts the long walk to shul.

As Lilly walks, she thinks about all the things that have happened to her over the years. She thinks about being a little girl who wanted a Christmas tree more than anything in the whole world. She thinks about how ashamed she was to take peanut-butter-and-matzo sandwiches to school, and about all the years she spent trying to diet and straighten her hair. Lilly walks quickly through the streets of her town, not paying much attention to the cars that pass her, all the while thinking. She thinks about marching with Angie in the Gay Pride March and she thinks about fighting with Bernie over Christmas. And she thinks a lot about Nina; how she offered to go to shul with her that morning and how sometimes she asks Lilly to sing her to sleep. "Sing me a Hebrew song," she says to her. "Your voice sounds so beautiful when you sing in Hebrew."

Lilly walks and walks. Tucked under her arm is her tallis, in a little blue velvet bag she has sewn herself. She wonders what her mother would think to see her daughter carrying a tallis. Lilly remembers how happy her mother was last year to receive a New Year's card from her. The card had a picture of a woman with a shawl on her head chopping apples in her kitchen, and Lilly had written inside "Thank you for never letting me forget who I am."

Lilly also remembers her first day of college when she told her three roommates that she wasn't a Jew and how she hadn't said anything to Eddie whenever he told his awful Jewish American Princess jokes. Lilly is thinking about all of these things as she turns onto Elmwood Avenue and the synagogue comes into view. She notices a young couple across the street and smiles at them, knowing where they are going. The young woman calls to her son not to run so fast and to wait for his father before he crosses the street.

Lilly enters the shul and takes a prayerbook from the shelf in the lobby. She is too shy to put on her tallis. She goes inside and sits down, holding the prayerbook and the tallis on her lap. The rabbi is reading in Hebrew. Lilly looks around to see if she can find anyone she knows. Her friend Barbara is sitting two rows in front of her, with a bunch of women Lilly doesn't know. One of the women is wearing a yarmulka on her head. When the Ark is open, Lilly tiptoes down the aisle and squeezes in next to Barbara. Barbara smiles; she is happy to see Lilly here. Barbara is wearing a grey sweater and a black skirt with little grey elf boots. She has a gold labyris with a Jewish star cut out of one of its blades around her neck.

The rabbi begins to sing and the congregation sings with him. Lilly sees that Barbara can read Hebrew. She is moving her finger right to left across the page. Her voice is loud, strong and beautiful. Lilly cannot read Hebrew, but she sings along, surprised that she remembers so many of the words and tunes. Lilly feels like a little girl again, and she half expects to see her mother and father sitting in front of her in the next aisle.

The rabbi and the cantor sing the *Shema* in loud clear voices, and Lilly feels her heart swelling inside her chest. She repeats the *Shema* along with Barbara and the hundred or so other people in the small synagogue, letting the tears run down her cheeks like rain. Barbara turns to face Lilly and Lilly does not turn away. They smile at each other and Barbara squeezes Lilly's hand. She understands. Lilly has come home.

LIBBI MIRIAM

TAKING THE BUS

I tell you I'm removed from both of you   no longer have to please you
You can never share my inner world   You know nothing about
me   How will I mourn you when you die

 As she watches them deplane Nina relives the old fear: They'll gobble her up; she'll become their good little girl. The fear quickly dies. Her parents look old and fragile; she's shocked by the sight of them bobbing down the ramp.

By the second day the fear's gone. Still, they're her parents all right. As if she'd never left them. Though they've been through heart attacks, tumors, hernias, cataracts, God knows what, Nina manages to direct their care from a safe distance. And she's never exposed them to her turmoil during those long child-rearing years. At last she knows what parenthood means.

Ma Pa why were you so ordinary   so middle class   not political rebels
artists so I'd know how to live my life   You tried hard   Everything for
the kids   You lived for us   Why didn't you teach me how to be a parent
and a person

This visit she'll spend less time with them than last, just enough to satisfy her sense of responsibility. Vivian and Davey accuse her of being their parents' favorite, the good one.

She sees her parents twice a week: at their rented apartment on Tuesdays before teaching and at her home for Friday-night dinner as she half-heartedly performs food rituals for them and the grown kids, in case they pop in. On Fridays Mom attacks Nina's kitchen with her old cleaning mania. But those meals together prove easier than the treks into town — haunting malls, comparison shopping, Dad talking to every stranger, telling them he's from New Jersey, and Mom complaining about her feet; both of them bickering over what time to eat,

Mom announcing, *It's noon, I want a nice place this time,* Dad insisting, *Wait 'til one and then we'll go to Burger King, I got my Senior Citizen's discount. Besides they grill the fat out of their hamburgers, and McDonald's doesn't.*

Then Dad turns to Nina. "I can wait an hour. Your old man's a trooper, kiddo, don't you forget it. You don't have to help me for another ten years," he adds, pushing away her arm.

Dad's more stooped than last year. Despite his soft chin, he still has the appearance of a man who's done physical work most of his life. He looks good for eighty, not as if he's been through three major operations, and suffers from sudden attacks of weakness.

How hard you push yourself until you're exhausted Pa   You don't know how to save your energy   'Father,' what does that mean   What does eighty mean

Mom still dresses in a light corset and pants suit, her face powdered and pencilled, her hair tinted to brassy gold, her skin unwrinkled from staying inside. Nina knows she'll wrinkle more than Mom by seventy-seven. Will she let herself go gray, or have Mom's vanities?

Ma I'm afraid of becoming you, of turning into you   I see you in my mirror living in your world   Don't let Pa go first

Elevator music filters through the furnished apartment Nina has rented for them. At first Mom complained about the place until Dad threw a fit. Now she wistfully sighs, "It's nice, very nice. It just takes me a while to get used to it. It's hard for me to pack up and leave my home."

Dad responds on cue: "For God's sake, Pearl, you've got to roll with the punches. Adjust to new places. It's gorgeous here."

The two of them glance from Nina to the view of the soft hills against a clear sky after the rains. Mom likes the hills but complains wildly when it rains. She wants them covered with constant sun.

"Pretty out there, Nina, but it rained again last night."
"It'll clear up in an hour or so, Mom, you'll see."

Sorry Ma no more guilt about weather   I didn't make the rain   Don't talk about it   It gives me a headache

They lunch on tuna casserole and cottage cheese. Mom insisting, "Eat a piece of cake, Nina." They make their usual conversation about the view, about the grandchildren. Dad laughs, "I tell you, those kids must have landed on earth from spaceships." And hesitantly Mom asks the question Nina's been waiting for: "Is Amy still living with that goy?"
"Amy doesn't say much about her relationships."

She's distant Ma   cold the way I was toward you   We can't break that chain   Goy   she still uses that word

"Never mind, she's a smart cookie with a good mind and a good job," says Dad. "Maybe she'll change her mind. And Jon, twenty-four, a pisher with a gorgeous car. I didn't have a tin lizzy until we were married seven years." Dad shakes his head.
Mom grimaces, examines the living room, not listening.
"Nina, before I leave, take some money and get rid of that hideous lamp on the piano."
"Don't talk like that; Nina could care less about lamps," Dad bawls.
"Are you angry, Nina?"
"Not at all."

It's true Ma   I don't care   Really I don't even hear you   I don't listen either

The three of them talk about Ma changing her will again.
"Nina. Are you paying attention? There are the grave sites, the

federal notes, the jewelry. Vivian wants the piano, the charm bracelet. . . . "

Ma I'm you   Quick-tongued   self-important   Taking your glasses on
and off   Reading your will in your orator's voice   What's wrong Pa

Nina watches the expression on her father's face go dead. "Are you
okay, Dad?"

"I'm okay. Ya got an aspirin?"

The veins in his left temple protrude. Ma gets up to bring him one.

"Better get one for me too," Nina says.

"Just like your father. "Now *you've* got the headache. Wait, I'm not
finished. I want to do this fair and square. After I'm gone, no one will
accuse me of playing favorites."

"Dad, are you sure you're okay?"

"Everything's fine, everything's dandy, like sugar-candy. Just finish already, Pearl. Make sure Nina gets my mother's samovar from
Russia. She's the most like my mother. The other kids can have
anything else. The rest doesn't matter. I'm too old. Let them make the
decisions themselves. Now tell me, are we moving to California or
not?"

"You know we can't leave our home, Morris; Vivian needs us too
much." Ma says firmly.

"Don't fake, Pearl; you're the one who can't get used to new
places. That's the reason. Just say so."

Are you fake Ma   Am I   I don't remember how you took care of me
only your worry over how wild Davey was   how Vivian wouldn't clean
up her room   Can't we laugh   reach out like Pa   Something about
being a woman   Ma you made such good lunches for me   You loved
Jon so much when he was born   Ma

Nina changes the subject; she knows they'll never make the move.

"There's a new queen-size dress shop in town. Why don't I pick
you and Mom up after my class and drive over to see if she can get
something. This will be her chance to bring home a dress from California."

Mom's face brightens, then pouts. At home Dad still chauffeurs her everywhere in their old Ford; she sits in the back seat with an unfastened seat belt.

"How will we get back here?"

"I'll take you and bring you back."

Dad looks at Nina sharply. "No, you're always tired after teaching. We'll take the bus. Just tell us where the shop is."

Your're right Pa   I'll be tired   I give it my all like you   It would be easier Ma if you took the damn bus

"No big deal."

Dad beams. "A chip off the old block. Just like my side of the family. Nothing's too hard for Moe Harris's daughter. We can take the bus."

Mom's face reddens. "Just forget the whole thing. I don't need to go," she huffs and clears off the table.

"Whadda ya mean, 'you don't need to go.' You'd go if Nina drove, wouldn't you? Don't be selfish; think of Nina."

Ma bursts into tears. "I *am* thinking of Nina; this could be the last time we're together for another year. Who knows if we'll make it back. Are you in one of your crabby moods again? I don't have a selfish bone in my body. Don't I visit your old aunt in the nursing home when her own children don't come? Every time I go, I bring a batch of home-made cookies, a bottle of cologne, a . . . ."

Dad pounds his fist against the kitchen table. A cup jumps in its saucer. "Do you know the meaning of the word 'selfish'?"

"I'd do anything for Nina, you know that, Morris." She turns to Nina. "Your father has been badgering me all morning."

Pa why are you so hard on Ma   crabby   Trying to make her strong for when you're not here   Your hand's shaking   What's wrong

Nina watches them play out the same roles she and Hal play with their children. Something in her throat tightens.

Stop it Pa she's not going to change   Ma please Don't you see his ashen face   He pushes too much   Pa she keeps your house cooks every meal How could you get along without her   How long before Hal and I become like both of you

"Answer me. Tell me the meaning of 'selfish.' You don't know. You visit my aunt because you want to. But taking the bus, something you don't want to do, means putting yourself out. That's a different story."

"Morris, after fifty-three years you don't know anything about me. Tell him he's wrong, Nina."

No Mamma he's right   Forgive me Mamma   I'm not fair   Don't linger with illness like Hal's mother   Go quickly together   An airplane crash   I'm growing older by the minute

"I don't want to take sides."

"Morris, why do you always test me? Do you want to show that you love Nina more than I do?"

Yes Ma a contest and women get gypped   Daughters admire their fathers   It's not fair Ma is it

Dad slumps into his chair. His head begins to shake slightly. His eyes close; a single teardrop falls from them.

What is it Pa   Should I come to you and kiss you   we'll both break into tears   hurt Ma   make her feel outside our love   Damn it don't make me break down   Pa you hold me on your black hairy arm   I finger your mustache   You sing an off-key lullaby   dream I save you from robbers who break into your store   We're walking through snowy city park on New Year's Day   Ma you're cooking   Everything's so clean You're worrying about money about Davey   Vivian   inviting those fat ladies with make-up for mah jongg   Ma do something else you won't be depressed   I won't come to you   never changing your talcum   wanting Pa to speak better English   Pa   laughter hugs   You want Ma to be strong   I am both of you   Both

Mom gets up from the table. "Finish your coffee, Nina, I'm cleaning up."

Dad stands. "She doesn't have time. She's gotta go to her class. She loves teaching those people from Pakistan to talk English."

"They're from Afghanistan, Dad."

"Okay, Afghanistan. Are we taking the bus or not?"

"Only if you apologize."

"For what?"

"For what you said to me just now."

"All right, all right." He leans over and kisses Mom. She beams.

Ma I carry you in my bones   Don't die Pa   I love you too much

"Can I buy my bride supper afterward?"

Do you sleep together   Ma do you take off your nightgown in front of Pa

"Only if you don't tear your roll into pieces and stuff it into a napkin to bring it home."

"You do the same."

"I do not. I cut my roll neatly."

Nina shakes her head and laughs. "Do you have the bus schedule?"

"Sure. I got it the first day we moved in here. Do you think your father's an old man?"

"The shop's behind Macy's."

"What side, left or right?" Mom frowns at the sink.

"For Chrissake; we'll find it. We're no dummies. You worry about every little thing. Let her go; she's late to her class. You know she loves that class."

"Maybe we can have a little outing Sunday," Nina yells from the doorway.

"Don't do it if you're busy."

"Oh, Moe. You *know* she wants to take us."

They both come rushing out to the car. "You're going to miss my Tuesday lunches, aren't you, Nina?"

Yes Ma   No I don't know Ma   I don't know   Don't ask me that

"You were a help to me while you were here. Mom, the way you'd clean up after dinner and bake things —"

"Oh, Nina."

"No, really."

"Aren't you going to say you'll miss me?"

"Don't put words in her mouth. She doesn't have to miss you. This is the best part of her life. It's for enjoyment, not missing old parents."

"That's all right, Dad. I'll miss you both.

I'm removed from you   I no longer have to please either of you   win your love   You're choking me   Let me go   Let go   I rehearse your deaths

Nina starts the motor.

"I wish the weather had been better; Hal and I could have taken you to Yosemite. We usually have better winters than this."

"It would have been nice." Mom looks like she'll cry any second.

"Never mind Yosemite; it's plenty nice right here. A few drizzles are nothing," Dad says.

Mom's turn. "Nina, you and Hal should go out together more now that the kids are grown. Do you really need to teach now?"

Dad's angry again. "Don't ask her that. She knows what to do."

"It's all right if I tell you, Nina, isn't it? It's for your own good. And for Hal too. Women know."

"Yes, Mom, it's fine."

How much you want my approval Ma   You knew I withheld it all these years didn't you   What's this emotion   this tightness in my chest Breathe it out   blow it out   Force a smile   don't disappoint them

"I don't know about you, Pearl, but next year, I'm taking Greyhound cross-country, yeah, with a little pack on my back like a hippie. You can stay home in the snow. If I go bye-bye on the way, I won't know the difference. Just fly the body back home."

"Moe, stop that foolishness."

"It's not foolish, it's real."

From the car window Nina reaches out and pecks them each goodbye. They stand in the driveway shouting, "Drive carefully," as she pulls away.

MARCIA TAGER

COUSINS

Her name was Lillian but we called her Lilo. Lillian was too ordinary a name for her. Lilo had something slightly exotic about it, faintly foreign, although she was no more foreign than I. I sat next to her at the cousins' table for years. The cousins' table was where the children sat at family functions — weddings, Bar Mitzvahs, anniversary parties. All the cousins sat there, the poor ones as well as the rich ones. It was about the only time I saw Lilo. She was always wearing an elegant dress that curdled my heart. We were separated by unbridgeable gulfs. She was fifteen. I was twelve. She was the pampered, petted, only child of Uncle Joe and Aunt Ida. They were rich. They had moved into a green suburb while we remained in our crowded, rented apartment in the city. In less than twenty years Lilo and I reversed the process, I living in the suburbs, she in the city, each pretending to misunderstand the other's choice. At just about the time Lilo would have graduated from the cousins' table to sitting with the adults, she dropped out of sight. I heard she had gone abroad to study. Wisps of outrage floated about her name, for Lilo hadn't chosen a very acceptable place to study. Paris was acceptable. London, Rome, Florence, Oslo, Tokyo, Honolulu, Tahiti, Reykjavik, any of these places would have done, but Lilo had gone to Heidelberg. Now why would anyone in our family choose German as her major and go to *Germany* to study? In actual fact Lilo was a linguistics major but that fact was totally obscured by the fact that she was studying in Germany. Parents sighed, shrugged, lifted their eyes heavenward, asking God to witness the madness of their young, asking for the strength to bear the terrible burden of their children's lunacy. From under lowered lids they looked over to the cousins' table to see if they could predict who would be the next to embrace mania and flee. I felt a contemporary's sympathy for Lilo — an us against them feeling. I saw the adults hovering about Aunt Ida and Uncle Joe, commiserating, offering comfort, especially to Uncle Joe for we all knew Lilo had been Uncle Joe's darling. Going home after these parties my parents turned to each other, and one of them said with relief, and a little satisfaction, "Thank God she isn't ours," to which the other replied, "So what good does all his money do him? In the end he's got the same aggravation we've all got."

Lilo's defection made everything a little easier for the cousins. No matter how far we went, none of us (thanks be to God, they sighed) went as far as Lilo. Getting out of town to college was much easier than it would have been if Lilo hadn't gone to Heidelberg. For how could they complain about Michigan or even California when they had Heidelberg staring them in the face? It was all too much for Aunt Ida. She was a frail, tentative woman who bounced for years between Lilo and Joe, like a tennis ball whammed off the catgut of their fury, pleading first with one then the other to have some heart — *rachmones* was the term she actually used. She was a small person with a quiet voice. Lilo and Joe were shouters. My mother, having grown up as Joe's younger sister, had plenty of practice in standing up to Joe. This practice made her tough and wary and taught her that the best defense is a good offense. My father sometimes never knew what hit him. He'd hardly have time to get his hat off his head or his feet inside the front door, when my mother, no mean shouter herself, would come blazing out of the kitchen to fling down the gauntlet. He was no slouch in the ring either. He had a wild sense of humor to which my mother was fatally susceptible. In the midst of her fury she often, wholly against her will, disintegrated. I could see her fighting to keep her lips straight. You couldn't take her fury seriously. It was too ephemeral. In this way she was very different from her brother Joe, who remembered a snub, real or imagined, for thirty years. My mother said, after the beginning of the Lilo *skondahl,* that if only Ida had stood up to Joe once in a while maybe Lilo wouldn't have done it so often.

My mother failed to take into account Aunt Ida's perfectly valid sense of survival. People who live in the eye of a hurricane figure out their best defense against the wind and fall into the same position as soon as they smell it coming. Aunt Ida did survive Heidelberg. Lilo's return was a quiet affair. Aunt Ida went alone to meet Lilo's plane. Her strategy was that their prodigal daughter had come home and she and Joe would be very happy to have her back, without ever mentioning where it was she had been. I don't know exactly what happened when Lilo and Joe confronted each other but I am certain, knowing them both and knowing the ineffectuality of Aunt Ida's stratagems, that confronted is the right word. Lilo left home again very quickly. She went to graduate school to get her Ph.D. in linguistics. There was a lull in the war between Lilo and her parents. Getting a doctorate wasn't as good as getting a nice Jewish doctor, but it wasn't as terrible as Heidelberg.

I had my own life to attend to and I lost track of Lilo's for a few years. I married and was then living in Allentown, and although my mother sent long, detailed letters about who was doing what, I was too absorbed in my own affairs to pay much attention to news from home. I had started my own family, and my old family with its dramas, gossip, and tensions seemed blessedly remote. But one day my mother phoned to tell me Aunt Ida had died. I cried when I hung up the phone and was surprised to discover how much I had loved her. My mother took it for granted that I would come home for Aunt Ida's funeral. Her assumption that I would do this made me realize that in her eyes I was finally grown-up, for the children had always been shielded from funerals. There was the cousins' table at weddings and anniversaries and birthday parties — *simchas*, happy affairs, where they paraded in new clothes and got their cheeks pinched by aunts and uncles. Nobody ever brought the children to funerals.

Lilo was the star of Aunt Ida's funeral. And she wasn't even there. She had been forbidden to attend by Uncle Joe who trumpeted forth the news to the world and the assembled family that Lilo had killed her mother and that he never wanted to "lay eyes on her as long as he lived." Why Lilo accepted this ban I never understood for I know she loved her mother and although, to the world, Aunt Ida appeared weak it was that very weakness that gave Lilo her strength. It was Aunt Ida and not Uncle Joe who made Lilo powerful. What had Lilo done to kill her mother? Why, Lilo had married out. She married a gentile. My mother, realist that she is, had told me on the phone that it was cancer that killed Aunt Ida. What my mother found shocking and hard to forgive was Lilo's timing. "She could have waited a little. It wouldn't have been for more than a few months. She could have let Ida have a little peace at the end." Lilo had known her mother was terminally ill and would not live very long. But Lilo was nearing thirty when she married Patrick Lanahan. It was hardly an act of youthful rebellion or spite. She had fought her battles with Uncle Joe and she had gone her own way. She loved Aunt Ida too much to be spiteful. Lilo simply fell in love and in that state a week can be an eternity, a month a millenium. I'm sure the real difficulty for Lilo lay in admitting that she loved someone, that *she* needed someone and that for her religion had nothing to do with it. This was hard for the family to accept. Religion, they think, has everything to do with everything. If it was not for their religion, they ask, why else were six million Jews killed?

The day after the funeral Lilo called me and asked if we could meet for lunch. It was the first time Lilo and I would be meeting on our own, more or less as equals, both married ladies — and who had been older, who younger, who rich, who poor, who thin, who fat, wasn't going to matter any more. Uneasily I thought Lilo might want to hear the details of her mother's funeral, might want comfort (which I prepared myself to give). I tried to recall who said what to whom, who cried, who didn't, what the rabbi said in his eulogy. I was totally unprepared for the self-possessed young woman who met me for lunch. Lilo was radiant. Lilo was keeping her grief to herself. What Lilo wanted to share with someone was her happiness. She had a very simple, wide gold wedding band on her left hand. She kept looking down at it and smiling. She slipped only once, when she said, "I *know* my mother would have liked Pat. If only she could have gotten to know him." She reached into her purse and took a picture of Pat and herself out of her wallet. I remembered the excitement of my own wedding, how beautiful my sister looked in her long dress, how angry my brother was about being in a tux, my father's arm shaking under mine as we walked down the aisle, tears in my mother's eyes when she kissed me goodbye. I remembered standing, in white lace, under the ancient, flower-adorned chupah and I looked down at the snapshot of Pat and Lilo in street clothes outside City Hall, and I thought she had been cheated. Lilo, of course, thought I had been conned.

It was not a successful lunch. It left neither of us anxious to repeat the experience, in spite, of course, of our goodbye promises to meet again soon. I admired Lilo, maybe I even loved her. But Lilo never seemed to understand that you have to have things before you can throw them away. It's easy for Lilo to turn up her nose at the suburbs. To Lilo the word suburban is pejorative. But Lilo grew up in a suburb, in a white house guarded by a velvet lawn. I think you have to grow up on city streets to want lawns for your children. I suppose my own children, growing up on lawns, will one day prefer concrete and find a cold-water railroad flat desirable. Lilo is much too intelligent not to understand this.

I returned to my suburban split-level and for the next few years was totally absorbed in raising my own children. When the children went off to school I returned to graduate school. Coming out of the cocoon of childrearing back into the world and into the light I discovered that my parents had suddenly gotten old. It seemed to me that one day they were young or at least only middle-aged and now they were old. On a trip home for the holidays I noticed that my mother was wearing what I used to call "old-lady shoes." My mother had a great pair of legs. My sister's are too thin, mine too heavy, but my mother's were once really perfect. When I was little I used to say to her, "Ma, promise me you'll never wear old-lady shoes." She had written to me about her arthritis but until I saw her in those sensible, low-heeled oxfords, it had no reality for me. I knew my parents' forty-fifth wedding anniversary was coming up shortly and I knew that I wanted to give a big party for them. I wanted my children to sit at the cousins' table. I called my sister and then my brother and we three decided that we would toss one smashing party for them and we would invite everybody in the world. But not Uncle Joe *and* Lilo?

Uncle Joe remained true to his word and in the fifteen years following Aunt Ida's death, never laid eyes on Lilo. Lilo and Pat Lanahan had two children, a boy and a girl. Uncle Joe had never seen them. "But they belong at the cousins' table," I insisted. "They *are* cousins." My sister replied, "But Uncle Joe won't come if Lilo comes. He's Ma's only brother. You know she'd want him there." I countered, "Well, Lilo's her niece." Trying to figure out the importance of brothers versus nieces irritated my own brother and he left the room. I won. We invited Uncle Joe and Lilo and her husband Pat and their two children.

There is a unique talent in this family for dramatic non-entrances. Uncle Joe was the star of my parents' anniversary party. He wasn't there. He got wind of the fact that Lilo and her husband (whom he had never met) and her children (whom he had never seen) were coming and he never showed up. My mother looked weepy and woebegone. She had for years explained Uncle Joe to us. Yes, she conceded, he was a stubborn man but he really had a good heart (hadn't he always lent us money when we needed it most?) and Lilo had hurt him, hurt him badly. She was his one and only child, all he had, and look what she did to him and who were we to judge him, were we God? My father joked and tried to jolly her out of it. He loves parties, and he was moved by the trouble we had gone to and was determined to enjoy this party. We are not a notably polite family. Everyone at the party was very polite to Lilo and Pat. They handled them with delicacy, as if they were fragile and might break if you got too close to them. Nobody pinched their children's cheeks.

Shortly after this party Uncle Joe had a massive coronary. He died instantly. No one told Lilo not to come to her father's funeral. She was not there. She didn't call and ask to meet for lunch the next day. When Uncle Joe's will was read we discovered he had disinherited Lilo. Uncle Joe had a competent lawyer and his will was very specifically and very precisely worded.

I won't beat about the bush. Uncle Joe left $300,000. He divided that amount equally among his ten nieces and nephews. Each of Lilo's cousins got $30,000. I felt it was an extremely unfair will and deep in my heart wanted none of it while my head kept thinking of all the pleasant uses to which I could put $30,000. Uncle Joe was a stubborn man, an unforgiving man, even a vindictive man but he was smart. He knew us *all* better than we knew ourselves. How could I give my share back to Lilo if none of the others did? It would make me look like a saint and if there's one kind of person in this world who makes other people feel miserable it's a saint. I wasn't sure I was willing to bear the hostility of my own brother and sister as well as that of all my cousins.

Besides saints don't run in our religion. There were my children to consider. Did I have the right to deprive them of Ivy League schools?

We talked it over, my sister and brother and I. We talked for hours and hours over numberless cups of coffee and some apple strudel my mother sent over. But she and my father stayed out of it. What it all came down to was, we wanted the money but we also wanted Lilo to have some. Finally we decided that if each of the cousins would give up only $5,000 that would come to $50,000 for Lilo. She would have what we all had and a little more. To the three of us, this seemed to be a reasonable, sane, and satisfying solution. So we divided up the seven remaining cousins. We each took the cousins we felt closest to. I got Bella and Carol. My sister got Rose and Sheldon and my brother took Alan, Jack and Sarah. We put our reasonable, sane and satisfying plan before them, and while none of the cousins said no outright (although Cousin Bella came pretty close), none of them said yes either. Then Cousin Sheldon took it upon himself to call Lilo. When she heard what was going on she flew into a rage, a rage that forever demolished Uncle Joe's reputation as the supreme rager of the family. Lilo said she wouldn't spit on a dime of her father's money.

GLORIA L. KIRCHHEIMER

A CASE OF DEMENTIA

My father, who is not given to introspection except about his pension plan, came to believe that my mother was having a breakdown.

How did he reach this conclusion? His prior experiences with breakdowns were mechanically or municipally related: toasters, subways, the work ethic of civil servants. Within his category of mental aberrations, disrespect for one's parents or husband ranked high. Anyone who sought help from a psychiatrist had to be crazy.

He whispered over the telephone and I had to strain to hear. Mother had been "hysterical." She had called him names: "tyrant," "dictator," "monster."

In a household where contrariness on the part of its females was regarded as a sign of grippe (the culprit was offered a glass of water and made to lie down), outright criticism was unthinkable. I feared for my father's sanity; Mother was on the road to health. With delight I pictured the scene. Mother brandishing a pot in which she had cooked thousands of delicacies for him, or waving a slipper or—most appalling—rending her clothes after the fashion of her countrywomen.

Mother was born in Egypt, a polyglot like all Sephardim of her generation. She often told me stories about the bazaar, the Arab quarter, the harems, the Arabic girls who taught her to put *kohl* in her eyes and henna in her hair and amulets around her neck. She swore to me that she had given up her Egyptian ways the moment she touched Ellis Island. But I wondered. Her eyes were so large, so dark. She could play the tambourine and gyrate demurely in a rudimentary belly dance.

And now, forty years of submission to my father had finally erupted, accelerated by his retirement. A man who had commanded a large staff on three continents was now reduced to questioning my mother on the wisdom of refrigerating a grapefruit and interrogating her about every telephone call she made or received. To a man who had championed raises for his staff (but not coffee breaks), the sight of Mother leaving him in the middle of the day to attend a meeting of the charitable organization of which she was president constituted dereliction of duty.

I asked if I might speak to her. I wanted to congratulate her. For her benefit he said heartily, "Everything is fine, fine." Then again in a whisper, "Don't say anything." Then, "Honey, it's your beloved daughter," a curiously archaic mode of referring to me.

"Leave me alone." I heard Mother's voice in the background. "Leave me in peace."

"Everything is under control," my father said loudly. Then, *"Ne dis rien,"* as though with her reason, she had also lost one of her mother tongues.

To me Mother said, "Is this a life?"

Ignoring the question, I said that it was all to the good that she had finally exploded.

"I'm sick. It was terrible."

"Yes, but—"

"I was tearing my hair," she added as if to convince me of her dementia. She had in fact said to me recently and quite cheerfully that I must not be surprised if she should go berserk. "Berserk," she had repeated, relishing this exotic word which she knew only from newspaper accounts about seemingly normal persons like herself. "This is Alcatraz," she said, perhaps confusing the George Washington Bridge, which she could see from her window, with the Golden Gate. Earlier she had prepared a six-course meal for my father, with instructions, before leaving for a meeting. He had accused her of abandoning him and threatened to go on his own to the old-age home. "I prepare everything for him. Hand and foot. . . . Is this the thanks? No, I don't want coffee now—" He must have made her some, a peace offering. "Half a cup then. Hmm. Not bad. How are you?" she asked me. "You're lucky. You can come and go as you please. Women's lib."

"Women's lib," Father echoed gaily over the extension phone. "Didn't I just make her a cup of coffee?"

» «

"For better, for worse, and this is worse," he complained when next I phoned. "Of course I didn't say anything, I didn't want to upset her. Monday a meeting, Tuesday a benefit, Wednesday a luncheon—"

What energy, I thought, picturing Mother in her rakish felt hat, those great dark eyes, the snappy leather briefcase.

"What would public opinion say? A wife who leaves home every day." Public opinion meant my father's brother for whom he had the requisite family feeling but mostly contempt. "I ask you, is this natural? She is so high-strung. What should I do?" And lest I think he was actually consulting me, he said, "I will speak to the rabbi."

Ah, not that: an unctuous, platitudinous man whose yeshiva was Madison Avenue. But so great was my father's reverence for "the office" that it did not matter what kind of person filled it as long as he displayed the appurtenances. I pictured Claude Rains, *The Invisible Man,* playing the part, skull cap bobbing merrily, prayer shawl sweeping the furniture. Respect for the office was what mattered to my father. Thus when ex-President Nixon was forced to resign, my father felt sorry for him. After all, he was The President. The only office exempt from respect was that of Labor Leader, for to my father it was synonymous with Racketeer, his memory still fresh from the unionization of his clerical staff. This rabbi had already proven himself a keen judge of the human heart by recommending a Caribbean cruise to an insurance agent whose wife's derangement was clearly manifested in her refusal to prepare a box lunch for him every day.

How was mental illness treated in the old country, in Turkey, Greece, Egypt? The afflicted person was said to have had the evil eye cast upon him or her. By having a special incantation performed, the person lost the hex and was cured. The incantation, in Hebrew and Ladino, was first a recitation of all the victim's maternal forbears, followed by a heavily symbolic story about the prophet Eliahu. The person administering the spell must always be a female. It must be learned not through instruction but through eavesdropping while it is being performed. If the woman reciting it begins to yawn uncontrollably, the spell is working. During my childhood it had been performed with great efficacity by my mother as an all-purpose cure, equally good for melancholia and viral infections, though over the years it had gradually been replaced by penicillin.

One day I discovered, tucked into the drawer where I kept my tennis socks, a gaudy glass bead which I recognized as the charm against the evil eye. It was crudely painted with concentric circles, in the middle of which was a blue dot, presumably the iris, rimmed in (blood-shot) red, the whole resembling a bulging eye suffering from glaucoma. Designed to outstare the evil eye, it had been hidden there for my protection by my mother.

To my father's great relief, the rabbi renders the verdict that my mother is suffering from overwork and needs to curtail her activities outside the home. "Psychiatry shmuckiatry," my father says. "A racket. They make money so families can split up. Look at the divorce rate."

I look and wonder how my parents have stayed together for so long. Was she ever truly happy? Was he ever different? Always the despot, benevolent but always contemptuous of any ambition she might have entertained (though he boasted of her capabilities behind her back). A woman who might have gone to college or held an important position. Now she administers thousands of dollars, super-vises dozens of volunteers, a woman who writes and edits reports, deals with printers, rabbis, caterers, immigrants, and bureaucrats. Why has it taken her so long to revolt?

"Everything is under control," he says suddenly, signaling my mother's arrival home. "How's the weather there?" as though I were in Palm Beach instead of three miles downtown. "Darling, I was just saying that your daughter is almost as pretty as you." He laughs that nasty laugh I have heard so often.

"This is not a life," she says to me, answering her own question of an earlier conversation. "You know your mother is nothing but a vegetable? Come for dinner or I won't be responsible. . . . "

No help for it. I leave my office early and rush uptown to pay my call on the unhinged one.

A barefoot woman opens the door and greets me by singing a song in Italian. Not Hello, glad to see you, but instead a song about a sprig of violets plucked from a mountainside, sung in a strained alto — she has never reconciled herself to being a soprano manquée. She is braless and disheveled, her slip hangs down below a crooked hem. She sa-shays across the room, ending her song, and with scarcely a pause for breath, starts reciting a long poem in French about a noble wolf. On the table there is food for ten though we are only three tonight. One never knows who will drop in and truth to say, in the old days people were always dropping in and staying. "Is this my daughter?" she asks after ending her poem, upon which my father gives me a meaningful look.

A loud street noise startles us and Mother quickly licks her index finger and touches her throat three times, uttering a few expletives in Arabic.

"Isn't she cute," Father says to me with an agonized smile.

Mother points to him, "Dr. Jekyll and Mr. Hyde."

I am very relieved. There is nothing untoward in her behavior. She is quite herself. "How like yourself you are," I say, quoting Strindberg to her.

"I knew you would understand." Tucking her arm under mine she says, "Only what is written in French is poetry, and only what is sung in Italian is music. The rest is holy — the Hebrew — or harsh — the German." Her cultural cosmos has no room for the Scandinavians.

"Strindberg was a Swede, Mom."

"Smorgasbord," she says, leading me to the kitchen.

"When do we eat?" Father taps on a glass with a fork. "Let's have a little service around here."

"Do you know that he can't even boil water?" Mother asks.

"What good is boiled water?" he says.

"A boire, à boire, par pitié!" she cries. (A drink, a drink, for pity's sake.) Father pours some wine. And not to be outdone, recites a short poem in French about a shipwreck. The dinner ends with conviviality. They appear to be making eyes at each other and I leave soon after dinner, not wishing to be de trop.

» «

Distraught, my father has violated the hallowed custom of the parent waiting for the child to call and phones me to say that in his time women were stoned for desertion.

"Desertion? You mean adultery."

She phoned him from the street and refused to say where she was.

We must call the police. This is alarming.

"All she said was she had a ticket."

"A ticket? Train, bus, plane — ?"

"A matinee. I ask you, is this right? Without consultation?"

"Without permission you mean," I say, emboldened.

"Of course I would have given my permission. I am a reasonable man. I don't know what to do any more."

"Perhaps — " dare I say it? " — it would be good for you to talk to a psychiatrist."

"God forbid. Charlatans. They are worse than chiropractors. They are all in cahoots. No. I have an idea. You are going to laugh at it." He hesitates while I clear my throat. "My father, may he rest in peace, would turn over in his grave if he were alive. But I am a desperate man."

Not a Caribbean cruise.

Not garlic hung around the neck.

Not a walnut shell inscribed with Hebrew characters, to be placed under a pillow.

His solution is that I, the daughter, must perform the evil-eye exorcism upon my mother. Ah, no — this is the twentieth century. I remember myself as a scoffing, irreverent child, sick with stomach aches, chicken pox, strep throat; giggling as my mother performed it at my bedside, tolerant and loving even as I mimicked her yawning.

"Really, Dad — "

"It worked for you, didn't it? You got rid of the measles. And when I had pleurisy — "

Yes, this is our answer to the Ashkenazim. The evil-eye incantation in lieu of chicken soup. "But I don't know it. I never memorized it."

"If you are not willing to help your own mother — "

"All right, but it's absurd. In this day and age." My bravado masks the strain of superstition which prevents me from ever breaking a chain letter (the last person who broke this chain suffered a cerebral hemorrhage). Why take a chance?

» «

One late afternoon, a stylish woman in her mid-thirties, dressed in a suit and carrying an attaché case hurries to — a board meeting? A conference? A senate subcommittee hearing or a lecture hall to address a gathering?

This woman is going to cast a hex over the evil eye. Not in a village hovel or a stucco house with no plumbing, overlooking the Mediterranean, but a thirty-five-story apartment house with the thin walls, plastic palms and peeling paint that are *de rigueur* in new buildings. Closed-circuit television reveals to the doorman a professional woman of the new breed, the kind who understands corporate law and makes decisions affecting his life. The woman's lips are moving. She is babbling a spell whose origins are lost in twelfth-century Spain.

The victim opens the door cheerfully. How to reconcile polyester with exorcism? Is there a connection? Mother shrugs. "If it will make him happy . . . I threw him out. We can't have a man listening. What a lovely evening. What a shame to stay home. I would rather go to Lord and Taylor. You need a new raincoat. Why do you wear such dark colors?" She fingers my suit. I am reminded of my father's "You are almost as pretty as your mother."

"Now Mom, you know I think this is ridiculous. All this ancient mumbo-jumbo."

This unleashes a monologue in French by Racine, about honoring one's ancestors, all while she plies me with food.

"And besides," she finishes, "it always worked when *I* did it."

I pick up the gauntlet and stamp around. "Well I suppose it can't hurt."

We lower the blinds and take the telephone off the hook. I feel as though I am about to perform the Black Mass. Mother lies down on her bed. The Arts and Leisure section from last Sunday's *Times* is on her night table, along with a dog-eared copy of proverbs by La Rochefoucauld.

"Salt," she prompts me.

I go into the kitchen and pour about half a teaspoonful into my right hand.

Mother's eyes are closed. Will something dreadful happen if I don't do it right? *The last person who broke the chain died a horrible death.*

"Take your time, honey," she says. "I'm very comfortable."

I raise my right hand and make a pass over her face. I begin to recite in Ladino, with my American accent: *"Vida, daughter of Allegra, whose mother was Miriam . . . "* I feel a lump in my throat. I am blessing my mother. *"Before her was Fortuna who was the fruit of Esther . . . "* A veritable Amazon land from which men are excluded. Women's lib, I hear my father say. Mother sighs. Words come into my head, Hebrew blessings learned as an unwilling Sunday School student. I am swaying now as I chant. Twenty floors below us, trucks rattle down the avenue, a few bars of disco music float up and die away.

There is a smile on Mother's face, her eyes remain closed. Now again in Ladino: *"Eliahu walked down the road, clad in iron, shod in iron. Three keys he carried: one to open the gate, one to lock it, and one to ward off the evil eye."* I smother a yawn and repeat the line about the three keys. I see him clanking down a country road, dusty trees — poplars, cypresses — the prophet in medieval garb, fooling the authorities, fooling the evil eye, casting away doubt and evil from the people of Israel. *"How many are the daughters, how many are the names, how many the signs and wonders?"* I am so tired. I can hardly raise the hand holding the salt over Mother's face. Wearily, yawning, I trace a six-pointed star across her face, a name for each point of the star, a blessing for each name, miracles for each succeeding generation, a logarithmic explosion of miracles for my mother.

She opens her eyes and nods kindly at me, at my hand. I open it, press the index finger of my left hand to the salt so that some grains adhere to it. She sits up and I place my finger gently in her mouth, applying the salt to her palate. I do this three times, reciting a threefold blessing in Hebrew which I do not remember ever having heard before. My eyes are tearing. Violently I throw the salt over her left shoulder. I am yawning uncontrollably. Mother reaches out and embraces me.

"How do you feel?" I ask, not knowing what to do with the rest of the salt on my palm.

"Wonderful," she says. "For once your father was right. I never felt better in my life."

ZENA COLLIER

PASSAGE

Every year, on the first night of Passover, we gathered for the Seder at my grandparents' house in the far reaches of north London. The house was tall and narrow, made of beige stucco and not particularly attractive, but it was more inviting on the inside than you would suppose from the exterior. My favorite rooms were the kitchen, where on all but the warmest days coals burned in the grate of the fireplace, and the cavernous, rarely used room at the top of the house called "the billiard room." It had been so equipped by my uncles Leonard and Jack when they lived there.

Everyone — my mother's three brothers, their wives and children, my parents and I — would arrive at the house in the late afternoon. Soon, the men and my older cousins would depart for synagogue, while the rest of us milled around the kitchen, helping with final preparations for dinner. At sundown, when the men returned, we would all sit down at the dining-room table that was set with my grandmother's best china, Madeira lace tablecloth, silver candelabra, flowers in cut-glass vases, and wine glasses which, in the course of the Seder, would be filled the traditional four times.

My grandfather would sit at the head of the table, in an armchair with a single cushion, and all the men would sit grouped together at that end. The women sat together at the other end. Whether this was cause or effect, I don't know, but while the men recited and sang the stirring account of the flight from slavery, the women, while joining in the blessings and adding "amen" at appropriate moments, would gradually begin chatting in undertones as the service continued. When we reached the break for dinner halfway through the service, the women would rise at intervals to bring in the various courses of the lengthy traditional meal.

Nothing about this procedure ever varied. I loved it — the conclave, the service, the entire occasion — and never tired of its sameness. On the contrary, its attraction lay in its unchanging nature, affirming verities as fixed as the tides, constant, eternal. Never mind that my cousins were inclined to be pests, their scornful tolerance of me — the only girl and youngest grandchild — infuriating. Never mind that my grandmother, with rouged, pouched cheeks, hair swept high with combs, was more severe than fond toward me; I was, in fact, a little afraid of her. Never mind that I was mostly bored by my aunts' conversation. (My aunts reminded me of the fairytale about the king who, about to depart on his travels, asks his daughters what he should bring them. "Bring me the finest, richest gowns," says the eldest — Aunt Muriel, obviously. "Bring me sparkling jewels," says the next — Phyllis. "Bring me just one perfect rose," says the youngest — who but vivacious, slender Poppy, my favorite?)

As for my mother's brothers, I never thought of them in those days as anything but *uncles*. As such, they dwelled on a lofty pinnacle, to be viewed with respect, while they treated *me* with somewhat formal amiability. Only Jack, the youngest, tended to be more genial and relaxed. He was a solicitor. Saul, the oldest, weighty in girth and manner, was for some reason considered the family sage. Leonard, nearsighted, wore a perpetual look of slight worry. He and Saul ran the wholesale shoe business that my grandfather had founded.

As the years passed, however, one aspect of the Seder had begun to trouble me. It was this: all through the first stages of the service — the lighting of the candles, over which my grandmother recited a blessing, my grandfather's chanting of Kiddush, the drinking of the first glass of wine, the eating of parsley dipped in salt water symbolizing gratitude to God for the earth's products — I would sit with mixed feelings, waiting for the *Ma Nishtana,* the asking of the Four Questions. When we reached this point, the company would listen attentively as my cousin Paul, preening with odious self-importance, would begin to recite in his still-piping treble, *Ma nishtana halila hazeh.* . . . *Why is this night different from all other nights?* By the time he had finished the first Question, I would be squirming in my seat with private resentment — for, since the Haggadah said clearly that the Questions should be asked by the youngest member, why was it always Paul, five months older than me, who was chosen?

By the time I was eleven, I had been registering my dissatisfaction for three years. Not with any of the adults, of course—I wouldn't have dared complain directly to them. It was my rival, Paul, on whom ostensibly I vented my frustration.

"It's not fair!" I spoke loudly enough for the others to hear, though it was Paul I addressed as we waited in the kitchen.

"I keep telling you, girls don't ask the Questions."

"Why not?" I demanded, hotly. "Andrea Mills does. So does—"

"Not in this house—I won't have it!" My grandmother stood at the table shelling hard-boiled eggs. "In this house, young ladies *behave* like young ladies. Now make yourself useful; fill those dishes with nuts and take them inside. Eve, look in the oven and see if the chicken needs covering. Do you hear?" she asked my mother.

"I covered it five minutes ago," my mother told her, quietly. "Where are the fish plates?"

"In the scullery. They need rinsing."

"You're looking very chic tonight, Eve," Muriel said, graciously.

My mother gave her an absent look, as though wondering for a moment who she was, then turned away silently. Muriel considered herself a fashion arbiter, and even I could tell she'd meant well just then, though she'd sounded patronizing. But I knew, of course, what was troubling my mother: my grandfather was ill. This would be his last Passover. We all knew this, and because of it, everyone seemed to be making a special effort. Phyllis, who usually talked endlessly of various maladies, steered clear tonight of the subject of illness and instead ran on about my cousin James who, still at Cambridge, had become engaged and was at his fiancée's parents' tonight for Seder. Poppy, who'd been heard in the past to say acidly that housekeeping, as some people practiced it, was sheer fanaticism, tonight made a point of praising everything lavishly. "The whole house sparkles! You must have worked like a Trojan. And those flowers! Did you do them yourself?"

"Eve did the flowers. All the rest, I did," my grandmother said, shortly.

"There." Muriel stepped back from the fruit she'd arranged. "Does this go on the sideboard?"

"Leave it here for now, there's not enough room."

Stephen, David and Wally clattered into the kitchen. "We're going to play billiards. Coming?"

I shook my head. Normally I'd have gone, but just then I preferred the warmth of the kitchen and the good food smells to the large, unheated room. "There won't be time for a game, anyway."

"Spoilsport. Coming, Paul?"

He scurried off after them, footsteps thumping on the stairs.

My grandmother looked at the clock. "They're late."

Every year she said this, but this time she spoke with real anxiety. My grandfather had insisted on going with the others. Saul had carried him out to the car.

"Don't worry," Phyllis said. "They're all with him. Anyway, they never get back much before this."

Ten minutes later, the men came home. Jack carried my grandfather in. My father helped settle him on the divan that had been moved downstairs and placed at the head of the table. He lay propped against pillows, looking ethereally frail, while we brought in the last touches for the table: the large plate containing the symbols — matzos, roasted shankbone, roasted egg, horseradish, haroset and parsley; the large silver goblet filled with wine for the prophet Elijah; the Haggadahs, one for each place, over which the men now conferred, deciding on certain cuts in the service so that my grandfather could get back to bed as soon as possible.

At last, everyone got seated and the service began.

As always, my grandmother lit the candles and recited the blessing. As always, I stared at the points of flame, caught by their leaping golden gleam.

We all stood. My grandfather, helped by Leonard and Saul, struggled to a slightly more upright position and, raising his wine glass, began in a voice thinned by illness to intone the Kiddush. *Baruch atah adonai. . . .* Saul took it up as his voice weakened. *Even this day of the Feast of Unleavened Bread, a memorial of the departure from Egypt. . . .*

The first glass of wine was poured. Together, we all spoke the blessing, and drank.

Soon now.

I sat keyed up through the blessing of the matzo. *Lo, this is the bread of affliction which our fathers ate. . . .* This year I didn't bother trying to see who hid the Afikomen; I was beginning to feel I'd outgrown that game.

Now.

As always, Paul cleared his throat officiously as he began to recite. *Why is this night different from all other nights?* As always, envy and resentment swelled within me as I listened. But tonight, as he reached the end of the second Question, something different happened: my grandfather raised a hand and interrupted. "Laura will ask the next two Questions." He gave me a nod and smiled, faintly.

Overwhelmed with surprise and joy, I sat up straight, drew a deep breath and began to read in a proud voice that sounded too loud in the silence. *She'bechol haleylot aynu matbilin. . . . On all other nights, we do not dip herbs in any condiment. Why on this night. . . .*

From the corner of my eye, I saw my mother, seated at my right, smiling as she watched me. It was the first smile I had seen on her face that evening. I suddenly realized to whom I owed this moment; she must have pleaded my cause with my grandfather. As I finished, she patted my knee. My father, seated at my left, leaned close and whispered, "Bravo!"

My grandfather proceeded to answer the Questions. *We celebrate tonight because we were Pharaoh's bondmen, and the Lord delivered us with a mighty hand. . . .*

Then came a favorite part, the responsive reading.
Had he brought us out of Egypt and not divided the sea for us —
Dayenu! We would have been satisfied!
Had he divided the sea and not permitted us to cross on dry land —
Dayenu!
Had he permitted us to cross the sea. . . .

From her end of the long table, my grandmother watched my grandfather, everyone, everything. Nothing escaped her.

An eagle eye and an iron hand, I'd once heard my mother say. My mother had stories to tell of her youth. From her mother, she had had unremitting discipline, instruction in housekeeping, and an injunction, on the day she married, always to rise promptly in the mornings and have hot meals ready at whatever hour her husband required. "She was surprised that someone like Ralph wanted me. After all, I was twenty-two by then and no beauty. I'd been on the shelf for a good few years, by her standards." She had given a little laugh — I can still hear the sound of it.

Tonight, my mother didn't say "amen" or recite the blessings. She didn't join in the half-whispered talk of the women. She was utterly silent as the service continued, lost in a dark contemplation of her own.

She had seemed subdued, though not quite like this, for several weeks now. Because of my grandfather, I knew. But my uncles weren't behaving this way, and he was their father, too. Still, it was probably worse for my mother, I thought. She had told me often how, as a child, she'd received from her father the embraces and kisses that her mother withheld. He had always spoken to her gently, even when rebuking her. Busy though he was in those days, working day and night to build up the business which later prospered, he had always found time for her as well as for his boys. When she became engaged, he'd told my father forthrightly that he was a fortunate man to be gaining such a wife. And now he was dying, this father, my grandfather.

I was suddenly glad all over again, for my mother's sake as well as my own, that my father was here tonight. Something had come up, some question of his not being able to manage it. It had to do with business. My father was a chartered accountant; he sometimes had to travel to see clients. He had been away a great deal lately. Because of his absences and my mother's sadness, our house had become depressingly quiet. There was something in the atmosphere I couldn't identify, but it made me uneasy; outside, spring was beginning, the plane trees lining our street had started to bud, but inside our house it felt more like autumn, a time of endings.

A fortnight back, just after my father had returned from a trip, I'd overheard them talking one Saturday while I was doing homework in the next room.

"You're definitely going, then," my mother said. It sounded half like a question, half like a statement.

Going where, I wondered. Scotland again? He had a new client in Scotland.

"Yes."

My mother was silent for a moment. Then she said, "Would you be willing to put it off until after Passover?"

"Eve—" He broke off. "It's no use."

"Just for the holidays," my mother said quickly. "Or at least until after the Seder. I don't want Father to know."

I could understand that. Certainly my grandfather wouldn't approve of my father's being gone at such a time. For that matter, I didn't like the idea either.

"All right," he said finally. "I'll come to the Seder."

"And—you won't say anything?"

"No."

"Well, I'm grateful for that much, anyway." But she didn't sound grateful. She sounded—what? I couldn't put a word to it.

In the pause that followed, I heard the slight clinking sound which meant she was lifting the lid of the teapot to see how much was left. "Do you want another cup?"

"Please."

I could picture her pouring milk in the cup, adding tea, passing it to him.

"I don't suppose—" She stopped, then started again. "Could anything make you change your mind?"

"Eve, we've been all through this."

They both spoke calmly, I noted with relief. Because several times lately, I'd heard their voices raised behind closed doors, though I couldn't make out what was actually said.

They made their lives bitter with hard labor in mortar and bricks. . . .

My grandfather, with fingers that trembled, made up tiny matzo sandwiches of maror, the bitter herbs, and the sweet haroset, and passed them out. As I ate, I thought as always how strange it was that these symbols of mortar, token of bondage, should taste so delicious. In union, we all spoke the blessing.

Then it was time to serve dinner.

Like puppets pulled by a single string, all the women rose.

"No need for everyone. Just Phyllis and Eve for now. You, too, Laura, lend a hand."

In the kitchen, my grandmother spooned gefilte fish onto plates. Phyllis bore off the first loaded tray.

"Wait, Eve," my grandmother said. "A little more juice there." She tilted the spoon. "Have you noticed how handsome Wally's become? Exactly the way Jack looked at that age. . . ."

My mother put the plate on the tray. "That's ready, Laura."

I carried out the tray, distributed the filled plates and sat down, listening to my father chatting with my uncles and grandfather, though my grandfather lay still, listening, rather than talking.

My father got along well with the family. He often played golf with Saul and Leonard; he and my mother went to the Continent with Jack and Poppy; my grandmother seemed to hold nearly as high an opinion of him as she did of her sons. But though he called my grandfather "Dad," he didn't call my grandmother "Mother," I noticed.

I'd once heard him refer to my grandmother as "The Gorgon." "Why do you let her talk to you that way?" he'd asked my mother. "Anyone would think she were *your* mother-in-law, not mine."

"It's hardly a matter of letting, is it?" my mother answered.

After fish came the soup. Then the chicken. My grandfather took a few spoonfuls of soup, nothing else. Slowly, the candles burned lower.

Saul tried to persuade my grandfather to go back to bed, but he wouldn't. "I'll finish the service. Anyway—" he looked down the table, towards my cousins and me, with a smile, "we must see who finds the Afikomen."

"No, Simon, listen, go up to bed," my grandmother urged, her voice softening. "It's not good for you to stay up like this."

"Tillie, please." His hand fluttered like a wounded bird. "I'm staying."

She sighed. "Saul, change his pillows. If he lies higher, he breathes easier. Are you warm enough, Simon? Another blanket? Leonard—"

"I'll get it." My mother stood up, went out and came back with the blanket which she tucked around him, then bent and kissed him, placing her hand against his cheek.

I was growing uneasy about my mother. Twice I had asker her to pass the matzos, but she hadn't seemed to hear. At one point, Phyllis spoke to her across the table, saying how light the almond cake was, she would like the recipe—but she, too, received no answer. My father, chatting with the men, didn't seem to notice.

My grandmother leaned forward. "Eve." Her voice was low but commanded attention. *"Eve."*

My mother focussed her gaze, finally.

"Such a long face. You should do better."

My mother gave a barely perceptible shake of her head. What did that mean? I can't? I'm sorry?

"You think it's easy for *me?*" my grandmother whispered. "Or for the boys?"

She was right. Everyone else was at least pretending. My mother ought to make an effort, dreadful though it was, her father dying. Dying. I tried to imagine how I would feel if it were my father, but my mind skittered away from the thought. I put out a hand and touched his sleeve, feeling the flesh and bone beneath, needing to know he was with me, alive.

He turned at my touch, eyebrows raised. Then he smiled, put out his hand and stroked mine reassuringly.

I suddenly noticed my mother watching. She stared at us both with a strange expression, then snapped her head away as though caught in the act of watching an indecency.

Across from my mother, Muriel and Poppy were discussing Wally's Bar Mitzvah, scheduled for June. How many were invited? Who was the caterer? What would Poppy wear?

My grandmother got to her feet. "Eve, come. A few things to fetch, and more tea."

"I'll help." Muriel started up, but my grandmother said firmly, "No, stay," and Muriel sat down again.

A moment later, I felt terribly thirsty. Wine always made me thirsty for water, but there was none on the table. I got up and went to the kitchen to fetch some.

Approaching, I heard my grandmother speaking in a tone of quiet fury. "A lot of help you are at a time like this! Aren't things bad enough?"

My mother shook her head, twisting her hands together. Her

mouth kept opening as though she were about to speak, then closing again.

"Look at you—a fish swallowing air!" Her voice grew thick with contempt. "Pull yourself together! Take a lesson from your brothers! They—"

"Don't!" Her face worked. "He's leaving me, Mother!"

My grandmother's face turned brick red with anger. "He's leaving us all! Do you think you're the only—"

"No—I mean Ralph."

My grandmother's expression changed. "Ralph?" She put a hand to her face, and took a step backwards. "*Ralph?* Are you saying—"

My mother nodded.

For once, my grandmother seemed at a loss. "Then—but what— how . . . ?"

"I made him promise to come tonight. So that Dad wouldn't know."

After a moment, my grandmother turned and went over to the stove. Absently she lifted the kettle as though to fill it, then put it down again. She turned and looked at my mother. "What's it about?" Her voice was flat.

My mother shook her head. "I don't know. He's stopped—he no longer loves me, he says." She swallowed, hard.

"There must be a reason. Another woman?"

"I . . . don't think so. He says not."

"What, then? A man doesn't suddenly, out of a clear blue sky . . ." She was beginning to sound angry again. "A man doesn't all at once . . ."

"Mother, please, I—"

"One day you're married, the next he's leaving. Not another woman. Not even that!" Her voice rose. "What did you do?"

"Do?"

"You must have done something! A man like that!" She was breathing heavily. "All I asked was for you to be married . . . a good man, children. Is that too much to ask? Look at your brothers—"

"Don't—don't—"

"—fine men, with beautiful sons! But you—no! You can't even stay married!"

My mother turned and started out of the kitchen, and ran blindly into me. "Laura!"

We stared at each other for what seemed an eternity. Then she seized me and pulled me into the kitchen.

She stood me in front of her, my back to her, and put her hands on my shoulders. "You see her?" she said to my grandmother. "My daughter, your granddaughter." Later, I found bruises on my shoulders. "We'll go back to that room and finish out the evening, and I will help put my father back to bed. So long as he lives, I'll pretend nothing's wrong. But after he dies," her voice shook — "be glad you have your sons and grandsons. Because this grandchild you won't see again. Nor will you see me."

She took my hand and led me back to the dining room.

The Seder had resumed. They were filling the glasses for the third time. Beneath the table, my mother still held my hand as they spoke the blessing over the wine.

"David found the Afikomen," Wally whispered. "It was on the floor, behind the curtains."

"I don't care," I muttered. Under the table I pulled my hand away and tucked it between my knees.

My father glanced at me, then at my mother. I looked away, at my grandmother's place. Just then, my grandmother came back, carrying the teapot, and sat down, stiffly. Her lips were compressed. She kept blinking rapidly. Over and over, her hand smoothed the tablecloth.

Poppy's glance went from her to my mother. "Eve?" she murmured. "Eve? Are you—"

I saw Muriel whisper something to Phyllis. Phyllis whispered back.

Let us now open the door that Elijah may enter.

Stephen went to the door and threw it open with a flourish. In the slight draft that resulted, the green velvet curtains stirred. We sat silent, waiting for the legendary emissary of hope and faith.

Who is Elijah?

He was a great prophet in Israel. On Mount Carmel, face to face with the priests of Baal. . . .

I do not see him.

He cannot be seen. He comes as the goodness that is in the hearts of men. . . .

I knew that, of course. Still, I had always waited with fixed gaze and bated breath, conjuring an ectoplasmic Old Testament figure, robed, bearded, coming through that doorway, footsteps soundless on the polished floor. I had stared intently at Elijah's goblet in the centre of the table, willing the level of the wine to drop, be it ever so slightly.

But not this time. Lost in absorption of my new knowledge, I was hardly aware of the door being closed. The voices resumed, faster now, like a speeded-up record, as Saul hurried things along.

At last, the end approached. My grandfather raised his glass. *As we offer benediction over the fourth cup. . . .* The hand holding the glass shook. His face was the color of wet blotting paper. *May God bless the house of Israel with freedom and keep us safe from danger. . . .*

For the last time, we recited the blessing, and drank. It was over, except for the songs.

But tonight Saul declared, "No songs, no songs." Cries of protest came from my cousins.

"Just one, then. Which? *Echod Mi Yodea?* Right."

Jack, who had a beautiful tenor, started us off. *Echod mi yodea? What is your one, ho? I'll sing you one, ho!*

One is God and one alone, And evermore shall be so! my cousins roared back.

My father joined in, but my mother did not. She was watching my grandfather, who lay back, eyes closed, lips moving soundlessly. My grandmother was watching him, too. She said something to Poppy, who stopped singing long enough to pass it on to Muriel, who spoke to Leonard, who stood and went to my grandfather and began to gather him up. But my grandfather weakly waved him off.

Hamisha mi yodea? What are your five, ho? I'll sing you five, ho! Five are the Books of Moses, Four are the Mothers of Israel, Three are the Patriarchs. . . .

Wally's voice, which had begun to break recently, went from squeak to baritone.

Shisha mi yodea? I'll sing you six, ho!

I did not sing. I was floating adrift in uncharted seas, where the tides had somehow cut loose from the moon, and there was no sight at all of a friendly shore.

All around, the voices continued, louder, faster. *Tisha mi yodea? I'll sing you nine, ho!*

Four more verses to go. Thirteen would end it. *Thirteen are the Attributes of God, Twelve are the Tribes of Israel, Eleven are the Stars.* . . .

If only they would keep singing, I thought — would continue on to an infinite number, all the disparate voices, Muriel's warble, my cousins' stridence, Saul's hearty basso profundo. . . . So long as it lasted, I could tell myself that nothing had changed, and that next year we would all be seated around this table, held safely in the protection of God and love's continuum.

AUTHORS' NOTES

MARSHA LEE BERKMAN, who holds an MA in English and Creative Writing from San Francisco State University, has published short stories in a wide variety of academic and literary magazines, including *Lilith, Agada, Western Humanities Review, Other Voices, Sonora Review,* and *Feldspar Prize Stories 2: An Anthology of Bay Area Women's Writing.* She recently completed a collection of short stories and is working on a novel.

E.M. BRONER is the author of five books, including *Her Mothers* and *A Weave of Women.* Her play, *The Body Parts of Margaret Fuller,* was produced at Playwrights-Horizons, and her stories and reviews have appeared in *Ms., Lear's, Tikkun,* and *Mother Jones.* She is a recipient of two National Endowment for the Arts Awards and a Wonder Woman Award given to women at risk in their lives and art. She has taught at Wayne State University, Oberlin College, UCLA, Sarah Lawrence, The Ohio State University, and Columbia University Center for American Culture. Currently, she is working on a novel, *The Repair Shop.*

ZENA COLLIER has published short stories in literary journals, including *Prairie Schooner, Southwest Review, Literary Review,* and *Southern Humanities Review,* and in magazines such as *McCall's* and *Alfred Hitchcock's Mystery Magazine.* Her novel, *A Cooler Climate,* has been published by British American Publishing. She has also published five novels for children.

LAURIE COLWIN is the author of three short story collections, *The Lone Pilgrim, Passion and Affect,* and *Another Marvelous Thing* as well as three novels, *Family Happiness, Happy All the Time,* and *Shine On, Bright and Dangerous Object.* She has also written a cookbook, *Home Cooking: A Writer in the Kitchen.*

LYNN FREED's second novel, *Home Ground*, is set in South Africa in the fifties and sixties. She has published short stories, essays, and reviews in *Harper's*, the *New York Times*, the *Washington Post*, and elsewhere and is presently working on a novel and collection of short pieces. She is writer-in-residence at the University of Texas at Austin and a Guggenheim Fellow.

JOANNE GREENBERG, who is probably best known for her novel, *I Never Promised You A Rose Garden*, is also the author of novels and short story collections, including *Age of Consent, High Crimes and Misdemeanors, In this Sign, The King's Persons, Of Such Small Differences, Rites of Passage*, and *Simple Gifts*.

CAROL K. HOWELL is a 1985 graduate of the Iowa Writers' Workshop. Her stories have appeared in *Redbook, North American Review, Crazyhorse, New Orleans Review*, and other quarterlies. Currently, she teaches in the Writing Program at Syracuse University and is finishing a collection of stories.

BETTE HOWLAND's short story collections are *Things to Come and Go, Blue in Chicago*, and *W–3*. She is a MacArthur Fellow.

GLORIA L. KIRCHHEIMER's short stories have appeared in *Carolina Quarterly, Cimarron Review, Kansas Quarterly, New Letters, North American Review*, and other magazines as well as in the anthology, *The Tribe of Dina*. She recently completed a novel and is currently working on a collection of short stories based on her Sephardic background.

LIBBI MIRIAM, who writes in several genres, often writes on the subject she finds powerful: the family.

FAYE MOSKOWITZ is the author of *A Leak in the Heart: Tales From a Woman's Life* and *Whoever Finds This: I Love You*. She is a member of the UJA Speakers Bureau, has been a commentator for "All Things Considered" on National Public Radio, and currently directs the writing program at George Washington University.

LESLÉA NEWMAN's books of fiction and poetry include *Good Enough to Eat, Love Me Like You Mean It, A Letter to Harvey Milk*, and *Heather Has Two Mommies*. She also edited a poetry anthology, *Bubbe Meisehs by Shayneh Maidelehs* and received a Massachusetts Artists Fellowship. She teaches women's writing workshops in Northampton, Massachusetts and around the country.

SHARON NIEDERMAN is the editor of *Shaking Eve's Tree: Short Stories of Jewish Women* and *A Quilt of Words: Women's Diaries, Letters and Original Accounts of Life in the Southwest, 1860 – 1960.* She is a member of the Jewish Welfare Board Speakers Bureau. Her articles and reviews have appeared in many national and regional publications, including the *New York Times, Boston Globe,* and *Christian Science Monitor.* She is currently working on an historical novel set in New Mexico and is Associate Editor with Johnson Books, Boulder, Colorado.

TILLIE OLSEN's books are *Tell Me a Riddle, Silences, Yonnondio: From the Thirties,* and *Mother to Daughter, Daughter to Mother: A Daybook and Reader.*

GRACE PALEY's short story collections are *Enormous Changes at the Last Minute, Later the Same Day,* and *The Little Disturbances of Man.*

NIKKI STILLER's poems, stories, and essays have appeared in a wide range of periodicals, including *The Hudson Review, Midstream, Response, International Poetry Review,* and *Primavera.* She is the author of *Eve's Orphans: Mothers and Daughters in Medieval English Literature* and the forthcoming book, *The Figure of Cressida in British and American Literature.* An associate professor of English at New Jersey Institute of Technology, she now writes primarily on Jewish subjects. She is also working on a novel, *Desperate Measures: The Life and Times of Luba Radisch.*

MARCIA TAGER's short stories have appeared in numerous literary reviews. She is presently at work on a short story collection.